KNIGHT

B.B. REID

DEDICATION

To Sunny, who listened to me moan about this book for six months.

Mian's name is pronounced
My-an.

THE BEGINNING

In 1812, Adam Knight died of consumption, leaving his wife and three children destitute. It was four years following Adam's death when Louis Wilde encountered Adam and Amelia's oldest son. Alexander's reckless attempt to steal a jeweled ring from the home of politician John Sullivan had been witnessed by Wilde.

But Louis didn't turn in Alexander.

Instead, he paid him for his enemy's ring.

And then paid him for his silence.

DUTY OF KNIGHTHOOD

The Knight is responsible for the well-being of each descendant of Adam. He will be known as the Bandit.

The Knight can only be the Bandit.

The Knight will keep a record of every job, bribe, and client in the book.

The Knight will never sell secrets.

The Knight will never sell silence.

The Knight will protect the book.

The Knight will produce a male heir to continue my legacy.

If the Knight fails in his duty to produce an heir, power will revert to the next eligible descendant of Alexander.

The Knight and descendants of Adam shall treat these rules as law.

Should the Knight break these rules, with the exception of producing an heir, his life will be forfeited, and power will be inherited by his executioner.

CHAPTER ONE

MIAN
Three Years Ago

I CAN STILL FEEL THE BUTTERFLIES.

Angel's midnight voice on the phone, making me wish him a happy birthday, and inviting me to his party tonight did that.

I never thought I'd see him again. I never thought he'd care if I didn't.

Mixing with the flutters in my stomach was the stabbing memory of his order to stay away from him. I tried to picture a girl he loved enough to hurt me, but I could only see myself as the girl he shared his kisses with—only and forever.

I sighed and fell back onto my bed. If he loved someone else, why would he purposely stir these feelings inside me by inviting me to his party?

A little hope and a lot of uncertainty wreaked havoc on my mind. I'd go to his party, but if he wanted me to stay, he would need to be honest about what he truly wanted—and if he wanted *me*.

Before I could get any answers, though, I'd need my father's permission to go. Angel might think he could control the universe, but so did my father.

He spent most of his time in the den during the rare occasions he was home. I rehearsed my lines as I made my way to his man cave. He'd definitely be suspicious of why I wanted to attend since Angel and I weren't exactly best friends. Any reason other than the truth would do.

I stood outside the den until the truth no longer sounded so distorted. My fist was poised to knock when I heard Daddy speak. His angry bark made me jump back from the door. I've never heard him speak in that tone before. Curiosity had me pressing my ear to the door.

"Why are you showing me this?" The long silence meant he was thankfully alone. I didn't want to know what he would have done if the person had been standing in front of him. I decided I didn't want to know what he'd do to me if he found me eavesdropping, so I headed to the kitchen for a snack. I wanted to go to this party more than anything and maybe dance with Angel. Getting on daddy's bad side definitely wouldn't get me there.

It was an hour before I heard his footsteps moving across the wooden floors my mother had loved so much. She spent a good part of her day watching home improvement shows after she'd fallen sick.

I jumped from the barstool where I'd been eating an apple and met him in the hallway as he was tugging on the distressed brown leather jacket he always wore. I think he's had that thing longer than I've been alive.

"Daddy, I need to talk to you."

"Not now," he answered in a clipped tone. He didn't bother to spare me even a glance as he shoved his phone in his pocket and moved past me.

"But it's important," I whined then winced. Maybe Angel had been right about me being spoiled.

"It can wait." His back was still toward me so he couldn't see my frown. Daddy was never short with me.

"Where are you going?" I demanded. I was tempted to stomp my foot and cry as I would have six years ago.

His eyes seemed to lose some of their jade as he said, "I've got a job, Mian. Go to your room."

"I'm too old to *go to my room*," I sassed. I've never openly defied my father before. I was accustomed to getting my way, especially after Mom died.

But when his finger jabbed angrily toward the stairs, and he bellowed for me to obey him, I stared back at him in shock.

I felt betrayed.

He's never spoken to me this way before.

Ever.

"I hate you," I lied on a broken sob. The truth was I could never hate my father no matter how much he hurt me, and maybe it was the reason Angel mocked us, but my father was all I had. I could see the jade in his eyes returning a second before I turned and ran.

I was staring in the mirror silently bemoaning my puffy eyes and hoping they'd return to normal before the party when the doorbell rang. When the tears finally stopped, I'd decided I wasn't waiting around for Daddy's permission. He'd be forced to deal with me when he found me at the party falling deeper in love with his best friend's son.

Still standing at the mirror, the visitor continued to ring the doorbell more rapidly until it became obnoxious. My phone then vibrated twice signaling a new message, and when I saw Angel's name at the top of the message, I quickly snatched up the phone.

Angel: Answer the door, Sprite.

I clutched the phone tight in my hand. It couldn't possibly be him standing on the other side of my parent's front door. Even he wouldn't be that daring.

Would he?

I ran, dangerously skipping steps on my way down. I thought of my puffy red eyes for only a second before I ripped open the door. I was wearing a smile I couldn't fight, but when I saw who was standing on the other side, my smile quickly fell.

The man standing on my front porch didn't have Angel's dark hair, imposing body, or eyes with depths no one could ever reach.

Instead, this stranger sported blond hair and impatient blue eyes. He was dressed in a navy sports coat with a simple white shirt underneath and dark gray slacks hugging his legs. Clutched in his hands were three boxes of varying sizes. The adrenaline that sent my heart racing with anticipation, fear and delight evaporated.

"Mian Ross?"

"Yes?" The confusion I felt was evident in my tone. He

held out his arms, indicating I take the boxes. I did after a moment's hesitation.

I put them on the floor just inside the door and turned to ask what the packages were. "Sign here," he instructed before I could question. He then thrust a tiny device forward, and I obediently scribbled my name across the screen. "Have a good day." He turned and left, leaving me even more confused.

I eyed the packages after closing the door. There was no labeling. The smallest box was made of light blue velvet. It looked just like a box to hold a ring. I took the boxes upstairs, and only when I was behind doors did I open the first box.

A ring was exactly what I found inside.

My eyes bulged at the size of the single diamond. With careful fingers, I plucked the ring from the bedding. The band was platinum, and a diamond twinkled brightly at the very top of the band even in the low lighting.

I didn't know much about rings, but this seemed like a ring a guy gave a girl when he wanted her to wear it forever. But that was impossible, right? I was only sixteen, and Angel didn't love me.

With shaking hands, I placed the ring back in the box and closed it gently. The possibility that it could be true was too frightening, so I decided not to open the rest until I had answers.

It took me four tries before I knew what to say.

I got your package, but somehow, I think you know that already... What does it mean?

My other problem occurred to me after I'd sent the text. A few minutes had already passed without a response, so I bit my lip and sent another.

Um…I may need a ride. My dad bailed a few hours ago, and he still isn't back.

Ten minutes later, I was still waiting on Angel's response when the front door opening and closing sounded as if it'd been kicked in by Big Foot. I could hear Daddy calling my name. His voice sounded desperate as he ran up the stairs. Seconds later, he was filling my bedroom door looking just as he sounded.

"I need you to pack a bag and come with me." When I didn't jump to obey, he snapped. "Now, Mian."

His mood obviously hadn't improved in the few hours since he left, but this time, instead of running away in tears, I stood my ground and crossed my arms.

"Why should I come with you? You're being kind of a jerk."

"Mian, I'm very serious." He brushed past me to my closet and pulled out my lime green Jansport. My arms dropped from my chest when he dumped my notebooks and homework from the backpack. He then crossed to the dresser and started pulling my clothes out randomly and stuffing them into the bag.

"Daddy, I'm going to the party tonight."

He twisted with my pink lace bra clutched in his fist. I don't think he noticed, so I snatched it from him and ignored his impatient scowl.

"You aren't going to any party," he dictated. "I need to leave Illinois. I'm taking you to my brother where you'll be safe."

My head tilted as I frowned. I was used to him coming and going, but this held finality. "What do you mean you're leaving Illinois?" The thought left a bad taste in my mouth, especially since he noticeably hadn't included me.

"Why wouldn't I be safe here?" Uncle Ben was Daddy's illegitimate half-brother after my late grandfather's affair with another member of their church. I didn't know many of the details, but I knew enough to know the end of the affair had been ugly. Uncle Ben and his wife, Gretchen, kind of gave me the creeps. Their religious views bordered fanatic.

"Later, baby girl. We don't have much time." He zipped up my backpack and moved to grab my arm, but I twisted my body, escaping his hold by a mere inch. I no longer had his attention when his gaze had fallen on the boxes.

I didn't try to stop when he plucked the tiny velvet box from the bed. He gingerly flipped open the lid, and when his gaze settled on the ring, his face turned to stone. I didn't know how to explain the ring's presence or what it meant. I braced for his anger and the questions.

I didn't expect him to place the box back on the bed carefully.

He grabbed my arm before I could think to escape and pulled me from my bedroom.

I never saw my home again.

A month after Daddy drove me to Tome and left me with my aunt and uncle, I learned he had been arrested.

I never expected his victim to be his best friend.

CHAPTER TWO

MIAN

Present

R UN.

I couldn't see past my tears. I couldn't feel past my heart clawing against my chest and his blood coating my hands as I ran. I could only obey fear's demand.

I pushed at the door, but my hands slipped on the first try. *There's so much blood.* I threw my body into the door the second try. The light from the sun was an unwelcome change.

I deserved darkness.

I used my weight to push the heavy door closed, shutting in death and mayhem, as hard sobs shook my body.

I killed him.

When my legs threatened to collapse, I surrendered and slid to the ground. I'd only just closed my eyes—I wanted to let the pain consume me—but then I heard the shout.

"Princess?"

Another kind of terror seized me when I opened my eyes and found Z running toward me. When they found their brother dead, would they know it was because of me?

"Son of a bitch!" I recognized the sound of Lucas's rage, but I didn't get the chance to react. His strong hands closed around my upper arms and gently lifted me from the dirt. His fingers bit into my skin as he held me up, but fear of what would come next distracted me from the pain. "What happened?" Lucas demanded.

"Are you hurt?" Z questioned at the same time. He pulled me away from Lucas and held my face between his hands. His worried gaze searched mine. I wondered if he could read my guilt. "Where's Angel, princess?"

My gaze slid away to fix on the dirt beneath us. "Inside."

"Why is he—" He paused when his mind started piecing the answer together.

"I—" If I told them he was dead, would they see my guilt and know it was me? My eyes drifted shut as more tears began to fall, but I ripped them open again when the vision of me plunging into Angel's knife that was inside him replayed all too vividly.

"Son of a—Is that *blood*?" Lucas blurted. My attention shifted to my bloodied hands at the same time as Z. *Oh, God.* They'd know.

They probably *already* knew.

"Fuck this," I heard Lucas growl past the drumming of my heart. The cry of the metal doors as he yanked them open drowned out whatever Z was saying to me. When the warehouse doors closed again, he cursed and dropped his hands from my face to look over his shoulder.

I didn't see them until they were already surrounding me.

"Take her and don't let her out of your sight."

Killing Angel didn't set me free. I was trapped now more than ever, and my prison was an elegantly decorated bedroom. Pacing the floor, I held Caylen in my arms as he screamed at the top of his lungs. I had no idea how much time had passed since Angel's band of less than merry men took me from the warehouse. They'd brought me to the estate—the perfect prison.

Already, the walls were closing in on me, and this time, there was no chance of escape or Angel to save me. The estate sat alone on land that stretched for miles, and the house was a maze. I'd never make it to the front door before I was caught. I was willing to bet it was heavily guarded after Victor's daughter, Eliana, so easily kidnapped me from Art's home. Angel, Lucas, and Z weren't men who needed to learn a lesson twice. I didn't often see the men Angel used for protection, but I guess that was the point.

I gazed down at my son, whose cries had stopped. He stared back up at me with trusting eyes. The day he was born, I knew I would give my last breath to protect him. A tear slipped down my cheek at the reality that it just might come to that.

It was only a matter of time before Lucas and Z came

to kill me. They had to know it was me who killed Angel. Water had washed his blood from my hands but not the feeling. I'd never stop seeing the blood.

Caylen mercifully drifted to sleep just as night fell. I had finally decided to give in to my own body's demand for sleep when the door slowly opened. I thought I might already be dreaming until someone stepped into the shadow of the room. I quickly sat up just as the light flickered on.

My body tensed even when my head screamed to hide my guilt. *Maybe they didn't know anything.* Maybe they'd *never* know.

"Princess?" The voice, soft and hesitant, was one I recognized.

"Z?" I quickly scrambled from the bed. If I had to fight, I needed the advantage of being on my feet. He looked completely burned out as he moved closer. The black shirt he wore was wrinkled and discolored with the stain of blood that likely belonged to Angel.

"Are you okay?" I could hear the fatigue in his voice.

I'd never be okay again. "Are you?" I questioned, instead, while managing to mask my confusion. I should have been fighting for my life. Instead, I was pulled into his arms.

"I don't think I'm going to be okay for a long time."

I don't know why. Maybe it was the way he held me or the pain we shared, but I found myself crying against his chest. My tears mixed with Angel's blood as I poured my soul onto Z's chest.

"We should have never let him go in alone. Angel wanted us to hang back, and we just followed his orders like we always do," he admitted bitterly. "He's been up against worse and survived with barely a scratch."

I didn't speak as Z carved out pieces of my heart with his pain. For the barest of moments, I considered asking him to end my misery forever.

"I can't believe he's gone," I heard myself say. It was the truth even if I had been the one to end his life. I felt his body stiffen just before his arms fell from around me. When he took a step back, I did the same. It was the frown on his face, however, that set my heart racing.

"He's not gone, princess."

It was my turn to frown. "What are you talking about?" My voice was steadier than it should have been.

His face relaxed. "Angel's really fucked up, but the doctor said he'll live. They're keeping him sedated for a few days while he heals through the worst of the trauma."

"H—how—" I cleared my throat to heal my broken voice. "How can that be? I—" I stopped short at the genuine confusion in Z's gaze. Suddenly, I was more certain than ever that Z had no idea it was me who tried to kill Angel.

"What?" he urged when I continued to stare with my mouth open.

"I really thought he was dead," I whispered instead.

CHAPTER THREE

MIAN

E VERY STEP FELT LIKE A STEP CLOSER TO THE guillotine. I focused on keeping my breathing calm when reasoning with myself had failed. Angel wasn't going to have me killed in a hospital, but it didn't make facing him any easier.

"So, what did you do with the bodies?" I questioned once the elevators doors closed.

"We took care of it," Lucas curtly answered. He stabbed the button to take us up and didn't elaborate. A hospital wasn't exactly the place to ask these kinds of questions, but it didn't stop me from voicing them.

"And Bea?"

They glanced at each other, the silent exchange saying enough when they didn't answer. The implication sent a shudder through me. "Oh, God." I held Caylen tighter to my chest. If they could be so callous with Bea's body, what mercy would they have for my son and me?

"We didn't have a choice, princess. The cops would have asked too many questions."

"But they're going to ask questions anyway when they realize she's missing. Does Angel know what you did with his mother?" It occurred to me that I didn't have the actual details of what they'd done, but I didn't need them. Bea made her mistakes, but she deserved the respect of a burial and for those who loved her to say a proper goodbye.

"He would have done the same."

"You mean, toss his mother's body to keep anyone from pointing fingers at him when his dirt blows from under the rug?"

"Bea knew the stakes."

"Did she?" I was willing to bet my life that Bea had no idea who Art would become when she fell in love with him.

Neither of them answered as the elevator finished its ascent. The metal doors soundlessly slid open, revealing the brightly lit floor and the hospital staff moving around each other in practiced chaos.

"Come on," Lucas muttered. His hand dropped to the small of my back to steer me down the hall past nurses and doctors and concerned family members of other patients. We stopped in front of two double doors at the end of the hall. The nurse at the small nurses' nation casually glanced our way before pressing a button I couldn't see. A soft buzz sounded, and then Z quickly grabbed one of the large gray doors and pulled it open.

"Go on." Lucas pushed me forward gently.

"Aren't you guys coming with me?"

"He's still in critical condition, so only two visitors are allowed in at a time."

I glanced past the door down the short hall. There was another nurses' station to my right and rooms that lined the far wall.

"It's okay," Z implored. "Doctor says he hasn't been awake since we brought him in."

"But if he is awake," Lucas added, "I'm sure he'll want to talk." His voice held a weird note, and I could swear something peeked from behind the veil in his silver gaze. Just as quickly as it happened, however, his signature indifference returned making me wonder if I had imagined it.

"Okay," I agreed reluctantly. I had a feeling I never had a choice. The nurse was now watching us with interest, so I slowly walked through the door Z still held open.

"His room is the third on the left," Z called. I looked back in time to see him let go of the door. They both continued to watch me, Z with sympathy and Lucas with curiosity, until the door clicked shut.

I took a deep breath and returned the nurses' smiles as I passed. My skin grew colder with each step. The air smelled like death. I made the mistake of looking in the first room I passed. Inside, I glimpsed a man with a hospital tube protruding from his throat, and a frail woman bent over his bedside. Her lips moved rapidly, but no sound came. I glanced away and quickened my pace.

I reached the third door just as a young nurse, not much older than me, emerged. "Oh, hi," she greeted kindly. "Are you here to see Mr. Knight?"

"Um…yes." Her perfect smile made me fidget. I bet she'd never stabbed a man she once believed she could love. "Um…is he awake?"

"He was moments ago, but we keep him heavily medicated. I've just finished giving him a sponge bath." Was it incredibly unfair and immature for me to feel jealousy at her touching him in such an intimate way? It was her job. Point understood. But Angel was a man who could make women's hearts and other parts flutter even when he was weak.

"I guess I'll be quick then." I'd take any excuse not to stick around.

Still blocking the door, her eyes dropped to Caylen. "Oh, my goodness. Is this your brother?"

"He's my son," I said on a curt note.

Her happy mask fell for a moment as she sputtered her apology. "I'm sorry to assume. You're just so young," she quickly explained. She didn't say anything I haven't heard many times already. At the grocery store, in the doctor's office, on the street… it was always the same thing.

I was too young to be a mom.

What a shame to grow up so young.

It's not too late.

Is the father around?

Your mother and father must have been heartbroken.

"I'm not that young," I flatly stated. My driver's license may have said I was only nineteen, but my soul had already lived a thousand lifetimes.

I pushed forward, not giving her any choice but to move out of the way. The moment I was alone, I set Caylen on his feet. He didn't seem to mind at all when he immediately tottered over to Angel's hospital bed. The bed was too high for him to climb, so I picked him up and set him on the bed by Angel's side.

Stepping back, I watched as he stared at Angel. He

seemed uncertain, and a moment later, he reached out. "Anggg," he called as his tiny fist pulled at the sheet. When Angel didn't stir, Caylen tugged again. "Anggg."

Oh, God.

My vision blurred, and I quickly wiped at my tears before more could fall. I looked around, desperate to focus on anything but the bond that had been unintentionally forged between my son and my enemy. I blamed Angel. I blamed myself.

How could we have let this happen?

I was grateful the room was dark even if there was no one around to witness as I broke apart. Because I didn't know what else to do, I took a seat by his bedside and waited. Caylen's eyelids eventually grew heavy with sleep. He curled against Angel's side, leaving me alone with my thoughts. My fingers itched to draw them, but as heart-wrenchingly beautiful as they looked together, I didn't want to keep the memory. It would have only been a reminder that Angel had taken my soul.

Unable to deny the resentment burning in my heart any longer, I scooted closer and bent low until my lips were level with his ear. He might have been in a drug-induced sleep, but it didn't stop me from saying, "You were supposed to die." My woeful whisper was drowned by the steady beeping of the machines surrounding him. I watched his chest move with each breath he took as he slept. "I'm not sorry for what I did…" I'd always believed Angel was larger than life—someone who couldn't be hurt or killed. He was always so fast, so strong, so cunning. Until *I* almost made him a corpse. "It's not fair that it hurts me to see you like this." *He* was the one who betrayed *me*. "The pain is deeper than even you could have caused. It's not fair."

I shoved my hands under my thighs to keep from touching him and closed my eyes to hide my unshed tears even though we were alone. I wanted to kiss his lips and watch him come to life, but I kept my kisses. After all, this wasn't a fairy tale.

"His doctor says he'll be out for a while." The sound of Lucas's voice jarred me. Twisting to look behind me, I found him leaning a powerful shoulder against the door. "But I'm sure if the sound of your voice could numb the pain better than any drug." His eyes bore into me from across the room. The chill in his gaze couldn't be mistaken.

"I've said all I have to say to him."

"Are you sure?"

"Do you have a suggestion?" I shot back.

His smile was chilling. "I don't care to meddle in a lover's quarrel."

Wisely, I didn't take his bait, although I was pretty sure not doing so implicated me just as well. I hadn't admitted the truth to him, but I didn't call him a fool, either.

"I don't know what you mean," I attempted too late.

"Funny," he popped a stick of gum in his mouth, "I think you do."

"Can I help you with something?"

"It's been a couple of hours. I came to see if Caylen needed anything."

Caylen. Not me.

I used the moment to turn away and stroked my fingers through the soft wisps of Caylen's hair. "He's fine."

"And you?" he questioned after a brief pause.

"I'm fine, too." I kept my tone level and my gaze from straying away from my son. It worked for only a moment. I couldn't stop my head from turning, but it didn't matter.

He was gone.

I glared at the spot he had abandoned and dug my fingernails deep into the meat of my thigh. Lucas and I could never be friends, and now I knew why. He was too much like Angel. But Lucas and I didn't share a burning desire to own the other completely. It would be a lie to deny Lucas was sexy as hell. He'd also expressed with his eyes, mouth, and hands that he wouldn't mind fucking me… but he wasn't Angel, and that made his arrogance and dominant personality intolerable.

It was becoming clear that Lucas suspected something. Could he know it was me who stabbed Angel? I shook the thought off as soon as it formed. If Lucas was sure I had tried to kill Angel, he wouldn't have let me near him. He would have killed me by now or locked me in a place where I'd never see daylight again.

Either way, I had to be careful. I may not be locked behind a door anymore, but I was far from free.

Lucas didn't wait long to return. This time, he chose to sit quietly in the corner. I had lasted five minutes before his scrutiny got the better of me, and I left Angel's room in search of fresh air. I left Caylen napping by Angel's side because, even though Lucas didn't trust me, I knew he would keep my son safe.

I pushed through the double doors and headed for the elevator. I was too distracted to notice them at first as I neared the end of the hall.

"Where you headed, princess?"

My head turned sharply at the sound of Z's voice. In a hidden corner a few feet away, he stood in front of the nurse who had been attending to Angel. Her back was against the wall, and only a few inches of space separated them. I could see the blush that had yet to fade from her cheeks and took a guess at what I'd interrupted. I refrained from an eye roll at Z's lack of shame. The glossed over look in the nurse's eyes told me she was far from thinking clearly either.

"I'm taking a walk, *Zachariah*." His gaze narrowed at my use of his full name. "I need some air."

"I'll come with you."

"I prefer to be alone."

"I'll come with you," he repeated. He was already backing away from the nurse who was now pouting. She made her displeasure known when her pout turned into a frustrated glower.

I nodded to his companion. "Don't you need to finish up?" I should have been appalled that he could flirt with a nurse while his best friend was in critical care, but I had been around them long enough now to know she was somehow a pawn for something.

There was a twinkle in his eye and a smirk on his kissable lips before he turned back to the nurse. "I'll call you, Carly." He didn't waste time taking my hand and leading me past three of Angel's men and to the elevator.

"I can walk and breathe on my own, you know. I don't need you to hold my hand."

"What are you saying?" He waggled his eyebrows. "All the girls wanted to hold my hand in school."

"Look around you, Zachariah. This is real life." I pulled my hand from his and stepped inside the elevator.

He followed me in and said, "Then I should tell you that I never got to finish school. My mother was a druggie and needed to be taken care of more than I did. The system came and took me, and when I met Lucas, we ran away from the group home and lived on the streets until Art took us in." He stopped walking and turned to face me with a pitiful look in his eyes that I suspected was all an act. "So you see, I never got to hold hands with a girl and walk the school halls or steal kisses between boring classes or feel her up in the girl's—"

"Seriously, Z? All of that just to hold my hand?"

"Whatever it takes." He winked. "Besides, it's all true."

"And so you share your sad story, so girls will pity you and let you touch them?"

"Of course not." He frowned deeply, and this time, I had the feeling it was real. "I let girls touch *me*. Not the other way around." His voice had dropped to a whisper at the end. He kept his past buried deep, but it still tortured him. His easygoing nature was nothing but a camouflage for his pain.

I placed my hand on his shoulder to comfort, but the flinch he tried to hide made me drop my hand and wondered what demon rode the back of someone seemingly carefree. As the elevator descended, he backed away when he didn't think I was looking, putting an infinitesimal amount of space between us.

I was all too willing to give him the space he sought when we reached the ground floor. Witnessing him so vulnerable made me feel like I stepped out of my own skin. Surprisingly, though, he walked next to me until we stepped into the sun. "Don't stray," he ordered in a thick voice. "I need to make a phone call." He walked away assuming I'd obey. I watched as he stepped under the shadow of a tree and lifted his phone to his ear. Turning away, I drunk in the fresh air, ignoring the feel of his gaze following me.

Breathe and walk.

One breath and one step at a time.

My mind sent my life scattering in pieces for me to sort through.

Angel had framed my father.

As hurt and angry as I was at his betrayal, it was my father's betrayal that festered in my heart.

It had been hard to forgive my father for giving up even when a part of me had been afraid he really was guilty. But to find out he'd given up knowing he was *innocent*?

I wasn't sure how I could forgive him a second time.

He'd left me to the care and mercy of two people who hated me. Most of all, he'd lied to me. Somehow, I'd figure out how to visit him soon. I needed to hear the truth of his betrayal from him. I spent too many years enabling him and telling myself grief was the reason why he couldn't love me after mom had died.

So who do I blame for my spiral downward? Angel? My father? *Myself*?

"You are a beautiful one."

The familiar voice sent my heart plummeting into my stomach. Fear rooted me to the spot. I was afraid to turn around and see the monster attached to the voice. The air didn't seem so fresh anymore. It was too thick to breathe in and was pungent with the stench of evil. I looked around for the best escape route and realized I was now in an unfamiliar part of the grounds. I hadn't realized how far I'd wandered off. I could no longer see Z or the tree he stood under.

"My son isn't always intelligent," the voice continued, "but he has good taste." I felt a crawling sensation on the bare skin of my arm and realized it wasn't phantom. He was actually *touching* me. I spun around then, but the sickening feeling piercing my skin didn't dissipate when his hand fell. I opened and closed my mouth several times but words—all words—escaped me. "What am I doing here?" the senator offered.

I could only nod.

"I'm here to see Angel."

"You're out of your mind." I was startled by the threat in my own voice.

"You mistake my intentions, Ms. Ross. I simply want to call a truce. Angel is more valuable to me alive than dead."

"You mean because he's still alive, he's more valuable to you as an ally than an enemy. You're afraid of him."

Angel was undoubtedly someone to be feared, but it still amazed me that he could hold someone as powerful as a senator under his thumb. And then came the reminder that I'd tried and failed to kill him. What would he do to *me* once he'd gained his strength back? My death could reinforce their allegiance if Angel took his revenge.

"Don't be so smug, Ms. Ross. I'm not the only one vulnerable."

"But you're the only one afraid. Fear makes people desperate. It breaks them."

"And what does fear do to you, Ms. Ross?" His voice had lowered, and though no one paid us any attention, he stepped forward to ensure I would be the only one to hear his next words. "When someone threatens your life or the life of your child, will *you* break?"

His challenge hit its mark and the need to vomit built. *He's never going to leave us alone.*

"Mian!" The senator's deceiving smile dropped as he

looked over my shoulder. I knew that voice, and I knew Z was closing in. I could hear his footsteps pounding on the pavement. The senator, unfortunately, still had me under his spell.

Suddenly, I was being shoved behind a wall cloaked in a black hoodie I recognized. "You want to die, senator?" I could hear the leashed rage straining in Z's voice.

"Dear boy, it is not as if you are going to murder me in broad daylight. There are witnesses mere feet away." His gaze returned to me, his smile indulgent, and I knew it was the only reason I was still alive.

"Then you underestimate my ability to not give a fuck, Staten. What are you doing here?"

"Paying my respects."

"Angel isn't dead." He snarled. "You're going to have to pay your respects another time… if we don't kill you first."

"It is well within my power to have you arrested for threatening death to a senator." Staten coolly dangled Z's freedom in front of him like a leash.

"Then do it." Z took a step closer to the senator, and my heart stopped when I saw Staten's two-man guard reaching for their guns.

"Z, take me inside." There was no way I could risk seeing Z gunned down. I've had enough death for a lifetime. When my plea failed, I grabbed his hand to get his attention and dug my fingers into the warm skin of his palm. He trained his frown on me, but there was no longer murder in his eyes as he stared back. "I want to go inside," I repeated. "Now."

His hand tightened around mine, and after one last warning glance at the senator, he led me back inside with his body shielding me the entire way.

We didn't return to the estate. Arturo's home was much further from the hospital, but maybe that was why he chose this place for us to retreat.

"I can't believe anyone voted for that ass!" Anna paced the room that had once been my prison with a deep scowl twisting her soft features. This was becoming a too often occurrence—bad things happening to me and me bringing them to Anna's doorstep. For Christ's sake, she's just a kid. This shouldn't be her world. "What are you going to do?"

I purged my answer quickly so I wouldn't back out. "I'm going to run." After Z had recounted my run-in with the senator to Lucas, Caylen and I were driven to Crecia under guard. Running had been all I could think about since. It was scary and reckless, but it was also my salvation.

I once read in Homer's *Iliad* that it was better to flee from death than feel its grip.

"Run?" Anna squeaked.

"I can't fight, and I can't hide here. They'll find me." If I ran, it wouldn't just be the senator looking for me… Angel would also stop at nothing. The truth burned in my gut.

"But you can't run with a baby. Jesus, Mian! We can try going to the police." I studied Anna's bright blue eyes, her golden locks, and her red puffy cheeks stained with tears. She was biting her lips, the only sign she was keeping the fiercest of her emotions reigned in.

"And tell them what? That my son's father, the son of a senator, wants to kill me and my baby, and that another man wants revenge he doesn't deserve?" In a way, I envied Anna's naiveté. That level of innocence was something I would never possess again.

Her eyes filled with more tears. "It's better than never seeing you again." I forced my gaze away because I couldn't bring myself to offer promises I couldn't keep. "What if I came with you?" she offered.

"You're seventeen and still in school. Taking you with me would be stupid and selfish."

"But leaving me behind will hurt." Her voice cracked, and her body threatened to collapse. I jumped from my seat at the foot of the bed and pulled her into my arms. "It will hurt so much, Mian."

"It doesn't have to be forever," I caved. Angel lived a life that would eventually claim him, and maybe just maybe if I disappeared the senator would eventually wash his hands off me.

"Don't say that if you don't mean it."

"I mean it. Whatever the chances, I'll come back for you."

She lifted her head from my shoulder. "Where will you go?"

"I don't know, but anywhere has to be safer than Chicago." I hesitated to deliver a blow that would hurt me as much as it would her. "I won't truly feel safe unless I leave Illinois."

"But that's too far!" More of her tears fell, and I rushed to erase them.

"I have to be sure, Anna."

"You won't get far without money," she tried to reason.

"I have money," I answered. "I just have to get to it."

"What are you talking about? What money?"

"Angel gave me the money the senator paid him to kill me—"

"Oh, God," she groaned and turned so I could only see her back. I waited until her sniffling died before continuing.

"It's locked in a safe that only I know the combination to. I can get to it, but I need your help."

"I don't understand, Mian." She turned, her mouth agape and her tears dried. "What safe?"

CHAPTER FOUR

MIAN

Two Weeks Ago

I WOKE UP DISORIENTED AND SORE IN PLACES I'VE NEVER been sore before. One glance through the parted curtains and moonlit windowpanes told me it was still night. My body and weary mind begged me to drift back to sleep, but then Aaron, the senator, the money, and the touching… it all came rushing back vividly. I wasn't sure if it was the threat of death or the memory of what Angel did to me afterward that caused my heart to race.

Batting away the cobwebs of sleep, I moved to get out of a bed I should have never been in. I had one foot on the carpet when fingers grabbed my hair, and I was pulled back across the mattress until I collided with a hot wall of muscle.

Gasping from surprise, I felt his heat blanketing me.

"Where are you going?" His voice sounded like he'd been eating gravel.

"I need to check on Caylen."

"He's fine."

"I'm pretty sure that's not for you to decide." I tried to leave his bed, but he simply locked his arm around my waist. I could feel his dick pushing against my spine and every other hard part of him molding against my own body.

"I checked on him an hour ago and brought back his baby monitor. He's fine," he insisted a little more forcefully.

"How long have I been asleep?"

"A few hours," he grumbled before having the audacity to *snuggle* into me. I wanted to kick my own ass for almost leaning back into his chest. It would be exactly what he wanted—me, dependent and helpless against him. "How were you planning to get to him, anyway?"

Because Angel still kept him behind a locked door.

I didn't hesitate to answer truthfully. "Whatever it took."

He grunted his agreement because we both knew it wasn't an empty threat.

Sleeping was no longer an option, so I did a slow sweep of his room. The space took me back in time to when life honestly wasn't much simpler than it was now. I didn't find peace or a weapon I could use to knock him out. The lamp on the nightstand would do the trick, but I knew I wouldn't get to it in time. The monster would probably break my fingers before I could even wrap them around the black base with a silver skull painted on it. My gaze fell to the baby monitor lying next to the lamp. I could hear the faint sound of my baby's breaths as he slept and felt myself relax.

"If this is going to work, you're going to have to trust me." Angel's sleepy voice drowned the only sound I cared to hear.

"Well, maybe I don't want this to work." I sounded like a brat to my own ears. I had to make this work. For Caylen's sake.

"Then you'll both end up dead. Is that what you want?" It wasn't a threat.

"Of course not," I whispered defeated. He didn't respond as his arm released my body, and I listened as he heaved his powerful body from the bed. It was hard not to stare at the muscles in his ass bunch and release as he stepped into his pants. When he turned and held out his hand, it was all I could do not to retreat.

"Come with me."

I didn't move. "Why?"

"The window on my mercy is closing," he warned. I didn't know what his idea of mercy was, but I knew I would be sorry if I didn't accept it. His hand quickly closed over mine when I placed my palm in his as if he were afraid I'd change my mind and bolt. It was frightening sometimes how well he could read me.

It made it impossible to hide from him.

We started for the door when he suddenly stopped and bent to pick up his discarded shirt. "Put this on." It was then I remembered my nakedness.

I took the shirt with hesitant fingers and slipped my arms through the dark gray sleeves. He barely gave me time to button more than two buttons before he took my hand again and pulled me into the dimly lit hallway. I wanted to ask again where he was taking me, but the stiff set of his shoulders told me he wasn't in the mood to indulge me.

My heart rate picked up as we ventured through the west wing. *He was locking me back up.* I tugged against his fingers and berated myself for trusting him for even a moment. He didn't break his pace or acknowledge my resistance other than a hard squeeze of my fingers. When he stopped in front of the doors to his father's office, confusion replaced anger. My feet were like lead, so he all but dragged me inside and closed the door before letting me go and making his way across the room. His long strides ended in front of the painting of him.

"My father had this painting made weeks before Theo killed him," he said with his back facing me. "I didn't care much for the tradition, but he told me duty is something we rarely understand or agree with but something we must do all the same."

"Why are you telling me this?" I wasn't exactly in the mood for a family history lesson.

"Because the first duty he ever gave me was to protect you," he answered. "I never stopped."

"If I hadn't broken in here to rob a dead man, you and I would still be pretending we don't exist. I haven't been yours to protect for a long time, Angel."

He turned around then. His eyes were a storm, but his voice was composed as he said, "Do you think your life would have been any better if I hadn't stayed away? I claimed you when you were sixteen fucking years old. Your father would be in a grave instead of chains if he had tried to say otherwise." He took slow, careful steps toward me, but I refused to back down. "My ring would be on your finger, you'd be in my bed, and Caylen would be mine." There was a deep ache low in my belly that I shouldn't feel. I couldn't deny his words because I knew those words were true. He would have claimed me, and for a while, I would have believed it was what I wanted. "You wouldn't have wanted for anything except me. You would have been miserable. Stuck in a big castle in a faraway land with only your dreams to keep you company."

"Because that's what your father did to your mother?"

His eyes narrowed. "You know the tale."

"Maybe it's just the ending I don't quite get."

"As it turned out, it wasn't a fairy tale after all. Happily ever after isn't real." He turned and stalked back to the painting. This time, he lifted it from the wall with little effort and set it aside, revealing the safe that started this war when I broke into it. He keyed in the combination before pressing a few more buttons.

"Come here," he ordered with his back still turned. I approached with wary steps as I considered what he intended to show me.

What if it was the book? The perfect twist to a bad dream?

I closed my eyes and pinched myself.

When I opened them again, Angel was still there brimming with deadliness, and I was still his captive. He stepped around me, placing me between him and the safe.

In the safe wasn't a leather bound book inscribed with two-hundred years of deadly secrets. Inside were piles of neatly arranged stacks of money.

This definitely wasn't a dream.

The book was gone, the senator wanted me dead, and my son and I would never be safe.

"What is this?"

"It's the money the senator paid me to kill you. All accounted for and yours. All it needs is a code to protect it."

I turned away from the money to look into Angel's eyes. There was no deception in the mahogany depths, but still, I wavered. "What do you want?"

"Trust."

Instead of feeling free, I felt the walls closing in and my shackles tightening. To bestow trust is welcome deception. What if Angel's offer of control was nothing more than an illusion to gain my trust? He was willing to risk losing so I wouldn't fight him.

What would he be willing to risk so I wouldn't *win*?

I turned away so he couldn't see my doubt. I closed the safe door and keyed in a new code that only my eyes could see.

Angel wasn't the only one who could create illusions.

CHAPTER FIVE

MIAN
Present

M Y ARMS STRAINED AS I LIFTED THE PAINTING OF
Angel. Deja vu slammed into me when I almost
toppled over under the weight. I managed to hold
my footing and blinked away at the sting of sweat pouring
into my eyes. I didn't have much time to get into the safe
and out of the house with Caylen. Anna was currently
keeping Z and two of Angel's guards distracted, but it
wouldn't be long before Z would get suspicious. Lucas
had fortunately stayed behind at the hospital with most of
Angel's guard.

My fingers trembled as I keyed in the combination I
set the night Angel took me to his bed for the first time.
It took me three tries to calm my nerves enough to key
in ten-thirty-one—his birthday, and the night my world

crumbled around me.

I unhitched one of Angel's old backpacks from my shoulder and quickly filled it with money.

My money.

Caylen's money.

The money Senator Staten paid to have us killed rather than use to help feed his grandchild. The reality that my son shared blood with someone so evil made me sick to my stomach.

Once the safe was empty, I zipped up his ratty backpack and quietly stepped down from the chair. I didn't have time to right everything, so I didn't bother. Angel would know I'd been here anyway. It was the very risk he took when he bargained for my trust, and I would never in a million years feel bad that he lost.

As I slipped through the office doors and made my way back to the guest room, I listened to the sound of Anna's giggles and the chatter as it drifted up the stairs. Every now and then, Z's amused voice would respond to something she said.

Caylen was sound asleep as I grabbed as many diapers, bottles, and formula as could I fit in the limited space of the backpack before carefully wrapping him in a blanket. I said a prayer he wouldn't wake before slipping out of the nursery. I strained to hear their voices, but in the matter of minutes it took for me to gather the supplies, the house had fallen deathly quiet. Part of the plan was for Anna to ask for a ride back home with the excuse that I had gone to bed early with a migraine, so I wasn't alarmed by the silence. Z wouldn't bother me until morning and Anna would be safely home. Before we put our plan into motion, she'd called Joey, who had agreed to pick me with the promise that he'd get a second date with Anna. It was even more difficult this time to convince her even though she'd swear it wasn't because of a certain brooding criminal with silver eyes and a killer smile.

I was able to slip from the house and immediately shivered from the cool night air. Wrapping Caylen's blankets tighter, I escaped into the night. I made sure to stay in the shadows as I made my way to the end of the driveway where Joey would be waiting for me on the other side of the gate. The path seemed to stretch forever, and every other step, I expected someone to jump out of the shadows to catch me. The gate finally came into view, and when I squinted, I could just make out the rusted metal of Joey's car waiting along the edge. He wisely kept the engine and the headlights off, which meant Anna told him just enough to keep him smart.

I quickened my step, eager for freedom, and after some fumbling, found the button to release the gate. The soft purr of the gate's automatic locks made me cringe.

I only had to walk through the gates to be free. Even if Z noticed now, it would already be too late.

I waited only long enough for the gates to part enough for me to slip through, but as soon as I did, the hairs on my skin raised. I stood in place as I looked around. Nothing immediately seemed out of the ordinary, but I couldn't ignore the warning trickling down my spine.

The clouds chose this moment to part. The moonlight shined over Joey's car, revealing an empty driver's seat. Slowly, I took a step back. The gates were nearly shut, but the gap between them would be enough for me to turn back if I hurried.

"Where are you going, princess?" Z stepped from the

shadows just as I was ready to bolt. He didn't appear angry or threatening, but his calm proved just as intimidating as I sunk further into fear.

"I'm leaving."

"Why?" he asked as if I were visiting for summer vacation instead of being his brother's captive. When I didn't answer him, he turned his head back to the shadows. "Bring them out."

Shuffling that sounded suspiciously like to a struggle followed. The next moment, I heard a soft cry followed by a masculine grunt and then watched in horror as my friends were forced from the shadows. All I could do was face the danger I'd put them in. Anna stood in front of the two guards while Z pushed Joey to his knees and promptly placed a gun to his head.

"Zachariah, don't do this."

He ignored my plea and pressed the gun harder against Joey's head. "What makes you think leaving will keep you safe? He'll find you."

"Maybe he won't, maybe he will, but I have to try. The only thing I know right now is that I'm a sitting duck. Angel can't protect me."

Z shook his head. "I wasn't talking about the senator, princess."

"Angel won't come looking for me," I said in denial. "He promised me I wasn't a prisoner."

"But he never said you could leave, either."

The knowledge that I had been right about Angel made me sick to my stomach. I held tight to Caylen to keep him secure as I trembled. He remained fast asleep, blissfully unaware of the danger.

"Don't hurt them."

"I won't hurt them, princess. Or you." Shrugging, he lowered his gun by his thigh, but his finger never moved far from the trigger.

"Then let us go."

I didn't expect his features to soften. He looked more like the Z I knew and thought I could trust. "If I let you go and something happens to you, he'll kill me."

I shook my head. "You're his brother. That means something to him."

"But you mean more."

"What if you're wrong?"

We stared at each other for a moment that lasted too long before he finally spoke. I knew I'd won when his shoulders relaxed and he pinched the bridge of his nose.

"Go." I didn't hesitate. I rushed to help my friends but stopped dead when Z's gun was back at Joey's skull. "But they stay."

"I won't leave them."

"You'll leave them because that is the deal, princess."

Silently, I pleaded for mercy, but when his gaze hardened, it was my turn to accept defeat. I could never run and leave my friends behind.

"Princess…" I brushed away the soft caress of his voice and glared. "Angel won't stop looking for you," he continued unfazed. "He'll come after them anyway, but if I offer him two bread crumbs, there will be less bloodshed."

That may be true, but he was asking me to offer up my friends like sheep for the wolves. Neither of us moved. Neither of us broke focus. He'd made his compromise. I just couldn't make mine.

"Go." Anna's whisper faded into the dark, but I heard it as if she had screamed the command. I was taken aback by the fearless gleam in her bright, round eyes as she said, "We'll be okay, but you won't. *Go.*"

I shook my head. "I'm not leaving you. It's not worth it."

"That's for us to decide," Joey argued through gritted teeth. "Just go."

I shook my head again and backed away until the iron gate forced my feet to stop. No matter how much fear pleaded with me to run, loyalty wouldn't allow me to leave them.

"This is your last chance, princess."

I didn't recognize my voice in the cry I released when he pressed the muzzle of his gun harder against Joey's head.

"Run…or he dies."

CHAPTER SIX

ANGEL
Three Years Ago

DIDN'T WANT TO SAY I HAD BUTTERFLIES, BUT THAT'S what the light feeling in my stomach felt like—a million butterflies.

Little Mian Ross gave me fucking butterflies.

Smiling around the blunt I had lit as I stepped outside, I dropped down on the stoop of the brownstone I now lived in alone.

Tonight wouldn't be special because it was my birthday or because I was finally taking my place as the Knight. No, tonight would be special because I would finally have the only two things I ever wanted: power and Mian.

This morning, my father and godfather sat me down and told me that I would not only protect the family but the girl who consumed my every waking thought. I will give her my name and my life if need be. He went as far as to threaten my crown, but I knew it was to keep Theo in the dark about my feelings for his teenage daughter. I was taking her with or without her father's permission. My father had known all along and had found a way to give me what I wanted without bloodshed. Theo accepted everything my father offered him with the promise that I wait until she turned eighteen before I actually touched her.

I may not have been able to keep from feeling for his kid, but I was still very much aware of my physical boundaries. Theo told me he would be bringing her to the party tonight. Of course, I hadn't bothered to let him know I already invited her. I was too close to making her mine to screw it up now.

The party would be starting in a few hours so I made a few calls. It wasn't just my birthday party or transfer of power. It was also an engagement party, and my kid fiancée would need a dress. I smiled again as I took a drag from my blunt.

"What the fuck are you smiling about?" Lucas spat with a grin. I was so caught up in my head that I hadn't noticed my two best friends approaching. They hadn't been allowed at the brownstone when Mian lived here, and now that she was gone, they almost never leave.

"I'm engaged." They both laughed it off without even considering that I might be serious. "I'm not joking." I enjoyed watching the grins on their faces slowly fall and smiled harder at their matching expressions of horror.

"Dude… why?" Z questioned. It wasn't often Z didn't have a smile on his face. This was one of those rare moments.

"She's a birthday gift from pops."

"So, basically, he's making you marry some girl?" Lucas was the shrewdest of our group, and while most cowered under his interrogation, I met his gaze.

"Sort of. He's protecting his interests."

"Why aren't you upset? Is she hot?" Z's grin was back full force.

"Wait…" Lucas' eyes narrowed. "Is this fiancée the mystery girl you won't tell us anything about?" I passed him the cannabis-filled cigar since he looked like he needed it more than I did.

"Holy shit," Z exclaimed. "It's her, isn't it?" His bright green eyes shone even brighter with mischief. "You got her knocked up, didn't you? All that in-house pussy you've been secretly getting finally caught up to you."

If he weren't my best friend, I would have decked him. He threw up his hands and backed off at my look. "She's not pregnant," I answered eventually. "I never touched her." But my dick sure wishes I had.

"What's her name?" I shook my head at Lucas's question. "We still can't even know her name?" Mian has been my secret for six years, and I selfishly wanted to keep her that way for a little bit longer.

"She'll be at the party tonight. You'll meet her then." To save myself from more questions, I made excuses about shit to do and left my friends on the stoop smoking the last of my stash.

I was five minutes from Crecia when my phone rang. There was a sinking feeling in my gut when I read the name on the caller id.

"Hey." I figured now would be the time Theo would threaten me regarding the well-being of his daughter… off the record. It was cool. I had a few things to say too… off the record.

"Son." I sat up straighter at the unfamiliar grimness in Theo's voice.

"What's going on?"

"I wanted you to hear this from me before…" His voice trailed off, and all I could do was listen to the broken cries of a man I considered indestructible. It was the moment I knew whatever had broken him would do the same to me. I was already doing the impossible and trying to take back words I hadn't even heard yet. "Your father is dead, Angeles." There was a brief pause as my mind replayed these four words. "I'm sorry."

And just like that, the line died.

Soon after, my phone was ringing again. This time, I answered without checking because I already knew who it would be.

"Oh, God. Angel," my mother wailed. "Arturo is dead!" Before I could speak, she cried words I never expected to hear. "I killed him. I killed him! God, please help me."

The line didn't die this time, and my mother's screams continued. The emotions you're expected to feel when someone you love is killed—sorrow, anger, vengeance— eluded me. I was numb. I don't remember hanging up on my hysterical mother. I don't remember the next five minutes. I don't even remember walking up the stairs and finding my father lying in a pool of his own blood.

Years ago, my father insisted my mother learn to shoot if an enemy were ever bold enough to knock down his front door. To my father's pleasure, my mother had been a natural shot. I'm sure it made his many days away free of guilt. He'd gotten her a revolver since they were easiest to operate, and made sure she stayed in practice. It was because of his insistence that my mother's aim for his heart was true, and laying a couple of feet from the door was my mother's revolver.

My next move should be to avenge my father's death, but killing my mother would never be an option. I could only protect her from what happens next. My father's death wouldn't be an insignificant event overlooked by the police.

There were too many of them in his pocket.

"Sir, I've called the cops," an unfamiliar voice called. I turned and found a short African American woman in a white dress shirt and black tie. She looked scared as her eyes nervously shifted from me to the corpse behind me. "They're on their way."

"Who are you?"

"I'm Tanya. I'm filling in for Milly while she's on vacation." I shut my eyes tight to hide the internal war inside my head. If she was just a temp, then my father likely hadn't bothered to pay her off, which made her a witness. "I saw a man leave—"

She stopped speaking with a squeak when my eyes opened. "What man?"

"I'm sorry. I—I don't know." Her voice carried a desperate note now. "He was tall, light brown hair, green eyes…" Her frown deepened as she described Theo. "He was the one who shot Mr. Knight. He left in such a hurry after I heard the gunshot. Your poor mother was so hysterical. She must have witnessed the entire thing."

I wasn't sure if it was shock or betrayal responsible for the pain assaulting every cell in my body, but I recognized rage. Theo had run off rather than stand by my father's side, and I planned to find out why. "Thank you, Tanya."

Her eyes had glistened with sympathy before she hurried back downstairs.

I was remodeling the pieces of the puzzle as I calmly raided my father's stash of sedatives he used when he needed a job done quietly and headed back downstairs. My mother was still on the couch crying quietly. Tanya was kneeling as she rubbed my mother's back consolingly. As politely and unassuming as I could muster, I asked her to return to her duties until the police arrived. Once she was gone, I took the unknown woman's place, but I didn't offer my mother comfort. I lifted her head and gently stuck the needle in her neck. As I injected my mother with the sedative, I whispered three words in her ear.

Theo killed him.

Three months later, we sent an innocent man to jail.

I didn't feel the pain of my father's death until Theo was safe behind bars, and I was forced to accept that I wouldn't be able to avenge my father for a long time. I didn't feel guilt for what I'd done until three years later when I looked into the broken eyes of little Mian Ross.

CHAPTER SEVEN

ANGEL
Present

"WHERE IS SHE?" I WATCHED MY BROTHERS, MEN with the heart of a lion, fidget under my interrogation. I'd woken up to an empty hospital room and no memory of how I made it here alive. Lucas and Z had been MIA, but I'd learned half my men were on guard and now I knew why.

"We don't know," Z mumbled.

"She fucking ran," Lucas snarled. The phantom fist around my heart loosened. She wasn't dead.

"Why?" *Because she tried to kill you.* I waited for one of them to answer, but neither of them spoke a word. Z looked uncertain, and Lucas looked ready to explode, which meant they both knew something, but they were holding back.

"What do you know?" My attention focused on Lucas, targeting him first. "What are you hiding from me?"

"I could ask you the same," he shot back as he crossed his arms.

"Excuse me?"

"Who stabbed you, Angel?"

"Eliana." The lie quickly fell from my lips, but it was obvious they didn't believe me when Z's gaze narrowed, and Lucas scoffed.

"Why are you lying?" Lucas accused.

"Who are you to tell me I'm lying?"

"Your brother!" he roared. "She tried to kill you, and you're still protecting her."

"You don't know what the fuck you're talking about."

"Angel," Z called with less hostility. "We found Eliana dead ten feet from where you were with a perfect shot to the head."

"And it was *your* knife that had been used on you. It's also funny that the tape had been sliced clean through. Only a knife could have done that."

They watched me, waiting for me to trust them with the truth that would condemn her. I couldn't do it. They were my brothers, but Mian was… complicated.

Someday, we would finally destroy each other.

"Tell the attending he has ten minutes to have my discharge papers ready, or I'm leaving without them."

"You lost too much blood, and you'll tear your stitches."

"Am I a pussy? Have I *ever* been a pussy?" Neither one of them offered an answer, but one wasn't needed. "Brothers…" I stood carefully from the hospital bed. There was a burning pain in my gut that I ignored as I rocked to steady myself on my feet. "We have a runaway to find."

"We can't."

With barely suppressed rage I said, "Why the fuck not?"

"Because an hour ago your family showed up demanding answers."

Two days later, I sat at the head of the table in the estate's library. Lucas and Z stood as silent forces behind me while each presumptive heir surrounded the table. This was the last place I wanted to be with Mian on the run and me still in pain, but this meeting could not be avoided.

I was on trial.

"I assume Victor and Eliana are dead." Alistair was the first to speak after I gave a quick recount of what had happened four days ago. He was a direct descendant of Alexander, which made him as much an enemy as an ally. His entire line resented mine ever since my great-grandfather, Adan, took Archibald's life and inherited Alexander's legacy.

I met his assessing gaze. "You assume correct, cousin."

"We were sorry to hear about your mother," stated Aldric, a descendant of Meredith. I nodded, believing his sincerity.

"Thank you."

Reginald, a descendant of Alexander and first in line to succeed me, leaned forward, and I knew whatever he had to say would tempt me to kill him. "Why do you think Victor would betray your father after all these years? First, there was Theo," he continued before I could speak, "and now Victor. I'm not sure the family shouldn't be concerned about the betrayal your father's rule has bred."

"Well, my father doesn't rule anymore. I do."

"Yes, but I'm not sure how far you've actually fallen, Angeles."

More than a dozen gazes settled on me, waiting. "If your next stipend isn't to your satisfaction, we can revisit this conversation."

"The money is good. I cannot deny you that accomplishment, but it's not enough. We need protection and to believe you won't be the end of Alexander's legacy."

"Has anyone broken down your door and harmed you?"

"Fortunately, that has not occurred…yet."

"Well, then you shouldn't incite fate. Victor kidnapped my mother so he could get me alone and kill me." It was at least part truth. "He's been taken care of without any harm to the family."

"Except your mother," he cruelly reminded. "Or have you forgotten?"

"She was also Victor's *wife*." No one regretted leaving her vulnerable to that asshole more than I did. Lucas and Z shifted behind me. One word from me, and they would make sure Reginald didn't overstep again.

"Reginald, I believe you're being a bit too hard on the boy," Alistair valiantly admonished. "Shit happens."

"Yes. Just as long as Angel understands that *shit*," he mocked, "cannot continue to happen. I see no reason to continue this meeting."

Augustine and I locked gazes. He rolled his eyes with a smirk as our kin continued to argue. I held back my own and called the meeting to an end. It would take more than the actions of a traitor to dethrone me. Augustine, the descendant of Meredith, hung back as the rest of them filed out. We collided in a brotherly hug and exchanged grins when we pulled apart. "Try not to take their scrutiny too personally," he said the moment we were alone. "They're time is running out. They'll look for any excuse to take your place."

"And you, cousin? Don't you want to reap the glory of being the Knight?"

He shrugged. "I've got my own thing going, and I answer to no one."

I wanted to ask about his little venture, but I knew he wouldn't tell me anything even if I ordered him. He was even more stubborn than I was. "How is your mother?" His shoulders relaxed at my change in subject. "I noticed she didn't come."

"You know Mother. She hates anything to do with Alexander and his legacy."

"She would have run away with you years ago if Alan hadn't kept her under lock and key." Augustine may not have wanted me dead, but his grandfather was another story. I could never prove my suspicions, but I was sure he had been responsible for a couple of the attempts on my life. When you were a crime lord, people tried to kill you. Every job had its hazards, but when treachery is rooted from within your circle, it was more than just a hazard. It was a goddamn problem.

If I ever did prove Alan was behind the hit, I would have no choice but to make an example out of him. It was the very reason my friendship with Augustine skated on very thin ice. Killing his grandfather would no doubt make us enemies.

"Alan won't just need to kill me for the legacy."

Augustine chuckled. "That old bastard doesn't have much time left, and he knows it. You better watch your back," he warned good-naturally, although we both knew it wasn't an empty warning. Alan wasn't the only one who wanted control. He was just one of the few willing to kill me for it.

Nodding to Lucas and Z, who watched our exchange silently, he didn't stick around after that.

"I don't trust him," Lucas said as soon as the library door closed behind Augustine.

Z, still staring at the door, nodded his agreement. "He's got too many secrets."

"Let him have his secrets for now. It's not him I'm worried about. Reginald is getting bolder in the quest to dethrone me. I want you to find out what he's up to." They didn't hesitate and stood from the table. "Oh, and Z?" I called, stopping him in his tracks. Lucas paused too, his frown deepening. "Where are they?"

"Where is she, Anna?" I stood in front of Mian's friends ignoring the burning pain in my gut and praying I had the patience not to harm them. Mian would never trust me again if I did. Maybe it was why both of them were refusing to talk.

By now, I would have started lopping off body parts when someone refused to talk. Because they meant something to her, I held back. Z stood back observing with a careful eye. Lucas, however, never strayed too far from Anna. He stood behind her seemingly detached, but I knew instinct would make him protect her from me, brother or not. I would have questioned his loyalty if Mian hadn't stirred the same need in me.

"She's far away from you, and that's good enough for me." Her arms closed tight over her chest as she pierced me with her stare. Her friend, however, didn't display the same bravado.

"And what about you?" I challenged as I moved to stand in front of him. "Is dying good enough for you?"

"Don't say anything," Anna ordered. One look from me had her lips pressing in a tight line and the color draining from her face.

I gripped the back of his neck and leaned into him as I brought my knife to the side of his throat. "So?"

"I don't know where she went," he stumbled. "She just took off."

"It was *your* car she *just took off* in. Where were you planning to take her, hero?" I pressed the knife against his skin until I saw the first drop of blood.

"To the bus station and that's it. They didn't tell me anything else. I swear!" Anna's face twisted with disgust when she turned her glower on Joey. Fortunately for him, I believed him.

"Do you believe us now," Anna demanded. I shrugged and put my knife away as I stepped back.

"Are you going to let us go?" Joey questioned with hop.

When I shook my head. She surged forward as if to attack, but Lucas's hands closing over her arms stopped her. "Why not?" she growled. "You have no reason to keep us."

"You're her friends. She trusts you, which makes you valuable to me."

"My mom will be looking for me," Joey threatened as one of my men dragged him off.

"Then you better pray for her sake that she doesn't find you."

Another stepped forward to take Anna away, but one look from Lucas had him quickly retreating.

"Why can't you just leave her alone?" Anna fought to free herself from Lucas's hold. He looked as if he had more trouble keeping control of his patience. "You're going to get her killed!" Lucas tossed her over her shoulder and stormed from the office. We all listened as she spewed curses and threats until a door slammed, cutting off her screams.

"We need to talk," Z spoke from the corner. He had been silent as always during the interrogation, but this time I knew was different.

"Yes, we do." I leaned back in my chair and regarded him. "You let her go."

"I did."

"Why?" I forced myself to keep a level head long enough to hear his answer. It had better be good.

"Because I thought she was better off away from Chicago."

"Why shouldn't I kill you, brother?"

To my surprise, he cracked a smile. "She had it on good authority that you wouldn't."

"And why is that?"

"Because I mean just as much to you as she does." He waited, willing me to tell him if she had been right. His betrayal made me reluctant to confess the truth.

"Find her, Z, because if you don't, brother or not, I'm killing you."

I held my head in my hand once I was alone and breathed through the pain in my abdomen. Moments later, my phone was ringing, and I thought about letting it go to voicemail when I noticed the number of the family attorney.

"This is Knight."

"Mr. Knight, I'm so happy to catch you. I have some additional paperwork that we forgot to transfer to you during the reading of the will."

"What paperwork?"

"Your marriage certificate."

"My what?"

"After your father's death, we were entrusted by your grandfather to keep the certificate in our possession. Of course, now that you've inherited from him, the certificate can be transferred to your possession if you wish." I could tell by his tone that he found it all strange, but it wasn't his job to ask questions beyond legal necessity. "I assume you were aware of this?"

I was ready to tell him it was a mistake, that I couldn't be married. The only girl I ever intended to marry disappeared three years ago until she'd broken into my father's home and forced me to kidnap her son. But just as the words formed, I quickly pieced the puzzle together and realized what my father had done.

There could only be one name next to mine on that certificate.

CHAPTER EIGHT

MIAN

R UNNING WAS EXHAUSTING, BUT I KNEW IT WOULDN'T be easy. Two weeks have passed since I took Joey's '96 Caprice and left my friends at the mercy of my monsters in order to save them.

I didn't know which direction was safe or how far to go. I just ran. For the first three days, when I couldn't reach Anna or Joey, I considered turning back around and shoving Z's deal down his throat.

Somewhere in Kentucky, I finally learned from Anna that Angel had let them go after threatening to cut Joey's tongue out if he told anyone. I didn't want to be grateful to Angel for anything, but I was glad he hadn't hurt them. I had warned Anna that letting them go didn't mean he wasn't watching. I learned that the hard way when he took my son.

Paranoia forced me to hide in a different town every day for a week until I mentally collapsed in Mosset, North Carolina. The town had a population of four hundred and thirty-eight people in the middle of nowhere. There was nothing but swamp and woodlands surrounding three sides of the small town and only one road in and out. It wasn't big enough to get lost in, so I could only hope it was small enough to keep us under the radar.

I've also found that the people you meet in small towns are the friendliest I've ever met… even if they do ask a lot of questions. The first day of asking around, Caylen and I were offered a room above a small diner in the center of town. The room wasn't able to fit more than a bed, armoire, and chair. There was a small bathroom attached and a window overlooking the gas station across the street. Overall, it was clean, warm, and cheaper than a hotel.

Since I had waitressing experience, and the owners, Rebecca and Sam, needed help, they offered me the place in exchange for working a few nights in the diner. Without much being said, they also agreed to keep my employment and tenancy under the table. It was unsettling to think they knew I was running from something.

Mid-afternoon of my third day in town, Rebecca had demanded I stop looking over my shoulder. "Don't you worry about anything, missy. If he comes walking through that door…" she had pulled a huge shotgun from under the counter, "I'll blow him right back through it."

Rebecca Donaldson reminded me of a little dainty fairy… with claws and sharp teeth. The top of her head, covered with auburn hair, came only to my chin. She was curvy everywhere and had a commanding personality that she wielded on everyone in her path. Her husband, Sam, was a gentle giant and her complete opposite. Where Becky was small and plump, he was tall and hard. He was also the meeker and quieter of the two. I found it fascinating that, even though Becky was domineering and wild, with one shared look between the two, Sam could tame her.

He also hadn't seemed at all surprised by his wife's threats to murder a man on my behalf.

"I didn't say—"

"Oh, missy, you didn't have to. You don't get to me by age without learning a few things. Hell, every time that door opens you look ready to bolt. With that babe in your arm, it's obvious you're on the run from your man."

I'd started to argue, but Sam's gentle pat on my hand stopped me. "Don't bother arguing with my Becky. She's stubborn and is always right."

I had the feeling he was laying it on for her bene-fit. When she walked away triumphant, and he winked, I couldn't help but laugh.

Becky had given me a few days to get settled before showing me the ropes and putting me to work. The diner closed at nine every night and opened at six every morn-ing. Their rush, which wasn't nearly as heavy as the diners in Chicago were, only came during the lunch hour. I was more than able to handle it with my hands tied. Rebecca called me a godsend. I didn't know about that, but the work kept my mind off what waited for me in Chicago. Samantha, their twelve-year-old daughter, happily agreed to watch over Caylen whenever I worked dinner shifts. She said it was a better deal than working in the diner. When Samantha was in school, I'd keep Caylen on the far end of the bar away from the customers, although most of the women in town couldn't seem to stay away from him. I've had countless offers to babysit already.

By my second week in Mosset, I managed to find a routine and a small sense of safety. I would always be looking over my shoulder, but for the moment, I didn't have to run.

It was another week, while I was getting ready for my shift when I broke down and called Anna. "I was getting worried!" Anna shrieked the moment she picked up. "How could you go so long without calling?"

"I'm sorry. I had to make sure it was safe. Are you okay?"

"No, I'm not okay." I could hear her pout through the phone. "You almost gave me a heart attack, like, every single day. You can't just disappear. You have to call."

"I'm sorry," I repeated. What else could I say? It was hard to make someone understand your paranoia if they didn't fit in your shoes.

"You're not the only one scared, Mian. *Call.*"

"I will."

She didn't respond, so I listened to her sniff and huff while I searched for an excuse to hang up. "So where are you?" she finally spoke.

"Anna, I don't think—"

"No," she growled before I could turn her down. "What if something happens to you and Caylen? I won't know where to tell the police to look."

I gave in partly because she was right, but more because I felt guilty for scaring her this much. "North Carolina," I conceded. "Mosset is just a tiny piece of the world, Anna. You'd hate it." Anna was an undeniable city girl. "I got a job at the only diner in town and a place to stay. The people are so nice. I feel safe here."

"Are you sure?"

"I'm sure. No one will find Mian Ross here. To the good people of Mosset, I'm Alison Hill."

"Okay, *Alison*," she teased. "I love you. *Call*," she warned again.

CHAPTER NINE

ANGEL

I WAS GROWING IMPATIENT. LIKE A THIEF IN THE NIGHT, Mian had fled, and money, threats, and favors couldn't find her. Her little friends were loyal to a fault, even when I threatened death, but they were also her weakness, and I intended to keep them close.

After three weeks of no trail, trace, or cookie crumb, I paid a visit to the prison. Theo hadn't had a visitor since I told him his daughter had a price on her head, but maybe he knew where she would go.

"What are you doing here?" His greeting was about as inviting as crotch rot and he looked like shit. The bruises might have faded since I last saw him, but the weight he lost and the fatigue clouding his eyes were obvious.

"You look like shit."

"What do you want?" he demanded more forcefully.

"Your daughter is missing." I watched his pale face whiten even more. Unfortunately, I couldn't relish his suffering given the reason.

"You were supposed to protect her."

"Victor got to her. She vanished after that." I left out the part about her almost killing me.

"Victor," he whispered. His gaze lost focus as his shoulders trembled. His head lowered until his forehead hit the table with a harsh thud. Staring at the back of his head, I considered putting a bullet in it—damn the consequences. When he finally lifted his head again, his eyes were rimmed with red. "This is all my fault."

I ignored his plea for pity, and said, "He's dead."

"Then where is my daughter?"

"If I knew, I wouldn't be here." The day he had been led away, I dreamt the next time we met would be the day I put a bullet in *his* heart. "Where would she go, Theo?"

"I don't know."

"Think hard. The price on her head is high. There will be people who won't stop to find her." *Including me.*

"How do I know that debt isn't being paid to you?"

I ignored him again. "Who did she run to?"

"She has no one!" He then pointed his finger accusingly. "But she should have had *you*! I gave her to you because I thought you would protect her despite what happened between me and your father."

"She was always mine. My father knew I wouldn't let you stand in my way, so he made you an offer you wouldn't refuse. You should have thanked him instead of getting him killed."

"You don't know everything."

"I know about the marriage you and my father forged

between Mian and me."

Regret shone in his eyes as he shook his head and gazed at me with pity. "When it comes to Mian, you're a bigger fool than I had ever been."

"I know it was my mother who pulled the trigger, but you aren't innocent of what happened that night."

"He fucked my wife, but did you know he killed her too?"

I didn't react even as shock and suspicion ran rampant. "Your wife died from cancer."

"My wife had cancer, but she *died* from suffocation. All this time, I believed cancer took her earlier than we expected, but the truth was, he not only fucked my wife, he had her killed. Victor told me everything, and Art confessed that night. Ceci threatened to expose them if he didn't leave Bea, so he had her killed."

"Why did my mother kill him?"

"Why do you think? She overheard us. I went there to kill your father, Angel. If your mother hadn't—"

"You don't need to explain," I coldly interrupted. "I know what you went there to do." It was the other reason I didn't hesitate to frame him for my father's murder.

"What would *you* have done?" he boldly questioned.

"Nothing." He looked surprised by my answer. "*My* wife wouldn't need to fuck another man."

"Love is fickle," he shot back.

"Except your wife didn't love you when she spread her legs for my father. She probably never did. I was there when my mom told Mian about their history. Can you guess why she married you?" We both knew Ceci didn't marry Theo for love. He had been her ticket closer to my father's heart. She used him.

He cleared his throat and looked down at the table. "The reasons don't matter anymore. They're both dead."

"Your daughter will be too if I don't find her first."

He sighed, and for a moment, I thought I won. "Then so be it. She'll finally be free of you." He got up and walked away.

"He was either telling the truth, or he really did condemn his daughter to die," Lucas mused.

"Do you think Art really had Mian's mother killed?" Z questioned without a note of doubt. What Theo claimed was exactly what my father would have done to keep his secrets swept under the rug.

Lucas and Z knew it was my mother who shot my father. They had been the only ones I could trust with the lie I told to protect her. It hadn't mattered in the end. They'd found Theo as guilty as I and wanted him dead, as well. After all, he'd said himself he had gone there to kill my father. My mother's state of mind was never the same after she blew that hole in my father's heart... so I gave her another truth to live.

I shrugged my answer. My father would have done anything necessary to protect the family he neglected, but Theo's last day breathing was circled in blood. He had every reason to lie.

Would I still kill him without knowing the full truth?

Absolutely.

Theo knew the stakes just as I did.

"Anna's getting a call," Z suddenly announced. Before we let them go, he bugged Anna's phone, so we could monitor her calls. It's been more than three weeks since Mian's last call, and I had begun to think I underestimated her.

We were all tense as we listened to Anna tear Mian a new one. I held in a laugh at Mian's tone. I could tell she was frustrated with Anna's fussing but didn't want to upset her anymore. The exasperation on Lucas's face as Anna shrieked and shouted also made it hard to keep my composure. I was just glad she was his problem instead of mine. When the little bulldozer convinced Mian to tell her where she is, humor faded, and I went on alert.

Z didn't waste any time pulling up a map and finding the small blip I would never have thought to look if Anna hadn't led us right to her.

"Look's like we're heading to the swamps, boys." Lucas and Z wore triumphant grins while I sat as still as a statue.

Gotcha.

"The rock she crawled under is small as fuck," Z complained while tapping the screen of his phone. "There aren't even five hundred people living there. If we go there asking questions, she's going to know we're there before we even get to her."

"You don't need to ask questions. She's working at a diner. A town that small, my guess is you two won't have to look too hard."

"Wait… you're not coming?" Lucas baffled expression was priceless.

"I'm not the only one looking for her. I need to keep eyes on Staten. I can't do that while chasing her."

"Son of a bitch… Going after Mian will lead him right to her."

"Precisely." Their confused looks were expected. "When she sees you, she'll try to run, but if she knows the senator has found her too—"

"She's smart enough to know her chances are better with us," Lucas finished for me.

"There's one more thing." They leaned forward, taking cues from my tone. "She can't know I sent you."

My request earned a rare scowl from Z. "How the fuck will we get her to believe that?"

CHAPTER TEN

MIAN

I QUICKLY LEARNED THAT NOTHING EVER HAPPENS IN Mosset, North Carolina. Everyone here was born and raised here. There had been a few who hadn't been happy with small town living and made it out, but no one ever *moved to* Mosset. I was the first. The day after I showed up, I even found my picture and a three-sentence story of my arrival in the town newspaper. I had a panic attack in the middle of the diner, which had taken Becky almost an hour to calm me. No one here knew Mian Ross existed, and the senator would never bother himself to read a small town newspaper.

"So, did you hear?" Excited blue eyes twinkled from across the booth. Stephanie was another part-time waitress at the diner. She couldn't work many hours because of the bad knee she got from a car accident two years ago. She walked with a limp that she never seemed to let bother her.

"Hear what?" I asked with little interest. The good people of Mosset had a lot to learn when it came to juicy gossip.

"Some crazy hot guys drove into town this morning." I choked on the coffee I had been sipping. "Are you okay?" She quickly handed me napkins.

"What did they look like?" I said as I patted my mouth dry.

"Tall and *hot*."

"Stephanie," I took her hands in mine. I could tell I was freaking her out. "I need a little more than that."

"Ok, well, one was a gorgeous dirty blond with the brightest eyes and the longest lashes. The other cutie had long hair pulled back in a bun. I *really* need to ask who did his coloring. It's fantastic. Oh, and he had the greenest eyes I've ever seen. They're even greener than yours." She went on about how hot the two strangers were, but I didn't hear a word after I figured out they weren't strangers at all.

I don't remember leaving the booth with Caylen. I could hear Stephanie calling after me, but I didn't stop, not even to offer an explanation to Becky. I hurried up the stairs that led to the tiny apartment and threw open the door. A scream built when I saw my room occupied. Lucas had thrown his hand over my mouth before it could escape and tugged me inside before shutting the door.

"Don't scream. Don't you dare, girl."

Z took Caylen's carrier and moved him out of harm's way while I struggled against his partner. "Careful, princess. Don't make us do this the hard way." I struggled some more until I was too weak to fight anymore. Surprisingly, Lucas released me, and I didn't scream.

"How did you find me?"

"It's not what you think, princess."

"We're here for you," Lucas added.

"Yes, I figured as much," I answered sarcastically. I counted the steps it would take me to reach the bed and the seconds it would take to free the gun Sam loaned me from under the bed. There was no way in hell I'd let them take me back.

"I'm not going back," I voiced. I took another step and was surprised when they didn't pounce.

"We're not here to take you back. We're here to protect you."

My gaze narrowed. "Because he sent you?"

Z shook his head as his eyes pleaded with me to understand. "He didn't send us. We left on our own."

"You expect me to believe you left Angel broken in a hospital to fend for himself?"

"He was released weeks ago and is healing just fine," Lucas explained.

"We left because he hurt you."

"With your help," I pointed out. "Try again."

Lucas's nostrils flared, and Z's Adam's apple bobbed as he swallowed hard. "He lied to us too, princess."

"What do you mean?"

"We know it wasn't Theo who shot Art that night," Lucas answered. Before I could respond, he continued. "You don't have to believe us now, but you have to trust us."

"We need you to come with us, princess." The plea in Z's voice prickled the hairs on my skin. "We picked up a tail."

"Across the street," Lucas explained, "at the third gas pump, there's a black SUV that's been at the pump for an hour. Two doors east, there's a man in a blue and gray flannel standing by the lamppost smoking a cigarette. They're Staten's men."

My attention slid to the window on the other side furthest away from the gun. When I didn't move, Lucas reached behind him and pulled out Sam's gun. I recognized the custom oak handle.

"If you're wondering about this, don't bother. This isn't our first rodeo, kid."

Irritated at being bested, I stomped to the window and peeked through the curtains. True to his word, I peeped the large black truck and the man wearing the blue and gray flannel. He wasn't smoking, but from here, I could see several yellow buds littered around him. He'd been there a while.

"How did you find me?" I didn't turn away from the window. I didn't want to see any more of their false sincerity. I knew they weren't entirely truthful, but seeing the senator's men waiting for me out there left me no choice but to consider the lesser of two evils.

"It doesn't matter," Lucas evaded. "We need to go."

"I'm not going anywhere with you until you tell me how you found me."

"We bugged Anna's phone." Lucas sighed.

"And then you led them to me by coming here." They didn't try to deny it. "I was safe, and now I'm not because of you, and you expect me to just trust you?"

The loud knock on the door kept them from responding. "Alison," Becky called from the other side, "are you okay in there? Stephanie said I should check on you."

"Alison?" Lucas mouthed. He smiled faintly as he stared. I wanted to chuck something at his head.

I needed to do something and fast. The last thing I wanted was Rebecca or Sam caught in the crossfire of this standoff between Angel, the senator, and me.

"I'm fine," I called out. "I wasn't feeling well and didn't want to get sick in from of customers. I'm sorry for running off like that."

There was silence on the other side of the door. I held my breath, hoping she'd take my excuse and leave.

"All right, missy. I can bring you some tea if you think you'll need it?"

"No, I think I'll be fine." *Please go away.* We waited until Rebecca's footsteps could be heard moving away.

Z moved to the window and took a peek outside. "The guy in the flannel is moving in with two more guys. We need to go now." He turned green eyes on me. "You coming or are you staying to die, princess?"

They hadn't left me much choice when they came here. I ran to the bed and pulled the black duffel with our clothes and money from under the bed. Lucas took the duffel while I lifted Caylen, who passively watched us from his new carrier. As we made our way to the door, Z took point while Lucas brought up the rear, keeping Caylen and me in the middle. Once we were down the stairs, Z turned to lead us to the back door where the dumpster and Joey's car was hidden. We had only just made it out of the diner when we heard the unmistakable sound of a gun cocking.

"Don't you two take another step," Becky ordered. My breath caught, and my heart stopped. She moved from behind the dumpster where she had been waiting. "You're not going anywhere with this girl."

Lucas and Z didn't move. Even though the gun was pointed at them, my fear was for my friend. She may have the upper hand, but they were hardened criminals.

"It's all right, Becky. I want to go with them." I left out the part about not having a choice because I knew, if the wind even blew the wrong way, she wouldn't hesitate to blow them away.

"You don't have to lie for my benefit," she shrewdly shot back.

"We're not going to hurt her," Z dared to speak.

"I wasn't born yesterday, city boy. Now hand her the baby and back away real slow." To my surprise, they did as she ordered. I could no longer see them as they moved behind me. "Come to me, child." Rebecca's eyes never left them, and her finger never left the trigger of her shotgun. No sooner had I taken a step toward her, a shot rang out. The next moments passed in slow motion as Rebecca dropped to the ground. My scream was drowned out by more gunshots.

I shielded Caylen as best I could as I looked around for cover. The flannel-wearing shooter was laying face down a few feet behind Rebecca. I couldn't see where she was shot, but there was so much blood.

"We need to go now." I felt a hard hand close around my arm and jerk me up from the ground. Z grabbed Caylen's carrier, and together, we made a run for Joey's car. "Keys!" Lucas shouted in my face.

"We can't leave her!" I looked back at Rebecca's un-moving body. Guilt consumed me.

There were more shots and shouting. I felt my body being jerked as Lucas found the keys in my pocket and ripped them out before unlocking the Caprice and shoving me inside. No sooner were we all inside and bullets start-ed raining down on the car. Z was firing out the window while Lucas expertly maneuvered the car out of the back lot, running over the flannel guy and speeding around the corner of the diner.

"Oh, God. She's dead! It's my fault. Rebecca's dead. It's my fault. It's my fault." I no longer recognized my own voice.

"Shut her the fuck up!" Lucas yelled over my screaming. My screams mixed with Caylen's cries as Lucas drove us out of town.

"I'm sorry, princess." It was the last thing I had heard before my vision exploded and everything went black.

I woke up to a splitting headache and my hands tied. I could hear Lucas's low rumble as he spoke on the phone. "She's still out. We lost them."

I didn't move as I listened to his one-sided conversation. The only other sound was the television playing on low volume. I could smell the must from the old bed beneath me as I slowly opened my eyes. When the fog cleared, I noticed the stained green carpet first. A groan escaped as I moved to rise from the floral print bedspread.

"Whoa, princess." Z appeared in front of me and pressed me back down. "You took quite a hit. Take it easy."

"Where am I?" My voice sounded groggy, and I wondered how long I'd been out.

"You're safe."

"That doesn't answer my question, Zachariah. Where am I? Where's Caylen?" I swung my head in search of my son but ended up clutching the side of my head in pain.

"Damn it, princess." Z quickly knelt and pried my fingers from the lump. A guilty flush spread over his cheeks as he checked me out.

"You hit me."

He flinched and looked away. "I had to."

"You had to hit me?"

"We were on a high-speed chase, and you were hysterical," Lucas interjected. He was no longer on the phone, and he leaned against the paint-cracked wall.

"If you had left me alone, I wouldn't have needed saving."

"That's neither here nor there. You're dead without us now."

I turned away from Lucas to face his more rational partner. "Where is Caylen?"

He took my hand and helped me up from the bed. It took a few extra seconds for me to trust my balance before he led me over to the second bed I hadn't noticed.

Caylen was fast asleep on his blanket. I checked him over to make sure he was okay and turned toward my two *saviors*. "Why did you change his clothes? How long have I been out?"

"Only a few hours." Lucas nervously scratched his chin before answering my second question. "We changed him because he threw up all over his clothes. I think he got car sick."

"You don't say," I quipped. "A high-speed chase would do that to a baby."

"It's okay to hate us, girl, but we aren't going away, so deal."

I was across the room and in Lucas's stupid, smug face

before I had a chance to rethink it. "You led them to me."

"Does it matter now? If we walked away, you'd be dead."

"What do you want from me?"

"I don't want anything from you. Angel does."

"Then why isn't he here?"

"Because he's cleaning up your mess. That scrambled brain of yours refuses to see the whole picture. Staten was a *client,* not an enemy. If he walked away, and you and Caylen died, who do you think would have to live with that?"

"So, I'm supposed to thank him? What about Victor and his psychotic daughter? Was that my fault too?"

"But you already got your revenge in that warehouse, didn't you?" The knowing look in his eyes made me back down a little. Had Angel told them I was the one who stabbed him? Lucas's glare was full of accusation as if I were the one who did the betraying in that warehouse. I wasn't sorry then, and I won't apologize now.

"Not hardly," I answered coldly. After all, Angel was still alive.

I didn't expect Lucas's grin. It was cold and deadly. "You're a cold piece of work."

"Likewise."

"Are you two done?" Z finally spoke. He had been watching us argue from the far side of the room. "Princess, whatever happened in the warehouse is between you and Angel." His glower was trained on Lucas as he spoke.

"You told me he didn't know you were here." They both froze as I stood back. They shared a meaningful look I wasn't privy to before turning their attention back to me.

"He doesn't."

"Then who were you speaking to when you thought I was still sleeping?" Z's reaction would take a microscope to see unless you've been lied to enough times to spot it. "You lied to me, didn't you?"

"Princess—"

I held up a hand when he took a step forward. "Please just stop, Z. There's nothing you can say to make me trust you. For all I know, you're taking me back to him so he can finish the job himself, so give me one good reason why I shouldn't kill you both the second I have the chance?"

"The answer is irrelevant. You'll never get the chance," Lucas answered. He brushed past me, and it was a couple of hours before either of them spoke to me again.

"Pepperoni or Sausage?" Z quizzed.

I hesitated, not wanting to accept their help, but I was starving, so I said, "Both."

His grin was wide and bright, and I couldn't help but think how I could have fallen for a smile like his if circumstances were different. "My kind of girl," he praised before leaving the musty motel room.

Lucas rested his shirtless back against the headboard of the bed closest to the door and flipped through the channels. His jaw was hard, and his stare was steady, and I had the feeling he was trying to ignore me. I decided two could play his game, and I busied myself changing Caylen's diaper.

"You tried to kill him, didn't you?"

My hands paused from opening a fresh diaper. "You sound pretty sure of yourself. Why not just accuse me?" My lips were pressed tight as I turned my attention back to changing my son.

"I don't get what it is about you two."

"I don't know what you mean, and frankly, I don't care."

"Oh, you care. You want to know why he's helping you just as much as I do."

"You should ask him then. I'm not the one with the secrets."

"Angel keeps secrets to protect the ones he loves. What's your excuse?"

I didn't answer.

I was the one people kept secrets from, never the keeper. Lucas wanted an explanation that he wasn't owed. That was his problem. Not mine.

Z came back with pizza that smelled and tasted just right for my empty stomach. I ate silently while Lucas and Z placed bets and argued heatedly about a football game playing on TV. After I was full, I fed Caylen and cleaned him up. I wanted to go outside for fresh air, but knew it would be with company or not at all, so I passed and settled for taking a long, hot shower. It was the only alone time I was going to get.

I was alarmed when the shower curtain ripped back as I was shampooing my hair. Z then stepped inside wearing only a smile.

"What are you doing?" I crossed my arms tight to cover my breasts and backed away from him. The shower was tiny, leaving only a small space between our bodies, and leaving me under the spray.

"Wanted to make sure you weren't calling for help." He lacked the menace his brothers' wielded ruthlessly, but I had the gut feeling he was just as threatening and dangerous.

"In the shower?" I resisted the urge to knee him in the balls.

He shrugged powerful shoulders and reached for my soap. I watched him pop the top and take a sniff before waggling his eyebrows and squirting some in his palms. He then ran soapy hands over his body, but suddenly, stopped. His mocking gaze was trained on my arms still covering my breasts. "Are you shy, princess?"

"A little bit," I replied sarcastically.

"I've seen you… and felt you." His eyes trailed over my body slowly. "You have nothing to be shy about."

"That may be, but privacy is well appreciated."

He didn't respond, and I hated myself when my eyes dipped to his hard abs as he ran my peach-scented soap over them. The light scars made him look enticingly rugged. "I can pose if you like."

My gaze moved away to study the dingy shower curtain. "That won't be necessary." I turned my back on him to finish my shower as fast as I could. I could feel his eyes on me as I finished washing my hair and he continued defiling my soap.

"You didn't have to run," he blurted as I started running my sponge over my body.

"Yes. I did."

"The senator is powerful and relentless, and so is Angel. You can't run forever."

I forgot modesty when anger forced me to turn and face him. "Angel was never going to let me go after he kills the senator." Z glanced away, so I turned and finished my shower. I quickly wrapped my body in a towel and practically ran from the bathroom, but my escape was thwarted when I bumped into a very hard and hairy chest.

"Whoa." Lucas's hands closed around my bare arms. "Where are you going in such a hurry?"

"I was just going to check on Caylen."

He looked back at my son blowing spit bubbles and babbling happily at the dirty, cracked ceiling. When he faced me again, his frown was deeper than I'd ever seen. "I'd never do anything to hurt him."

"It's not that," I rushed to assure him. His face softened as he released me.

"Sorry," he mumbled before stepping around me and closing himself in the bathroom with Z. I chose not to fixate on them closed in the tiny bathroom together and hurriedly dressed while I had the privacy. Z emerged minutes later with his feet and chest bare and his signature black jeans riding low on his waist. He was scrubbing a white towel through his hair as he moved around the room. I hummed to fill the tense silence while rocking Caylen to sleep. When his eyes finally drifted shut, I put him down for the night.

Through the thin wall separating the room from the bathroom, I heard the shower shut off and listened as Lucas moved around. He came out moments later wearing less than Z had. The white fluffy towel was wrapped around his waist as hot shower water dripped from every tanned inch of him.

"You should get some sleep," he ordered when he found me sitting cross-legged on the bed.

"Afraid I'll run away?" I pretended not to notice the way the water glistened on his tan skin. I was pretty sure he had a thing for my best friend, and I was definitely sure she was in love with him.

"We won't be here past dawn."

I slipped under the covers and hoped there weren't any bed bugs or questionable stains. "Where are we going?"

He chuckled softly and shook his head.

"I can't sleep without knowing," I challenged.

His smirk made me realize my mistake a second before his hand moved. "Suit yourself," he grinned and unhooked his towel. I gasped and squeezed my eyes shut. I could hear his chuckle followed by the sound of his towel hitting the floor.

Moments later, I drifted off.

CHAPTER ELEVEN

MIAN

I WAS FORCED AWAKE IN THE MIDDLE OF NIGHT, COVERED in a cold sweat and trembling from the terror that had followed me into my sleep and stole my dreams. It didn't help when I realized I wasn't in bed alone. "Why are you in bed with me?"

"You didn't expect me to cuddle with Z, did you?"

"I don't care who you cuddle with as long as it's not me." I huffed and sat up. I was ready to kick him off the bed when he gripped the front of my shirt and tugged me down onto his chest.

"What are you doing?" I struggled to free myself after he wrapped his arms around me and buried his nose in my hair.

"Making up."

"I don't want to make up. I want you—*all* of you—to

leave me alone."

"Be a good girl, or you'll wake the baby again."

Suddenly, it dawned on me that we were molded together in the middle of the bed and my baby was nowhere in sight. I drove the back of my head into his chest, but it didn't free me. His pain-filled groan was muffled by my wild bed hair. "Where is he?"

"I put him in bed with Z," he growled after untangling his face from my hair.

"What if he rolls over because he doesn't know he's there? He'll crush him!" I hissed. The blanket slipped from our bodies and off the bed as we struggled. I was forced to stop fighting him when I ran out of breath.

He, on the other hand, had no trouble breathing as he said, "He's fine. Z's a sound sleeper."

"Lucas," I said slowly to allow patience to sink in. "Get out of my bed and give me my son."

"I heard him crying and found you thrashing in your sleep," he replied. He allowed me to turn in his arms after I relaxed. I could only see the silver of his eyes in the dark as he gazed back.

"Did I hurt him?" Worry was etched in every syllable. My fingers dug into his bare shoulders, but he didn't seem to notice.

"He's fine," he repeated. "He hung out with his favorite uncle for a little while until he went back to sleep."

"I can't believe I didn't hear him cry." My biggest fear had finally been realized.

I wasn't the mother Caylen deserved.

"You were doing quite a bit of crying yourself, girl. Don't be too hard on yourself." He pressed me tighter against him, and then I felt his lips brush my forehead.

Hours ago, we were at each other's throats, and now I clung to him while he kept me safe from the demons that chased me from my sleep.

After a while, Lucas rolled to his back, and my head fell comfortably on his chest. I listened to his heartbeat in the dark, afraid to go to sleep and face once again what could very soon become my reality.

"It was just a dream." I was startled by his whisper, thinking he had fallen asleep.

"It felt real to me," I whispered back. Suddenly, he rolled us over until he was leaning over me.

"There is more than one life he'll have to take before he can get to you, girl."

I wasn't a girl who swooned. Especially over words whispered by a man whose feelings were tangled with my best friend's, but he made it impossible not to.

"I'm not asking you to die for me."

His smile was leisurely, and he no longer appeared to be the brooding man I came to be wary of. "You don't have to."

"You wouldn't be doing it for me. You'd be doing it for Angel, and I'd still have to live with it."

"Well, then, I guess I better not die." He fell on his back again. "But I'll still do whatever is needed to protect you." He then ordered me to sleep.

I had awakened once more in the early hours of the morning by a different nightmare.

I was asleep in my bed, safe in the home I shared with my parents when I was awakened by Angel holding in the rotting flesh of his hand the bloody knife I used to kill him.

Z had been the one to wake me with tender kisses on my lips as he pulled me gently from my nightmare.

"Want to talk about it?" he asked.

"No."

We hadn't shared pillow talk like I had with Lucas, but he'd held me until Caylen had woken up with a hungry cry. Lucas was nowhere to be found as I fed and changed Caylen, and I found out why when he came through the door carrying breakfast and coffee.

Lucas handed me the largest cup after he set the food down. "Figured you might need a kick after last night."

My attention slid to Z sprawled in the room's only chair. He had been busy taking large bites of the burrito Lucas had handed him. When he noticed my worried looked, he mumbled around a mouth full of food, "Heard the entire thing, princess."

I groaned and wondered if these two had any sense of decorum.

"You shouldn't hide from us. We wouldn't be here if we didn't care."

My eyebrow quirked as I regarded them. "You mean your loyalty to Angel isn't the reason you hunted and kidnapped me?"

"We've never had a little sister," Lucas answered with a shrug and a mouth full. They had the worst table manners.

"Well, then, word of advice, *big brothers don't touch their little sisters* the way you two have touched me."

I happily watched them choke on their food as I sipped my hot coffee slowly. I rolled my eyes at their wide grins once their throats cleared. Perverts.

An hour later, we were checked out and on the road. I wasn't hysterical this time, but I did grow nervous when Z steered Joey's bullet-riddled car north.

"Where are we headed?" I tried to keep the tremble from my voice and failed.

"Indianapolis."

"But the city's mainstream. He'll find me." I was feeling the beginnings of a panic attack.

"Not if you know how to blend in."

I felt frustration bubbling to the surface. Instead of placing more distance between Chicago and me, they were dragging me closer to the senator's reach. I needed a way out of their clutches before they got me killed. "Angel's got bigger problems than me, don't you think? Victor is dead, but the book is still missing. Why is he so concerned with the senator when his precious legacy is still out there?"

"Angel decides what his priorities are, princess."

"Then why isn't he here?"

"He's keeping an eye on the senator while we keep you hidden."

"Why doesn't he just kill him?"

"The senator's murder would raise too many questions. The Knights have thrived as long as they have because they don't believe in sloppy work."

"How can I protect my son if the senator lives? You said it yourself—I can't run forever."

"He's going to die, princess. But it won't be murder."

My head spun. I didn't know what that meant. I didn't know what any of this meant. How could Angel kill the senator without killing him?

I stroked my sleeping baby's cheek as tears fell. "I'm

sorry I got you into this," I whispered to him.

I could feel eyes on me and looked up to find Z watching me. "You're a great mother, princess. If my mother had half the instinct you do, I wouldn't be screwed up."

I hesitated to enter dangerous territory but found myself more curious than afraid. "Tell me about her, Zachariah."

His jaw flexed. "She was a crack whore. There's nothing to tell." I was surprised at the venom in Z's tone.

"Was she always on drugs?"

"No."

"What about your father? Couldn't he have helped her?"

His laugh was dry. "He's the one who gave her the drugs, princess."

"He was a dealer?"

He shook his head, and when he turned his head to face me, his green eyes were nearly blackened with pain. "He was her pimp. He used drugs to control her. When she was strung out, he got bored and ditched her."

And you.

I couldn't help but feel pity for the man with an easy smile and anger for his mother who couldn't fight hard enough to keep him protected.

"No one's called me Zachariah since her."

My stomach ached at the thought of causing him pain. "I'm sorry. Does it hurt?"

"No." He turned to stare out the windshield. I wanted to ask if she was dead, but his wall was already up again, so I turned to Lucas.

"What about you, Lucas?"

"What about me?"

"Where are your parents?"

He snorted. "My dad already had a family, so he had no use for me, and my mom didn't either when she realized I wasn't enough to break up a happy home."

"When was the last time you saw him?"

"Nine years ago."

I frowned, not expecting the answer to have been so long ago. He was only eighteen the last time he'd seen his father.

"What happened?"

"He hired Art to kill my mother."

I couldn't catch my gasp of surprise before it slipped. "Why would he—"

"He paid her to make us go away. After she had collected, she ran and left me behind. I was found on the streets, placed in foster care, and eventually, a group home after I caused too many problems. When the money was gone, she wanted more, but my father refused, so she threatened to expose their affair to the rich heiress he married unless he paid to keep her quiet."

"So Art killed your father?" How much hate could Lucas hold for his father to work for the man who killed him?

My question was forgotten when Lucas's ringing phone interrupted. "Yeah," he answered gruffly as he steered with one hand. "Fuck!" he suddenly exploded. I had trouble following the questions Lucas shot at the caller rapidly. He handed the phone to Z and pressed on the gas. Z listened for a few seconds before cursing and pulling out his own phone and tapping quickly.

"Not a glitch. The tracking's stopped. He must have found it."

I felt my heart race as I tried to piece together what was happening. Z hung up and promptly smashed his fist into the dashboard. He then turned his green glower on Lucas and said three words that made my heart drop into my turning stomach.

"We're going back."

I wanted to scream at them not to take us back. Instead, my eyes shut tight as Lucas accelerated and drove us back to Attica.

CHAPTER TWELVE

ANGEL

MY PLAN TO KEEP MIAN AND CAYLEN SAFE AND FAR away from Chicago took a nosedive when the senator wormed his way from under my thumb and disappeared off the grid. The unsettling feeling in my gut wouldn't ease long enough for me to predict his next move. Calling Z only confirmed what I already knew, so I ordered them back to Attica. Without eyes on the senator, Mian was more vulnerable than ever.

Bringing her back to Chicago would draw him out. Using them as bait turned my stomach even more than the senator's disappearing act, but it was my only option. They were what he wanted.

It would be hours before they arrived, so I used the time to tighten security and figure out a plan. I had guards placed on almost every inch of the Knight estate. *No one* was getting in or out without my say.

I was barking orders at my men when my phone rang. The private number made me hesitant to answer, but instinct drove me to do just that.

"Knight," I growled into the phone.

"Mr. Knight, I'm glad to know you're doing well. I tried to stop by the hospital and wish you well, but the reception was a bit… tense." The senator chuckled as if we were old friends sharing a joke.

"That's disappointing to hear. Why don't you stop by now? I promise this time the reception will be a bloody one."

His tone was less pleasant when he spoke this time. "Your father was a business man and one I respected. He knew how to separate business from pleasure."

"I guess this apple fell too far from the tree. What can I do for you?"

"I want to make a deal."

"I'm not interested."

"You should really hear me out."

"My time is precious, Senator. You have ten seconds."

"I only need five. You want your book back. I want the girl and her kid. I'll call you back for your decision." The line died a quick death unlike the senator would when I finally caught him.

I calmly pocketed my phone and lit a blunt to keep me company as I waited out the final hours until the girl who complicated life arrived.

Mian and the baby were fast asleep when they arrived after night fell. I had Lucas and Z wait while I put them both to bed myself. She didn't stir as I put her in my bed. I then laid Caylen in the crib I had brought from my father's home. The crib was placed by her side of the bed so the moment she woke she'd know he was safe.

I memorized the peaceful set of her face because when she awoke, we'd be at war again. I lied to her, and she claimed my life for the betrayal. She would never agree to trust me without answers and possibly never trust me again when she had them. With a heavy feeling in my chest, I left them to sleep in peace, but I couldn't walk away before locking them inside. I told myself it was to keep them safe, but I knew it was to keep her from leaving. Mian was more re-sourceful than I would have given her credit for three years ago. She wasn't any easier to cage than she was to set free.

Downstairs, I found Lucas and Z raiding the bar with hard expressions. "I spoke to the senator." They froze at the same time, giving me their full attention. "He wants to make a deal."

"Fuck that," Lucas spat. "The deal is his head or no deal."

"My thoughts precisely," Z echoed with more menace than I ever knew he possessed.

"He has the book, and he wants to trade Mian and Caylen for it."

"How the fuck is that possible? Victor had the book, and now he's dead."

"There's obviously a lot we don't know, but my first guess is Victor tried to sell the book. He wasn't after power. He was after money."

"After all the shit he stirred for it, why just sell it?"

"The motherfucker was probably broke and was hiding it. I'll hack into his accounts."

"We're going to take the deal." I braced for the explosion my decision would cause.

"Why the fuck would we hand them over to him?" Lucas was the first to demand.

"He'll never touch them, but we'll make him think he's won for now. It's the only way to draw him out of hiding. I have no doubt he's going to try to double cross me and keep the book once he has them."

"What makes you think he isn't telling the truth?"

"Because he offered me a large sum of money to keep his dirty deeds out of the book. He's not going to hand that power back over."

"What if he's already destroyed the book?"

Duty should have meant doing *anything* to protect the family's interest, but it's become hard for me to care about legacies and power when I could have something much more potent.

I could have Mian.

She was a girl I craved.

A girl I didn't deserve.

A girl I'd crumble mountains to keep.

"I'll deal with that when the time comes." The truth was my priorities were changing fast.

"But your family—"

"They'll kill me. I know." If ever the Bandit failed to protect the legacy, by death he would be dethroned as the Knight. Reginald would make sure he was the one to take my life so he would inherit as well as his sons after him. He has been itching to take back what he claims is rightfully his. The feud between our lines started when my great-grandfather took over as the Knight after Archibald, Reginald's great-grandfather, tried to sell the book for profit.

"This whole legacy bullshit is seriously fucked!" Z seethed. I kept silent. I didn't agree with many of my family's practices but going against them would mean forfeiting the throne. A rule under Reginald would guarantee the downfall of the Knights. His entire line had been fueled only by greed and cowardice.

"How much do we tell Mian?"

"We tell her the truth. The plan doesn't work without her trust."

Lucas and Z weren't able to hide their surprise before schooling their expressions again. "She might run," Z pointed out.

"She might run even if we don't," Lucas argued. I nodded while hiding my surprise that he agreed with my plan.

Mian's trust in my ability to protect her was lost because of fear I helped cause. "We're a long way from Chicago, and every inch of the grounds is guarded to keep the senator out and her *in*. She's not going anywhere."

"When do we make the deal?" Lucas questioned.

I walked to the bar and pulled out a glass before pouring a drink and tossing it back. "Staten called from a private number. He wants to do this on his terms."

It didn't matter. His terms or mine, Staten and his piece of shit son were going to die.

"So then we wait," Z murmured and emptied his glass.

I returned to my bedroom and found them just as I had left them. I was partially relieved that Mian hadn't woken up. I wanted to avoid the questions and the fight we still needed to have for just a few more hours.

For Mian, I felt rage, possessiveness, and desire. When morning would finally come, I was afraid of which emotion would take dominance. I walked over to the crib and was surprised to find the baby awake and babbling quietly to himself. When he saw me, he showed off all four of his tiny teeth before crawling to the rails and pulling himself up. He held his arms out to me, but before I could pick him up at his request, he fell on his butt. The diaper cushioned his fall, and he seemed not to even notice. I watched transfixed as he carefully pulled himself up again using the rails and held out his arms to me again. He wobbled but kept his balance this time. My throat felt clogged as I lifted him from the crib.

"It's past your bedtime, kid. Playtime is over."

"No." He squealed and laughed as he smiled up at me, and I couldn't help but return the favor. I never grasped his effect on me—or why I didn't run away from it.

"You and your mother had quite an adventure, huh?" He babbled sounds that were strangely starting to sound like words as I sat us in the bronze love seat facing the bed. "She would have made me chase her to the end of the world to protect you." He trained blue eyes that haunted me on his sleeping mother as if he understood.

My phone's rhythmic vibration in my pocket alerted me to a phone call. I secured my arm around the baby as I dug it out. The screen flashed a private number as it continued to vibrate. A cold feeling rushed through my veins as I stabbed the green button.

"I don't have time for games," I seethed into the phone. I felt Caylen flinch in my arms at my sudden change in tone. He didn't cry, but his attention was no longer on his sleeping mother. He watched me now with uncertainty in his father's eyes. It should have been enough to make me hate him, but the connection he shared with his mother drew me to him.

"I trust you've made your decision then?"

I stared into Caylen's eyes and didn't hesitate. "When and where?"

"On a night of my choosing, my men will escort Ms. Ross and her child from your home to an undisclosed location. They will release your book to you once they are safely out of your gates with Ms. Ross."

"How do you know—"

"I know everything about this state, Mr. Knight. It's my job," he reminded unnecessarily. "We wouldn't want your family's lovely estate tarnished with blood because you tried to double cross me, would we?"

His threat didn't hit its mark, but I made sure mine would. "Make no mistake, the blood that will cover my walls won't be my own. Sleep tight, Senator... but you better leave one eye open. You never know what's hiding under the bed."

I ended the call and put Caylen back in his crib. He'd started to fuss, and I knew it was me who had upset him. Before I walked away, I covered him with a blanket. "Time for bed, kid."

It was a few minutes before he finally gave in and slept. I slid into bed and made the split decision to pull Mian close until her front was flush with mine. Her eyes opened just a crack, and her unfocused green eyes found me in the dark. There was a moment of clarity before her eyes drifted shut once more and her body relaxed against mine. I listened to her breathing before I touched my lips to her ear and whispered.

CHAPTER THIRTEEN

MIAN

"YOU WANT ME TO FIGHT THIS WAR TO KEEP YOU? *So be it."*

I'd heard the words Angel spoke to me when he thought I was sleeping. I had woken up when I felt arms close around me and a sudden flame of heat as he molded our bodies together. Even though I'd been in a fog of lethargy, I knew it had been Angel holding me. I should have kicked him out of bed, but the safety he offered had been too tempting.

But then he'd whispered those words to me, and I knew I was still living in his illusion.

Now it was morning. Angel was fast asleep. I was able to slip out of his arms and bed without waking him. I was surprised to find the crib I recognized from Art's home set up only a few feet from the bed. But this was definitely not

Art's home. The large room I unknowingly spent the night in surpassed the wealth and extravagance of his home.

We were back at the Knight estate.

It was a far reach from the dangers hunting me in Chicago, but it was also a far reach from escape. The land Angel now lived on stretched too far to run. On foot, I'd be caught before I made it off.

Shaking off the fear that I'd never escape, I plastered on a smile for my son that fell once I found the crib empty. I didn't panic. Insanity disguising itself as reason convinced me that Angel wouldn't hurt Caylen.

But that didn't mean he wouldn't keep us apart again.

As furtively as I could, I moved to the door. Angel didn't stir, and his breathing remained even as he slept. Fear that he could be faking it, as I did last night when his threat seeped into my skin and filled my blood with hate, made me pause with my hand over the knob. I waited only a second before making my decision and sneaking from the room. I stood in the middle of the empty hallway wondering where to look first. Far away, I heard voices and then the unmistakable sound of Caylen's babble. The voices grew louder as I moved closer to the double doors at the end of the hall. I finally reached a set of double doors that were closed. On the other side, I could hear the amused voices of Lucas and Z as they coaxed Caylen into walking.

My hand had only closed around the knob ready to push inside when another hand stronger than mine closed around my wrist and dragged me away.

"What are you doing?" I hissed when Angel turned me to face him.

"You surprised me." I could hear as much in his tone as he spoke. "I thought you were going to run."

"Not without my son." He looked over my shoulder at the closed doors. I expected him to let me go. Instead, he dragged me back to the room I'd spent the night in with him. "Let go of me, Angel. I learned to walk when I was ten months old. I don't need your help." I tugged to free my wrist, but he only tightened his grip. When we reached the bedroom, he pulled me inside before pulling out a key and locking the door from the inside. I rubbed my wrist over the red mark he had left behind.

"We need to talk," he demanded. He was always making demands but never giving in to them.

"We have nothing to talk about."

He ran his fingers through his hair. "You tried to kill me."

"And sadly, you aren't dead." His eyes narrowed as his hand fell to his side. He didn't move or speak after that. I don't even think he breathed.

"Do you want to do this, Sprite?"

"We're not doing anything because we're done. Didn't your little henchman give you the message? You can't protect me."

"The senator would have found you. *I did*, and he has even more resources at his disposal."

"Why do you care? I tried to kill you, remember?"

His smile was lethal. "Because you're my wife… didn't you know?"

I laughed even as I felt his poison percolating in my veins. "I'm done playing your games, Knight."

He didn't respond. With confidence, he walked to his suit jacket crumpled on the thick carpet. I couldn't hear the warning not to panic over the rapid beat of my heat as he pulled out a piece of paper. He moved in closer than he had been before until he towered over me. "I think you should see something." He lifted the paper for me to take. I didn't.

"What is it?"

"The last gift your father gave you. Your future."

I took the neatly folded paper from his hand with shaking fingers. *Curiosity killed the cat.* Breaking the red wax seal, I unfolded the cream parchment to reveal a marriage certificate. I felt punched in the gut when I read our names in a scrawl that didn't belong to either of us. The certificate was dated three years ago. Two days before my life changed forever.

"This is impossible. I was sixteen!"

"Your father signed the consent form and mine generously padded the clerk's retirement fund since neither of us could attend our own wedding. I imagine he retired early to spend the rest of his years traveling with his wife and taking couple's painting lessons."

"You didn't know?"

He shook his head slowly. "I didn't just inherit money and land the day I buried my grandfather."

The meeting after the funeral…

"We've been married all this time," I whispered in disbelief. Rage made me ball up the paper and toss it across the room. Angel's gaze never left me, even when the lie that was our marriage sailed past his head. "What they did isn't legal, which means we aren't married."

"Maybe not… but who is going to contest it?" he questioned calmly.

"I will," I growled.

He turned his back on me and walked deeper into the room. "Afraid not, Mrs. Knight. Legally, you are mine. And so is Caylen."

"His father is alive."

His chuckle sent chills down my spine. "Not for long."

"I'll file for divorce."

He watched me as he pushed his unbuttoned pants down his legs. "Hidden on every acre of land is a man who will drag you back to me dead or alive at my command. You aren't going anywhere."

His cock was impossibly hard as he closed the distance between us. I tried to keep a grasp on reality, but the desire was waging war with my head. "Victor said I wasn't supposed to marry you until I was eighteen. Why didn't he know about the marriage?"

"My father stopped trusting Victor long before he died." I felt as if I were going to drown when he crowded his large body in my space so I sucked in as much air as I could and held it. "He only told Victor what he trusted him to know, which wasn't much."

"But the contract said—"

He snorted as he lifted my sweater over my head. "Our fathers, on the other hand, trusted each other implicitly. There was no contract in the written sense. They gave their word that I would have you and you would have my protection when you turned eighteen. To them, it was more than any legal contract." His hands fell to my jeans and with skillful fingers, slid the button free.

"Something happened to make them marry us sooner than they had planned. You aren't curious to know what it was?" He pushed my jeans down my legs as he'd done his.

"No."

"Why not?"

"Because it's done. We're married, and nothing but

death can reverse it." He pushed his chest against me until my back hit the wall. Without warning, his hand slid inside my cotton panties, and I gasped when his skilled fingers skimmed my clit. "You've always been mine. I just wish I hadn't lost three years," he whispered against my lips. I shuddered as he pushed his finger inside me. "You'll always be ready for daddy, won't you?" I was so goddamn wet. His thumb brushed against my clit as he added a second finger, and I learned it wasn't by accident when he circled my clit and drove his fingers deep. Wrapping a hand around his neck, I rode his fingers. "So sweet and so willing."

I fought to get closer. I knew it was wrong for me to like his touch, but the feeling he stirred deep inside me felt so right. I felt grounded even when I was flying high.

"There's no price I won't pay to keep you, Mrs. Knight." I started to come just as he kissed my lips and drove his fingers deeper so his palm cupped my pussy. He forced my tongue to mate with his as my body came apart under his command. When my last whimper subsided, he gripped my soaked panties in both hands and tore it down the middle. I gaped down in shock as he let the scraps fall to the floor at our feet.

"Why did you do that?" I forced between pants. I wasn't talking about my ruined panties. Shame coursed through my veins as I leaned against the wall in order to stay upright.

"Because, wife, I don't need to tell you who you belong to. You show me every time I touch you."

"That's not true."

"The way you came on my fingers says differently." Crudely, he slipped the fingers he used to expose me past his lips as he watched me hungrily.

"You're disgusting," I spat to hide how turned on I was.

"And you taste amazing." He stepped back, and the phantom grip on my lungs eased the further he moved away. "Join me in the shower," he ordered over his shoulder. I didn't move. I had no intentions of showering with him. He disappeared into the bathroom, and I listened as the sound of running water soon followed. "You have about twelve seconds left before I come get you," he shouted over the running water.

I thought about making a run for it before I remembered he had locked us in. With only six seconds left, I quickly searched his suit pockets for the key but came up empty.

"Looking for this?" He stood in the door of the bathroom, wearing a smug grin, and holding the key in his hand. Neither of us spoke as he stalked across the room. I didn't cower, and his grin grew into a full-blown smile as he lifted me bridal style and carried me to the shower.

After we had showered, he gave me one of his shirts that fell to my knees and led me by the hand back to the sitting room. Caylen was no longer in a playing mood when we found him. He sat on the floor crying as Lucas and Z stood over him with startled faces.

"He just started crying!" Twiddle Dee accused. I shook my head at Lucas and picked up my hungry, red-faced son.

"Did either of you consider feeding him?" I hid my amusement when the light bulb flickered on and their faces relaxed. "I need my bag," I said to Angel, who shook his head as soon as I spoke.

"There's food in the kitchen. I'll take you." I decided not to argue when my son's cries threatened to blow my eardrums. Arguing would only take longer to feed Caylen, so I followed him downstairs. Each room was never more than a few steps away in our rundown apartment. The estate, however, was like a small city with walls built around it to keep us "safe."

As we made our way to the kitchen, I noticed the staff working in harmony. They dusted, wiped, and rushed from room to room to complete their tasks. It must take a small army to keep a place this size polished and running smoothly. I could easily get lost if I wanted to. The house wasn't any less intimidating without the music or finely dressed guests or Angel's grandfather. If anything, the silence was haunting.

The enormous kitchen was made up of stainless steel and white marble. Angel had, at his disposal, appliances fit for a world-renowned chef. He moved around the kitchen pulling pots from carefully selected spots and ingredients for breakfast from the largest pantry I'd ever seen.

"All of this is a bit much for just one person, isn't it?"

He set a bowl of applesauce in front of me with a spoon as he answered blandly, "I'm fully expected to produce an heir and plenty of back up heirs."

"What about heiresses?" I challenged as I fed Caylen.

"You tell me," he said, wiping the smirk off my face. His burning gaze met mine when I looked up. "Would you want that?"

I laughed to disguise my uneasiness. "You're delusional."

"Am I?"

"I won't have your baby," I denied with less aplomb. "This marriage isn't real." My gaze dropped to my empty finger. It was the only evidence I had that my father didn't betray me.

"Your father has had ample time to figure out his biggest regret in life." He turned the silver knob on the stove, turning on the flame, and setting a frying pan on top. "Are you curious to know the answer?"

"Why don't you tell me?"

"You," he answered without hesitation. He removed bacon from the packaging and placed the slices in the pan. "He doesn't regret not choosing you, Sprite. He just regrets *you*."

"Your parents didn't love you enough," I countered. "I get it. It made you sad, so I'll excuse your ignorance, but my father loves me."

"You've never considered that maybe he wishes he didn't?" He continued cooking as he coldly ripped apart my father's love—love that always made me feel safe without fail. "It would be easier for him to walk away and forget you. He's tried every day since that summer afternoon nine years ago."

"Stop it." My throat was clogged, so I had to force words through.

"He even married you when you were only sixteen fucking years old to a man he knew would corrupt you so he wouldn't feel responsible for you."

"Please. Just—"

"Would he die for you, Sprite?" I couldn't take anymore. I pushed away from the bar and stood up from the stool with Caylen in my arms. He was still hungry and started to cry and fight to free himself from my arms. I just needed to get away.

I hurried from the kitchen just as Angel snatched the pan from the burner and started after me. He caught me just outside the kitchen just as Z appeared. Before I could do anything, Angel gently pried Caylen from my arms and gave him to Z.

"Leave us alone!" He ignored me as he gave Z orders to finish feeding Caylen before dragging me up the stairs.

We were back in his domain, but this time, the air was heavier and more dangerously charged than before. "Why are you crying?" he demanded.

"You had no right to say those things!"

"Why? Because they were true?" He shoved all ten of his fingers in my hair and forced me against his chest. "Do the lies your father tell hurt less?" I pushed against him until he growled and shoved me on his bed. "Your father is not a man. He abandoned you when you needed him most, and who did he give you to?" I crawled through the rumpled bedding to get away from his possessive energy before it consumed me, but he caught my ankle and dragged me back as he growled, "You have no idea how hard I've tried not to hurt you." He lifted me up by the front of my shirt and nipped my bottom lip. "But what's control without a little chaos first?"

Brutally, he pressed his lips against mine. When I refused to kiss him back, he ripped open the shirt he'd given me. My lips fell open from shock, and his tongue found mine, coaxing me to play. We fell so deep that I feared we'd never find the surface again.

Eventually, I needed air, but the kiss went on until I was beating on his chest, begging for it. I drew in gulps of precious air when he finally let up.

"Every breath you take is a show of mercy, Mian."

"I hate you," I confessed to his beautiful, scowling face. "Why do you care if I love my father?"

"It doesn't matter anymore, does it? Your father will die, and you'll still be mine." I felt his promise seep into my veins and warm my blood. I was Angel's, body and soul. He'll possess one or destroy the other. "I want to hurt you for what you did in the warehouse." His lips coasted over my throat as he pushed me on my back and slipped my panties down my thighs. "I just might."

"You think I chose him?" I didn't recognize my quaking voice. "I love him because he's my father. I never had a choice. I've loved you since I was twelve. That was my choice. You were a choice." And a bad one.

"And what do you choose now?" His kisses trailed to my breasts, and then he slipped my nipple into his mouth as he moved between my thighs. He took my hands and moved them to his hips. My fingers had a mind of their own as they gripped the waistband of his sweatpants. Fucking was the only thing that could calm our storm. It was wrong, but it was ours. When his head lifted, brown met green. "Right now is when you decide how your life with me will be."

"I could give you what you want, but you'd never believe it was real." I didn't break our stare as I pushed his sweats down until they stopped under his ass. "You shouldn't."

"There's nothing about us that will ever be anything but real." Slowly, he slid inside me, making me feel every hard inch of him as he did. Soft lips brushing my ear, he whispered, "You wouldn't fit so perfectly if you weren't made for me." I didn't have time to argue his point when he flipped us over leaving me on top and him smiling sexily from below me. "Ride me, Sprite." He gave my ass a hard slap. "Fuck your husband."

I shouldn't have let his words get to me, but they did. My hands stacked on top of his chest for balance as I found a slow rhythm for my hips to dance. His cock filled me fully, and despite the ache left behind when he was no longer deep inside me, it felt good too.

His hands slid to my ass helping me move. The look of wonder in his eyes as I brought us pleasure was truly a Kodak moment. I could tell he was holding back, willing himself not to give in so soon. I was angry with myself for wanting it. But I remembered what it felt like to have him come inside me. It was hot, it was addictive… it was dangerous…

"Oh. My. God. *Condom*," I gasped. He drove deeper with a wicked look in his eye. I wasn't on birth control. I couldn't get pregnant again. I couldn't have Angel's baby and be forever tied to him.

"It's too late, Sprite. Not stopping."

I shook my head wildly and slowed my hips. I needed to stop this before it was too late. Angel growled and swiftly caught my hips before flipping me onto my back and driving even deeper.

"You want me to prove you're mine?" I scoured his back with my nails, and he smiled through his grunt. Maybe we were both insane.

"The only thing you'll prove by making me come," I panted, "is that you can fuck." I lifted my head. "But I already knew that," I whispered in his ear.

"Then maybe I should let Lucas and Z have a turn."

He wrapped his hand around my neck when I started to pull away. "See if they make you come as hard as I do." Next thing I knew, he'd lifted me from the bed and had me braced against the headboard with his knees digging in the mattress and my legs spread wide as he pounded me. "You hear that, Sprite?" My cries mixed with his grunts and the headboard banging against the wall as he showed me no mercy. "That's the sound of me owning you."

"Yeah?" I tightened my pussy around his cock, making him groan. "Is that the sound of me owning you?"

Angel's brutal kiss was heady. Addictive.

But Angel coming inside me?

It was the end of my world.

CHAPTER FOURTEEN

ANGEL

November 28th 2013

I COULDN'T BE REASONED, STOPPED, OR CONTROLLED. My ascension to power had been paved in my father's blood, but only with Theo's blood could I secure my place as the Bandit and the Knight. For a month, Theo managed to remain off-grid.

Until today.

I tailed the rust bucket he drove through the streets of Chicago. Two days before, he called Victor to set up a meeting in which Victor had relayed the information to me, proving his loyalty to my father even after he was dead. Theo, unaware he had fallen into a trap, had come alone because he had no options. Without my father, he was nothing, and he'd bit the hand that fed him. It took every grain of control to stay hidden and let the meeting happen without interfering. Victor was as clueless as I as to what the meeting was for. My guess was that he'd try to convince him of his innocence. It was too bad for him that Victor already knew the truth about that night and would protect my mother. He'd offered to kill him, but there was no way in hell I was giving him the honor. Letting some-one else avenge my father would be disgracing the birth-right my great-grandfather seized.

I've waited weeks to feel guilt for framing my godfa-ther, but my mother hasn't been the same since that night. The fragmented piece I had left of my mother was the rea-son remorse eluded me. I'd had to hire a nurse just to en-sure she wouldn't wither to dust. Lately, however, Victor had been overseeing her care. I had a lot to thank him for it seemed.

My thoughts drifted to Mian. Theo had hidden her well. The smartest thing Theo had ever done was keep his life before my father secret. Z had found his parents living on the outskirts of Illinois, but it had proved a dead end. A perverse part of me had entertained the idea of killing them an eye for an eye, but framing him and then killing him would have to be enough. When he was dead, Mian would need somewhere safe to go... if I didn't find her first.

I'd found the engagement ring and dress I sent to her for the party in their abandoned home. The ring was now tucked away in the locked compartment of my glove box.

We were ten minutes away from the outskirts of Chicago when Theo made an unexpected stop at a small neighborhood park. I strangled the steering wheel, eager to get him alone, but also hoping he'd lead me to Mian and save me the trouble of hunting her.

He unfolded his long frame from the car holding a

small duffel, and a few seconds later, shook hands with a man I didn't recognize. I'd only gotten a brief glimpse of him before he was hidden from view. Theo was out in the open, unaware and completely vulnerable. I could take the shot, leave Theo bleeding on the concrete, and get the fuck out of dodge. But then I remembered the other half of my objective.

To find his daughter.

The meeting between them ended quickly, and the man disappeared down the street. Theo watched him go until he disappeared around the corner. I noticed the slump in his shoulders and the worry in his eyes after he turned toward his car. His hand was on the handle when he stopped. There was tension in his body as his gaze moved around the busy area. He could feel me watching him.

I had a clear shot at him, but I knew I couldn't kill him here. I could hear my father's voice in my head, warning me not to be sloppy.

I made the decision to slide down in my seat and hide a moment too late. Theo was now staring at my car parked across the street. He couldn't be sure it was me. The tint was too dark, but it didn't matter to a man desperate to live.

He was already reacting.

Reaching behind his back, he pulled his gun and took aim. I was prepared to do the same when we both heard, "Sir, drop your weapon down and get down on the ground!" When Theo didn't obey, the officer screamed the command again. The other pedestrians screamed and ran to get away from danger. I watched, enraged, as Theo lowered his gun and the officer immediately cuffed him.

My only window to silence Theo forever was gone.

Present

"Why did you frame my father?"

I was running my nose over every inch of her skin, breathing her in and enjoying her scent, as she voiced her question. This wasn't a conversation I wanted to have naked in bed, but I could hear in her voice there was no avoiding it.

"There had been a witness that night who knew the only two people with my father when he died was Theo and my mother. Killing her wasn't an option since she had already reported the murder to the police. I had to protect my mother. My father wouldn't have expected any less. Even for Theo."

"So let me get this straight." She pulled out of my arms to face me. "Your father fucks another woman—my mother—your mother pulls the trigger, and my father gets screwed?"

"Theo wasn't just there to confront my father. He was there to kill him, and he succeeded. He also destroyed what was left of my mother, and I couldn't let her live with the consequences."

"My father didn't destroy your mother. Your father did. Why can't you see that?"

"When you thought you killed me, did you feel different? Like your humanity had been stripped from you the moment you plunged that knife inside me?"

Her gaze lowered, shielding the pain in the jade. "Yes."

"My mother loved my father, and not only did she kill him, but she learned he'd been unfaithful with the woman she used to call a friend. It changes you. The woman I was left with wasn't my mother. I had your father to thank for that."

"So your mother's mental state helped you feel less guilty?"

"I didn't feel guilty at all," I confessed. "Not until I saw you standing in my father's home ready to kill me to free your son." I couldn't handle the way her eyes bore into me, so I pulled her back into my arms and laid her head over my heart that didn't deserve to beat.

"I kept waiting for you to show up and tell me you didn't blame me, but then you never did, so I never let myself think about you."

My hand slid between our bodies until it reached her breast. I slid my thumb over the nipple and grinned at her gasp. "You weren't so easy to forget."

I was seconds away from pulling her under me and making sure she'd never forget me again when she grabbed my hand and laid it on my bare stomach. "My father wasn't the only one you condemned that night. Did you ever once consider what it would do to me to lose the only parent I had left?" I could see the answer she wanted to hear in her eyes, but I couldn't hand her the lie.

"Yes." She wasn't expecting my answer, and I wasn't expecting to give it to her.

"You're such a hypocrite," she breathed. She shoved me away, hopped up from our bed, and faced me with tears running down her face. "You hate my father for the same reason you betrayed me. You *chose* her over me. But why wouldn't you? She's your *mother*. Don't you see how unfair that is?"

"I didn't—"

"You did!" she screamed. "You put my father in prison knowing what it would do to me."

I sat up, ripped the covers from my waist, and stood on the other side of the bed facing her. "I knew I would hurt you, but I never meant to lose you. I searched for you, and after some time, when I couldn't find you, I figured your father hid you so that never would, and then I accepted that you'd be better off."

"Except I wasn't. Should I blame you for that like you blamed my father?"

"Being with me wouldn't have been any better."

"I know. Look how your mom turned out," she answered with a curled lip.

"Careful," I warned. My voice had gone deep, demanding submission. As always, Mian wasn't willing to give it so easily. We ended up in a staring contest that I broke. I decided I'd rather continue this argument without my dick out.

"Victor said he was the one to show my dad the video. That day, I heard my father speaking to someone just before he left. It all makes sense now." She paced the floor of my bedroom as I slipped into gym shorts. "It had to have been Victor. I was trying to ask him about the party, but he was so angry. He raised his voice when I asked questions. He *never* raised his voice to me. He told me he had a job, and a few hours later, he told me he was leaving Illinois. Not *us*. Him." I could hear the hurt and frustration she felt three years ago.

"He wouldn't have wanted you anywhere near him if I

found him, and I *did* find him."

Her eyes widened. "What happened?"

"I fucked up. He came back to Chicago to meet with Victor. I trailed him after the meeting, but he spotted me and pulled his gun. A cop noticed him before we could kill each other."

"I can't believe you were going to kill him after what you did." She looked at me as if she had only just realized I was a bad man.

I shrugged feigning casualness. "It needed to be done, Sprite. I didn't know if he'd talk."

"You mean prove his innocence?"

"Yeah." I held her gaze. She needed to know how ruthless I truly was. My family prospered by taking what we didn't deserve, and her father had been at the head of it all until the tables were turned.

She shook her head, and a single tear slipped down her cheek. "We can never be, Angel. There's too much bad history between us."

Was I mistaken or did she mourn the truth?

I wanted her father dead for causing my father's death and my mother's destruction, and now both my parents are dead. Theo was the only thing left to fuel my vendetta, but looking at her, I realized I had every reason to give it up.

"Come here."

"No."

I sighed. "One day, this cat and mouse game will get old," I lied. It would never get old. I'd always chase her, and she knew it too.

"It's not a game. You scare me, Angel."

I crossed the room until I towered over her and then slowly ran a finger over her naked hip. "My wife doesn't have to be afraid of me."

"But I'm not your wife. Our fathers were fools."

"They're far from it, Sprite. They knew exactly what they were doing when they forged our marriage. They used us for their interests, and now we're husband and wife." I wrapped my hand around her nape and pulled her body into mine. "Till death do us part."

Her green eyes blazed with irritation. "You should sleep with one eye open, husband. We wouldn't want to part sooner than later."

"I should heed that seeing as you've tried to kill me once before."

"It would be wise." I felt myself harden at the possibility of her murdering me in my sleep and chuckled. Her scowl deepened as my cock pressed against her bare stomach. She tried to pull away, but I swiftly wrapped my arm around her waist and pulled her closer.

"You don't need to run away from what's yours." I took her hand and slid it under the waistband of my gym shorts. Her small hand closed around my cock, and with her head tilted, keeping our eyes connected, she petted my beast with small strokes. I couldn't resist taking advantage and pressed my lips against hers. Her lips moved with mine, but she was still holding back. "Let me have that sweet tongue, baby."

"If I do, you'll fuck me."

"I'll fuck you harder if you don't." She couldn't hold back her reaction. Her body trembled in my arms, and I tasted her moan. "You want to sin with me, don't you, wife?"

Her answer was to grip my cock tighter in her palm. I backed her up to the nearest wall and lifted her. "Then again… it's not a sin for a man to fuck his wife."

"Unless she's unwilling."

"Are you unwilling?"

She answered by wrapping her legs around my waist while I pushed my shorts down enough to free my cock. "This doesn't mean anything," she moaned as I slid inside her. She was soaking wet and taking me greedily inside her.

"Is that right?"

"It's just sex. An itch to scratch."

I chuckled as I moved her hands from my shoulders to the wall above her head. The pain in my chest her words had created would have to wait. Right now, she was oblivious, completely vulnerable.

I moved inside her skillfully, drawing out her pleasure, and convincing her she'd do anything to have more. I tasted the sweat on her skin and smiled at the sound of her sweet moans. The sound was nothing compared to her screams when she was overwhelmed by what my body did to hers.

I wanted that again.

Before I could consider control, my hips moved with a mind of their own, turning our fucking from slow and easy to frenzied. "Am I scratching your itch, Sprite? Huh?" She could do nothing but take it as I pounded her. Her squeals of pained pleasure spurred me on. "Tell me, have I reached the mother fucking *spot*?" I moved my hand between our bodies and found her clit. Her mouth fell open, and her head fell back. She convulsed violently, shocking me and scaring herself. She had never come this hard before. I was forced to let her hands go and wrap my arms tight around her to keep from losing control.

"You…bastard," she gasped with harsh breaths. I could still feel the tight heat of her pussy pulsing around me.

"A bastard couldn't make you come that hard."

"Why did you—"

"Fuck you until you saw stars?" I was already moving inside her again. She gasped and clutched my shoulders.

"Don't make me come like that again." The tremble in her voice sounded like real fear.

"I wouldn't dream of it," I lied. It didn't take long before I felt my balls tighten. I was still feeling vengeful, so I waited until the very last moment before pulling her to her knees. I used her slender neck to pull her head back and came all over her pretty innocent face. Her mouth fell open in shock, and a drop of cum slid over her top lip. "Lick it up and swallow it," I ordered when she gaped. Her tongue obediently swept her lips, taking more of my cum when she closed her lips.

"Good girl." I pulled my shorts up and backed away from her before I gave in to the urge to take her again. "Let me know if you get an itch again." I headed for the bathroom. I needed a shower and space to think. I had a war to win and I all I've done was find my way between Mian's thighs.

"Asshole," I heard her mutter just before the door closed.

CHAPTER FIFTEEN

MIAN

"**W**E GOT A PROBLEM," LUCAS ANNOUNCED.

I'd fucking say.

After our fight, Z had brought a fed and sleepy Caylen upstairs for his nap, and the three of us spent the rest of the morning locked away in Angel's bedroom. Angel had his hand planted over my mouth, so I didn't wake the baby while he tortured me with his mouth and fingers. I was on the precipice when Lucas barged in with a scowl and a gun in his hand. Angel took his time freeing my nipple from his mouth and his fingers from my pussy, but when he saw Lucas ready for war, he was out of bed before I could blink. I scrambled to pull the sheets he'd kicked to the foot of the bed over my body and tried to act normal despite their casual disregard for my nudity.

"What's up?" Angel questioned as he stepped into his

jeans commando-style.

"Reginald is here."

Angel's mood shifted right before my eyes as he cursed, threw on a t-shirt, and stormed from the room with Lucas on his heels. Curiosity had me scrambling for our bags in the corner and quickly dressing. I checked to make sure Caylen was still asleep before following them. Guns meant this wasn't a social call, so I wisely stayed hidden near the stairs when I found Angel, Lucas, and Z in the foyer, towering in a circle around two men of middle height and build. The men didn't appear intimidated. In fact, the older man with a full head of thick, salt and pepper hair wore a smug smile and held his head high. The second man's back was turned. I studied his wavy, brown hair and broad shoulders that rivaled Lucas's, his waist narrow, reminding me of a football player in uniform.

"You want to tell me why you're here uninvited?" Angel growled.

"You know as well as I do that I have as much right to be here as you do. The estate is home to anyone with Knight blood." It was then I noticed the suitcases at their feet.

"You know the rules. I haven't welcomed you, have I?" There were only a few times I've witnessed Angel so menacing and none of those occurrences ended well.

"You should. My home was broken into and vandalized last night." He lowered his head and voice conspiratorially. "What do you think they were looking for?" I shook my head from the shadows. Baiting Angel was a bad idea, yet this man didn't look worried.

"Careful, cousin." I guess that would explain why he wasn't worried.

"It isn't me who should take care. We all know what it will mean for you if you cannot keep our family protected."

"There may be a time when your line rules again, but that time is not today."

Angel started to walk away when the older man shouted, "I demand your protection, Angeles! You can't deny me sanctuary. You know this."

From my vantage point, I could see Angel's jaw working before he turned on his heel, picked up the man's suitcase, and shoved it in one of the staff's hands. "Please, show my cousin and his son to a guestroom *for the night*." My gaze drifted to the son Angel referred to. He couldn't have been much older than I am, and he didn't possess the hard edge Angel did, though I could see a faint resemblance between them. Throughout the entire exchange, he hadn't spoken, but when he turned, I could see the same smugness on his face that his father displayed so foolishly.

Z repeated Angel's actions and directed the staff to take their bags. It didn't look like they were planning to stay long, but Angel was clearly not happy to have them here. I was ready to slip back upstairs, but I couldn't take my eyes away. The guys had already put their guns away, but their expressions remained hard.

"I was so sorry to hear about your grandfather," the son spoke. It was odd that he didn't sound the least bit sympathetic. "Did you ever catch who was responsible?"

"No, but I'll find them."

"Eventually. You've got your hands full already, don't you?" Angel's cold gaze sliced to the older man. I held my breath as I waited to hear his response or to see what he might do.

Suddenly, movement to my left caught my attention.

Lucas had somehow spotted me and moved unassumingly toward my hiding spot. "What are you doing," he hissed when he reached me. He grabbed my armed and pulled me deeper into the shadows. I could hear Angel speaking but couldn't make out what he was saying. Whatever they were discussing didn't sound friendly.

"Who are they?" I asked even though I already knew. Until the funeral, Angel's family had been but a myth. He'd barely spoke to any of them at the funeral, but even so, the hostility between Angel and Reginald was certainly a twist.

"Reginald and Andrew are father and son. They're also Angel's cousins."

"Why are they here?"

He took a deep breath and blew it all out at once. "It doesn't matter. They'll be gone tomorrow. You just need to stay away from them."

"It's going to be kind of hard with them in the same house, isn't it?"

"I'm serious, Mian. Stay away from Reginald. He's bad news, and you don't want him to find out about you and Angel?" His lips closed in a tight line.

"What is it that Angel doesn't want them to know?" I demanded. I was sick of them forcing me to live by their rules. If Angel was going to keep me here, I had a right to know what my father married me into.

He shoved his fingers in his hair before saying, "You should really be hearing this from Angel."

"Well, according to Angel, I'm his wife, so why don't I found out right now? Family should meet, after all." Before he could react, I walked around him and hurried into the foyer. I was met with surprised looks from Reginald and Andrew. Angel, Z, and Lucas, however, were not amused.

"Hi." I held out my hand to Reginald who was slow to get over his shock.

"I don't believe we've met," he said as he shook my head. "Who are you?"

"I'm sorry. My name is Mian Ross," I paused and peeked over my shoulder at Angel before saying, "Actually, I guess it's Knight now." If I thought I took him by surprise before, it was nothing compared to the startled incredulity taking over his face now.

"Come again, young lady?"

"Angel and I are married," I giggled, playing the role of a happy bride. I shouldn't have enjoyed pissing Angel off as much as I did. I felt fingers wrap around one side of my waist before I was pulled away from Reginald and Andrew. I looked up and found Angel's simmering brown gaze boring into me.

"What are you doing?"

"Honey, you didn't tell me we were having guests. I would have put on something more appropriate." His eyes promised retribution as Reginald introduced me to his son. Their gazes were curious and calculation as they sized me up.

"So when did this happen?" Reginald questioned while looking between Angel and me.

"Three years ago," I blurted before Angel could stop me. I was going to be bound and gagged to his bed later. I just knew it.

"My dear, you don't look old enough to have been married for three years. How have we've never heard about your marriage before?" Reginald directed the question to Angel, but it was I who answered.

"I was only sixteen when our fathers arranged for us to

be married against—"

I never got to finish that sentence when Angel picked me up and hauled me over his shoulder before walking away, leaving his perplexed family behind.

He carried me into a room, dropped me on my feet none too gently, and shut the door. He kept his back turned, and his hands braced on the door. His shoulders moved as he breathed in and out deeply. A few moments passed before he turned and regarded me with his back against the door, seemingly calm.

"What the hell was that, Sprite?"

"You insist that this marriage our fathers forged is real, so I'm just playing the part, husband."

"You think you can play this game, but let me enlighten you, *wife,* this isn't a chess board. When you move your pieces, you better be goddamn sure of the play."

"How can I be sure of anything if you keep secrets from me?"

"Reginald isn't your fucking concern."

"Then why does Lucas think I should hear it from you?"

He cursed and said, "What happens to you now is on you. Remember that." He then ripped open the door. "Go upstairs and wait for me." He didn't speak after that, and neither did I. He was wound tight as he held the door open. Upstairs, I held my son and waited for the consequences of what I'd done.

CHAPTER SIXTEEN

ANGEL

I t was all I could do not to follow Mian back to our room and forget about the problem that showed up on my doorstep and the one that waited for me beyond it.

Her stunt had written her fate in stone. Once a Knight, you die a Knight.

There had been a rumor among my family regarding my willingness to produce an heir. Mian was a threat to Reginald and all of Alexander's line. Not even Caylen was safe, even though the blood of Caylen's father running through his veins ensured he could never inherit from me.

I found Reginald waiting in the grand library, standing before the original paintings of the Bandits. The ones in my father's home were copycats he insisted having.

"Tell me why you're really here."

"I think I've been more than patient, Angeles. I suspect I've long had the right to claim your life. No one who carries our name will question my mercy when I do." He paused as if in thought while an evil gleam filled his eyes. "You aren't fit to rule, and once I prove it, your head is mine."

"Since when did your line care for tradition? What do you think will happen to you when you try to sell the book?"

"I'm not as foolish as my grandfather. I'm going to wield it just like you, only for a better profit."

"Getting fucked in the ass is okay as long as you're getting paid to bend over, right?" I grinned, but he didn't share my amusement. Instead, he turned to the makeshift bar my ancestors made out of the bookcase shelving and poured a drink.

With his back turned, he said, "Your friends Lucas and Zachariah are quite good at doing your job. Arturo trained them, did he not?"

I didn't need to guess what he was hinting at. "They'd never work for you. You'll be lucky if they don't kill you *if* I die at your hands."

"Every man wants money and power, Angeles. I'd be willing to offer them more than you've ever given them. What will happen to me then? Do you think your childish idea of brotherhood will survive when the worms are crawling from your skull, and you have only our dead ancestors to keep you company?"

He turned to face me with a confident grin curling the thin line of his lips. "The more you offer, the slower they'll kill you."

"Well, that's too bad." He shrugged. "I guess they'll

have to be taken care of as well. I'm a resourceful man. I may not have the muscle or skill for killing, but you shouldn't underestimate me, cousin."

"I make a point not to underestimate anyone," I assured him.

"Hm. So your father did teach you something after all," he whispered wistfully.

"Fuck. You."

"Angeles, I am not your enemy nor am I the villain." He slowly lifted the glass, but stopped just before the rim could touch his lips and said, "I am simply returning the mercy your line showed mine."

He took a slow sip of his drink before moving toward the door and bumping my shoulder lightly on his way out. I stood alone in the library and pondered my next move. The gazes of all the Knights before me, including my father, bore down on me with expectancy within the gold that framed the paintings, but I only had eyes for Archibald Knight. The painter successfully captured the cold greed in his blue eyes.

Reginald told the truth. He wasn't the villain of this story.

I heard a knock and then, "Penny for your thoughts?" Mian's soft voice went straight to my cock, and I didn't try to hide it from her when I turned away from my dead predecessors and faced my future. Her gaze dipped and then shifted as a blush spread over her cheeks.

"I thought I told you to go upstairs."

"I'm your wife," she sneered, "not your child." She moved around me, and I turned with her to keep her in sight and watched as her head tilted. "You had the paintings moved?"

"These are the originals," I answered, matching her bland tone. When she fell silent, I didn't bother to wait for her to reveal her hand. "How much did you hear?"

"What makes you think I heard anything?" she parried. I moved closer and watched her shoulders stiffen when she felt me press against her.

"Because you wouldn't be here if you hadn't."

"Does it matter? If I ask, you'll just lie to me." I wrapped my arms around her entire midsection and anchored her to me. To a perfect stranger, I was just a man holding his wife.

"Tell me what you heard."

She sighed and slammed her head a little too hard against my chest. I stifled a groan and waited. "I heard him say you shouldn't underestimate him."

"I don't intend to."

"I heard that too," she confirmed. She pushed to break free of my arms, and I let her, but then she surprised me when she didn't put distance between us. She turned and dug her nails into my chest, her eyes desperate. "Tell me that my son and I are safe here."

I took the pain because I deserved it. "You're safe with *me*."

Her gaze narrowed. "What were the two of you talking about?" I hesitated too long. "If you don't want to wake up one morning and find us gone, then tell me everything."

I had more men now than ever. She wasn't going anywhere, but letting her believe in her freedom was a step forward. I sighed and led her over to the dark oak table spanning almost the length of the room. When I pulled her into my lap, for once, she didn't bother fighting my possession. She stared into the windows of my soul searching for the truth before I could speak it.

"Two hundred years ago, Reginald's second great-grandfather, Alexander Knight, turned to petty thievery to help feed his mother, brother, and sister after his father died. It wasn't long before he expanded to robbing the homes of vulnerable merchants and wealthy politicians. Eventually, he crossed paths with the right people. People who wanted to keep their hands clean of their dirty secrets. His infamy spread, the rich got into his head, and he started stealing secrets. It wasn't long before dead bodies began to turn up."

"How did the book happen?"

"His clients were paying him so much they began to believe they could control him, and for a while, they did."

"So he wrote the book as blackmail."

"It worked like a charm for most. Those who sought to challenge him disappeared while others set a gruesome example. After that, my uncle was more than infamous. He was feared."

"And people still trusted him?"

"He was good at what he did. The promise of gain outweighed their fear of him. Some people even tried to bribe him with more money to keep their exploits from the book, but he wasn't willing to give up the power he held. By then, he'd lost sight of why he started stealing in the first place. He was addicted to his new life. So much so, he didn't produce his heir until he was fifty-six."

"How did he swing that?"

"He married a girl half his age and bred her."

"The men in your family really know how to woo," she drawled sardonically.

I pinched her thigh and continued. "Archibald didn't

inherit until he was twenty-five. Alexander was eighty-one and far past his prime, but it didn't hinder him. A few had entertained the thought that he was even immortal."

"Why didn't he pass the torch sooner?"

"Archibald was frivolous."

"His father didn't trust him," she stated bluntly.

"He was right not to. Archibald is responsible for this estate and as beautiful as it is, it plunged this family into a financial hole so deep, Archibald became desperate enough to bribe."

"He kept jobs out of the book?"

"Only if they could pay the price, but when it wasn't enough to cover the debt, he tried to sell the book."

She shifted, and I struggled to ignore what the feel of her ass moving over my cock did to me. "What happened?"

"Alec, my second great-grandfather, found out and confronted him. Archibald had him killed."

"I'm sorry," she whispered woefully.

I shrugged. Mourning was for those who had something to miss. Blood tied us together not affection. "Adan, his son and my great-grandfather, took his head." I left out the part about mine now being on the chopping block.

"And then he became the Knight?"

"It's as you said. Alexander didn't trust his son. Not only that, but Angelo, Alexander's brother, wanted his own son to reign. Alexander was too proud to dismiss his heir outright, so they made a pact, and Alexander included a clause in his will. His son would forfeit his place as head of the family, and that right would be transferred to Angelo's line."

"Why do all of your names begin with 'A' except for Reginald?"

"It's a tradition started by Alexander. Sort of like branding each firstborn son."

Her eyebrows pinched together. "What happens if you only have girls?"

"Then power—*the legacy*—goes to the next eligible heir. For descendants of Meredith and Angelo, the legacy will default back to Alexander's line."

I hid my smile when she rolled her eyes. It was a barbaric practice, but Alexander wasn't a modern man. "As for Reginald's name, his father wanted nothing to do with family tradition or our business dealings, and neither did his father."

"So, if Adan hadn't killed Archibald, wouldn't this whole Bandit business have died with him?"

I nodded. "Archibald was seventy years old and still in power when Adan killed him. He thought August was too weak, but I believe the truth was he didn't want to relinquish power. Fortunately, Adan had been well within his rights to kill Archibald and seize the legacy which didn't August wanted nothing to do with the family business and shielded Andrew from that life as much as he could."

"But he still named him Andrew..."

"Archibald's doing," I muttered. "Andrew shared his father's sentiments and named his son Reginald."

"And then there's Reginald who fell a mile from the tree." She seemed deep in thought as we shared the silence. "He knows the book is missing, doesn't he? He's here to kill you and take back the legacy."

I still didn't answer, but my silence was as loud as if I had roared. She shook her head and then dropped the weight on my chest. "I'm scared."

I stiffened underneath her. Was it possible that little

Mian Ross cared for me? I wanted to lift her head and stare into her eyes until I found the truth, but I didn't. My hands continued to clutch the arms of the chair we shared. I couldn't promise her nothing would happen to me, but I could make sure she was safe before I took my last breath.

"He's never going to touch you," I finally promised.

Her head lifted, and she met my gaze. "What about you?"

"What about me?" Her expression said she wasn't fooled, so I sighed and said, "I'm taking care of it."

"I don't think I can be like you. I can never be comfortable with death."

"What makes you think I'm comfortable?"

"You kill people and sleep well at night." The truth wasn't as black and white as she made it seem.

"I don't mourn those I kill because if I didn't mean it, I wouldn't do it."

"What about your mother? She just died, and it doesn't seem to have affected you at all."

"I lost my mother a long time ago, Mian." For the sake of not repeating an argument, I left out the fact that I blamed her father.

"So did I," she whispered. "It's been nine years, and while time may have numbed the pain, it hasn't ever gone away."

"We grieve differently, Sprite."

"Except you didn't grieve. You framed my father and ruined my life." She started to rise from my lap, but a soft touch to her waist, unlike the force she was used to from me, had her freezing in place.

"I'm sorry for what I did to you."

"But not my father." It wasn't a question. I swallowed

hard to keep the truth from spilling. I didn't want to fight with her, especially when my dick grew harder by the second.

"I wish I could be," I said instead.

She watched me. Her green eyes glowed with hate and disbelief. "I wish I could be sorry too." I didn't see it until it was too late. The light caught the metal as she swung the knife, aiming for my throat. I wrenched the knife from her hand and shoved her to the ground. She slid across the floor. I rose from my seat and flung the knife out of reach as I stalked after her.

"Are you completely unconcerned with keeping your life?"

She smirked, the bitch. "You're not going to kill me."

"No, baby, I'm not going to kill you." She started to rise from the floor. I quickly wrapped my fingers around her arm. "But I am going to fuck you." She didn't get the chance to struggle before I lifted her on the table. Mian made a lovely centerpiece.

She watched, frozen and fascinated, as I removed my shirt. Her gaze was stuck on my bare chest, so she didn't notice when I joined her on the table. It wasn't until I tugged that she realized where we were headed. "You think sex is the answer for everything," she griped. "It won't keep me from killing you."

"It will keep me from killing *you*." I needed to be inside her. It was the only way we could be free of hate without destroying each other. Besides…it wasn't fear that made her body tremble as I pushed her flat on her back.

She needed it too.

She didn't fight me as I finished removing her clothes. Didn't protest when my lips touched her hot skin. She didn't even try to pretend she didn't want it.

"That's the second time you tried to kill me." I kissed down her stomach.

"If you're not careful, it'll become a habit," she breathed. Her body jerked as if shocked by electricity when I licked the skin just above her pussy. Only Mian could threaten me and come apart for me simultaneously. God was feeling pretty self-indulgent the day he created her, and he secured my rightful place in hell when he placed her in my path. "I'm not afraid of you, Angel Knight."

"You don't have to be afraid of me." I yanked her panties down her slender legs and stuffed them in my back pocket. "But you should be afraid of what you'll become without me."

She gasped and shivered when my mouth hovered over her sex, and I inhaled her scent. Suddenly, I didn't want to breathe again unless it was her essence that filled my body with life.

"We aren't enemies." I placed a soft kiss upon her sex, and she jerked again in my arms. "That will never be us again." I crawled up her supple body and settled between her legs. "It's time you understood," I slid inside her slowly, "just how permanent we are." She sucked in a breath and held it. The monster prowling beneath my surface snapped at my restraint, challenging me to release it or to be forever ruined. "I need you, Mian." I slowly moved inside her. "Say you believe me."

Slowly, oh so slowly, she released the air she'd trapped. "I believe you," she admitted breathlessly. A smile of triumph teased my lips. Instead, I kissed her bare shoulder, rewarding her rather than gloating. I felt her soft hands run through my hair and then tug on the strands until our gazes were locked. "I just don't care."

Her gaze was both wary and defiant, expecting retaliation but refusing to fear it. Three years ago, I would have relished her fear because I couldn't have anything else.

But this wasn't three years ago, and she was no longer forbidden.

She was mine.

To have, to hold, and to ruin.

I kissed the generous slope of her breasts and watched her nipple harden. "I don't believe you." She cared. More than what was right. More than she would ever admit. She cared. She would always care because I belonged to her. That would never change.

"I don't care." Her voice broke when I shifted, brushing against her clit. I lifted her left leg over my shoulder and slid deeper.

"I don't believe you," I repeated unsteadily, my voice as unreliable as hers.

Her lashes lowered, shutting in the emotion she didn't want me to see. "I don't care."

"I *don't* believe you," I bit out slowly this time. The rabid beast I held at bay pulled at the restraints now, no longer willing to be caged. It wanted to claim her, make her bend to its will. I wanted to give her passion and leave fear in the past.

"I don't care," she shouted—not convincingly—at the filigree ceiling. I pumped into her, fucking her harder now. Faster. I was doing my duty while the Knights who ruled before me watched.

"You do care." I gripped her harder than I should have. My hands would no doubt bruise her soft skin with my mark and damn if that didn't just make me fuck her harder.

"You care so fucking much you'd risk your own life just to prove yourself wrong." She pressed her lips tight, cutting off the sob before it could release. The next moment, she was shoving me away and crawling backward across the table to put space between us. I could feel her arousal coating my dick as I tucked myself back into my pants and slid from the tabletop.

"What do you want from me if not my life? A possession? I won't be your trophy," she vowed before I could answer. "I'll never stop fighting to get away from you."

I didn't want to own her or strip away her most beautiful parts.

I wanted to protect her.

Nurture her.

Keep her, the beast hissed.

"Stay." It took everything I had left not to close the distance between us. "I just want you to stay."

"I'll try on one condition."

"Name it."

"There was a couple who took me in back in Mosset where Lucas and Z found me. When you led the senator to me, Becky got hurt. I don't know if she's alive and I—"

"Consider it done."

"But I didn't tell you what I wanted."

"I don't just know what's in your head, Mian. I also know what's in your heart."

CHAPTER SEVENTEEN

MIAN

I WALKED BAREFOOT DOWN A ROSE-LINED PATH, INCHING nearer and nearer to the end. Sunshine brighter than I'd ever witnessed surrounded me and warmed my blood. Birds with feathers the color of spring sang and danced around me, but instead of a happy, musical lilt, they screamed at me to turn back. Flee.

I wanted to.

But Angel's promise of beauty and pleasure pulled me closer to my doom.

"When you retreat inside your head, you let down your guard, and I can see everything you're thinking." He trailed a wet finger across my forehead, smoothing the frown lines before pulling away.

"What am I thinking?" I challenged. I was sitting in his lap, my back to his chest as we soaked our tired bones in the white marble tub. I committed to memory the hand paint-ed walls, marble floors, and the skylight above us because no matter what Angel threatened, this was temporary.

"You're thinking marriage to me is all you've ever wanted after all." I chanced a peek over my shoulder. His smile was quick and full of charm, but I wasn't so easily fooled. Not anymore.

"Not even close." I pinched his cheek and shook his face. "But you're cute when you dream."

He snatched his face away and quickly captured my fingers between his teeth. I yelped and scrambled away. Water sloshed over the rim of the tub and onto the marble. The predatory light in his eyes as I settled on the opposite side was a warning. *I could catch you whenever I want.* My fingers where he bit me throbbed. I glared. He smiled.

"You should keep your mouth to yourself."

The cocky bastard slid lower until he was lounging with one leg planted and his toes brushing my hip. I almost jerked away, but I didn't want to give him the satisfaction.

"But it's my favorite way to make you come."

My clit pulsed, and I wanted his teeth sinking into my thigh just before his tongue lapped up proof that I wanted him. My two-timing cunt always gave away my secrets.

"The water is getting cold," I said dismissively.

After an uncomfortable moment of staring he rose from the tub, dripping with lavender soap and water. It was glorious and gaudy, and it made me want to use my tongue to trace every path the water took until he was completely dry.

If he noticed my staring, he didn't let on as he helped me out and handed me a towel.

Back in the bedroom, he dug through my bag and

handed me a pair of my jeans and a shirt before dressing himself in dark jeans and white Henley. I followed him with his hand on the small of my waist down the wide hall until we reached the same room I had found this morning.

I could hear Caylen's laugh on the other side of the door and didn't wait for permission or for Angel to open the door. I pushed inside and felt Angel's hovering as he stood behind me.

Lucas and Z, crouching on their haunches in the middle of the room, hadn't seemed to notice us. Their attention was too focused on my son standing between them as he nibbled and drooled on his fist. "Come on, little man." Caylen grinned at Z. "You can say it."

My head cocked, wondering exactly what he wanted him to say.

"Say Daddy," Lucas gently demanded a moment later.

Angel swore though it sounded as if it were covering up a laugh.

Z frowned. "Do you think he won't say it because he knows we're not his father?"

I'd had enough. "What the *fuck* is going on here?"

Lucas and Z rose to their full height. Z tossed me an apologetic look while Lucas grinned and shrugged. Caylen noticed me and wobbled toward me as fast as his baby legs would allow.

"Mama."

"Oh, sure," Lucas drawled. "*That* he will say."

"Mama's boy," Z coughed. I picked my son up and glared at Angel's idiotic friends.

"What the hell is your problem? Why would you do that?"

"We thought we might help."

"His father doesn't even want him." Their gazes lifted over my head and their smiles brightened.

"Well, we figured with the marriage and all—" My growl was more than enough to keep Z from finishing that sentence.

"Stay away from my son." I turned to leave and glared at their leader when he didn't move. Wordlessly, he stepped aside. I met his gaze as I passed him, but his expression was unreadable, so I fixed my attention on Caylen.

"Did those bad men try to confuse you?"

He giggled and waved at them over my shoulder.

I was seething as their laughter followed me down the hall. This place was easy to get lost in, and with Angel's family in residence, I didn't want to chance running into any of them.

Especially his cousin.

According to Angel, he was greedy and desperate, and if what he told me about his family was true, then it was enough for me to believe him.

The library was the easiest to find, so I figured it was as good a hiding place as any. Caylen started to become restless without Lucas and Z to entertain him, so I skimmed the unending sea of spines until I found what I was looking for. Reading to him before his nap felt too normal for the situation we were in now. This wasn't our home, and we weren't a family, but Angel was committed to pretending.

When Caylen's eyes finally drifted shut halfway through the story, I laid him on the black love seat with gold trimming and covered him with a soft bronze throw that looked like it was purely for show.

My gaze was on the fire burning in the fireplace when the door opened. I didn't bother lifting my gaze from the flames when I said, "I thought you'd be busy playing criminal mastermind with your bonehead playmates."

A chuckle that wasn't rich and deep answered me. "I've become much too old for playmates, my dear." Reginald strolled inside with his hands casually resting in the pockets of his burgundy pants. "We haven't been properly introduced."

"I think we know enough actually. You're Angel's shady cousin, and I'm his unwilling wife."

I could tell I had said too much when his eyes lit with curiosity. "And what about this marriage makes you unwilling? I noticed my young cousin didn't shower that delicate finger of your left hand with diamonds."

Angel had warned me that Reginald couldn't be trusted, and at the first opportunity, I offered him our secrets on a platter. "Did I say unwilling? I meant devoted."

"I'm sure you did." I moved closer to my son with each step he took. "I was mistaken by your display earlier."

"How so?"

"I didn't peg you for the type to be trained."

"You think loyalty makes me a pet?"

"I think blind loyalty makes you a fool."

"And what exactly makes me blind?"

"My cousin is young, and at times, a bit too merciful, but he is also clever."

"What makes him clever?"

"His ability to make anyone believe what he wants." He studied me. "I assume he's told you not to trust me."

"I'm curious why it matters to you if I trust you or not. We're perfect strangers."

"With a common problem," he added. He took my silence as an invitation to continue. "When I take back what belongs to me, I don't want there to be any hard feelings. In fact, I have a proposition for you."

"You're right. He did tell me not to trust you, and even if he hadn't, I wouldn't." I lifted my sleeping child from the couch. "I'm not interested in a proposition. I'll be going now."

I was rooted to the spot, however, when I realized Reginald stood between escape and me. Would he try to stop me from leaving?

"What a beautiful child you've made with my dutiful cousin."

"Angel isn't his father."

He didn't look surprised by my admission. He looked pleased. "That's too bad. Your bastard child will never be his son in the way that matters."

I considered taking the iron poker by the fireplace and running it through him. "And what way is that?"

"He can never be his heir."

Was it the thought of Angel never accepting Caylen that made the knot in my stomach tighter or fear that, heir or not, if I stayed with Angel, this life would one day consume Caylen as it did Angel? "I would never let that happen," I vowed aloud.

Reginald's lips pinched. "Then I assume he hasn't explained your duties."

"I don't care," I snapped even as that knot tightened again. My duty was to my son. Fuck everyone else. Including Angel.

"It is said that when a lion takes over a pride and wishes to breed with a lioness, he will kill her cub to force her into heat."

Reginald's poison spread, curdling my blood and

stealing my breath. "He wouldn't hurt him."

"One day, you may give him no choice. Your refusal to give him an heir will force his hand."

"Angel knows killing my son won't make me give him one he can use."

"Don't be so naive, girl, or you'll soon discover how ruthless my cousin can be."

My naïveté was the very reason men like Reginald and Victor continued to underestimate me. Instead of crumbling under its weight, I used it as a shield until the right moment to strike.

"I think I'll take my chances."

"Mama!" Caylen clapped his hands and chased unsteadily after a red leaf blowing in the autumn wind. We found solace in the garden after Caylen's nap and my run-in with Reginald. So many rooms in this beautiful guarded home and none of them felt safe.

"Not so fast," I called when he almost stumbled.

He toddled around a bend of bushes and quickly disappeared from sight. I sped to catch up at the same time I heard the unmistakable sound of leaves being crushed. We had ventured deep into the garden because Caylen found everything fascinating, and now I was regretting that decision when it became apparent we weren't alone. When I spun around to see who was following me, I was met with thin air. Still, I searched the area, and when I didn't see anyone, I turned back and rushed down the path. I grew desperate, and my heart pounded faster each second he remained out of sight.

"Caylen?"

I was screaming his name by the time I rounded the third bend and came to a screeching halt when I found him. At the end of the path just before the last bend, I found him sitting on the stone path and crouched next to him was Andrew. His smile felt like acid on my tongue. I rushed forward drawing their attention. In Caylen's fist were pieces of the golden leaf he had chased. The brittle leaves must have crumbled when he caught it, which explained the fresh tears on his cheeks.

"Something seems to have upset the little guy," Andrew greeted when I stood in front of them. I didn't hesitate to lift Caylen from the ground and back away. "Whoa," he pleaded when he sensed my panic.

"Stay away from us," I warned when he followed.

"I'm not going to hurt you."

"Then why were you following us?"

He stopped and shoved his hands in his pockets. "I wasn't."

"Bullshit. I heard you."

"I wasn't following you. I swear. Your son found me not the other way around."

"I don't believe you."

"Look." He gestured with his head since his hands were still shoved deep in the pocket of his jeans. I stopped moving and forced my attention off the path near a low hedge where a gray stone bench was positioned. Lying on the flat surface was a well-worn book.

Reluctantly, my gaze returned to him, and I hoped my embarrassment didn't show on my cheeks. "Sorry."

He chuckled as he bounced on the tips of his toes. "Want to tell me why you're on edge?"

"I told you. Someone was following me."

His condescending smile stretched. "This is a big place on a very large property. There are servants and people who work the grounds all over this place. They know how to work and stay hidden, so I assure you we're never alone."

"Look, I said I'm sorry."

"And I accept your apology." His smile only grew, but it didn't feel harmless.

"Whatever." I turned to leave when his voice stopped me.

"Please don't leave on my account. I didn't mean to upset you, and I'm sure if my cousin knew I had scared you, it wouldn't end well for me."

Against my better judgment, I didn't leave. I turned and set Caylen on his feet, but captured his hand when he tried to move back to his crumbled leaves. He didn't seem bothered by Andrew's presence, so I told myself I didn't need to be.

"Why would Angel hurt you? You're his family."

His eyebrows rose. "We aren't the typical kind of family."

"What kind of family are you?"

He seemed to mull it over. "Competitive."

"You mean deadly. I know what your family is all about, so to answer your question, *that* is why I'm on edge."

Andrew simply sighed and lowered his long thin frame on the bench. "I was named after my grandfather. He was a gentle man. My father loved him, but he didn't respect him. We're not all monsters, you know." He picked up the book as his gaze met mine. "But my cousin? He's the scariest of us all."

"Are you trying to turn me against him?"

"No." He smiled again. "Scary is good. It keeps the others at bay."

"Except your father."

"My father is a foolish man."

"You're not on his side?"

"If I had a choice?" He shook his head and studied the bushes on the other side of the path. "No. I wouldn't be."

"And why is that?"

"My father doesn't just want Angel's power. He wants to kill him."

"I didn't realize you and Angel were close."

"We aren't, but my cousin has never wronged me."

"Your father doesn't seem to hold that same sentiment. Sins of the father and all that."

He looked at me then, studying me. "How much do you know?"

"Not much," I lied. If Andrew told me the same story as Angel, then it meant two things: Angel was telling the truth, and I might have an ally in Andrew.

"Alexander was my third great-grandfather. He started this legacy to help us prosper, but it's only driven us into wanting to kill each other for the right to control it. After Adam had died of consumption, Alexander tried to fill his father's shoes but found them too large."

"What do you mean?"

"Adam was a farmer. He didn't have much land, but he had a gift. Alexander was barely sixteen when he died. The little he'd learned from his father wasn't enough to keep the farm going and pay the few hands they had. It wasn't long before Alexander turned to petty crime to keep food on the table. When they were on the verge of losing their land that desperation made him reckless."

"What about his mother? Couldn't she have just re-married? Wasn't that the way then?" Hell, it was still the way now.

"Adam and Amelia's marriage was arranged, but there was a rumor they had actually fallen in love."

"She thought to remarry would betray their love."

"I don't believe in one true love. I think we're all in danger of falling in love over and over again." I stopped breathing when he focused on me. "It can happen any moment."

Um.

I was one more lingering gaze from leaving when I glanced away, and he muttered, "Frankly, I thought her children deserved better."

"So did she," I retorted. He held my gaze again and smiled. Clearing my throat, I looked away. "So what happened next? He steals to bring home cash. I could have guessed as much."

"Yes, well, one day, he decides to rob the home of John Sullivan. He was a young politician with little experience but gaining ground fast. I won't bore you with politics, but I will tell you his newfound popularity also made him enemies in high places."

"What kind of enemies?"

"Enemies who didn't wish to offer him the chance to make a difference. Enemies like Louis Wilde."

"What did he do?"

"He caught Alexander stealing Sullivan's family ring. When Alexander begged Wilde not to turn him in, Wilde offered him money in exchange for the ring and his silence. My third grandfather didn't know the kind of deal he was making until Wilde later visited him on his farm."

"Why?"

"He wanted Alexander to kill John Sullivan."

"Why would he think a petty thief capable of murder and why would Alexander trust him?"

"Men like Wilde believed money could buy anyone, and he was right, but he underestimated Alexander."

"How so?"

"The gun he used to kill Sullivan belonged to Wilde. The son of a bitch broke into his home, stole the gun, and killed Sullivan with it. Not only that, but he stole the ring back and hid it in a place that Wilde would never find, but it would also implicate him in Sullivan's murder.""

"Why go through all that trouble?"

"Men like Wilde don't get their hands dirty unless they've already found a way to clean them up."

"Alexander thought he was going to turn on him?"

"If he was or not, Alexander never gave him the chance to double-cross him."

"You sound like you admire him."

"He was a smart man. Cunning. Ambitious."

"I'm sorry to break it to you, but your great-great-great-grandfather was a murdering thief."

He chuckled. "That too, I suppose." He seemed so different from Angel who would have warned me to watch my mouth. It was almost astonishing how the two shared the same blood.

"So what happened after Alexander blackmailed him?"

"He hired him again. I guess he appreciated a man who was smart enough to best him. The jobs got bigger, more elaborate, and soon, he was getting his hands dirty for more than just Wilde." He angled his body, so he faced me, and I didn't miss how he moved closer. "It wasn't long before Wilde, and the others thought they could control him."

"So he started the book and took control."

"That's how the story goes," he answered smoothly.

"Why didn't they just kill him?"

"Ah." He snorted. "It wouldn't have mattered. In exchange for his protection and a piece of the pie, he secretly entrusted the book and its contents with Meredith and Angelo. Meredith was content with stability, but eventually, Angelo wanted more. He wanted to share Alexander's power."

"Let me guess… Alexander said no, so Angelo killed his own brother." It was a test, one I was hoping he would pass because I desperately needed an ally.

"No, actually. Alexander made a will, but it was more like a rulebook. Meredith's or Angelo's line could inherit if his own line broke any of the rules."

"What were the rules?"

He hesitated, and the moment he began to answer was when a voice deeper and deadlier broke the silence. "Don't you two look cozy."

I could feel Angel's anger washing over me, as unpredictable and wild as a tsunami, as I turned to face him. Andrew discreetly put distance between us. "Why are you sneaking up on us?"

He took his time answering when Caylen noticed him and excitedly ambled forward. Angel didn't waste time bending his magnificent body to pick him up. I used the distraction to check him out since he'd changed clothes. He was looking sinfully devilish in the dark gray three-piece suit with a black waistcoat and tie. Angel so finely dressed made me feel inadequate in my faded blue jeans and yellow smiley face t-shirt. It made me feel like I didn't deserve to be on his arm.

"I wasn't sneaking" he finally answered. "You didn't notice because my cousin seemed to have captured your attention so well." The jealousy in his voice did unexplainable things to my body. I wanted more of it.

"What can I help you with, husband?" I took delight in the way his eyes narrowed, and his nostrils flared. My smile was small, but he didn't miss it, and his irritation turned into exasperation.

"Anna's here."

Amusement faded, and I was standing up from the bench. "Why?" I haven't seen my friend in nearly a month, but worry over the reason she was here wouldn't allow me to be excited.

Angel's gaze flickered behind me where I knew Andrew watched us. "Come inside, and she'll tell you."

CHAPTER EIGHTEEN

MIAN

W E FOUND ANNA IN A ROOM WITH BLUE WALLS, GOLD rectangular molding, a cerulean love seat, and a fireplace. She was staring out the window pretending not to notice Lucas's attention across the room. The moment we entered, she shot to her feet, scowled at Lucas, and rushed towards us.

"You're really okay! Oh, Mian! I've missed you!" She bounced up and down in that adorable way only Anna could, but when I didn't return her joy, she paused. "Is everything okay?" Her threatening glare was back and directed at Angel when he stepped around me with Caylen still in his arms.

"I was going to ask you the same."

The question in her gaze had me stomping over to Angel with my hands on my hips. I waited as he set Caylen on his feet and ignored how my heart fluttered when he set a steadying hand on his back and didn't move away until he was sure Caylen wouldn't fall.

His back was still to me as he sighed and stood up straight. I couldn't stand the amused purse of his lips when he faced me.

"Yes, Mian?"

"Why is she here?"

His frown before he spoke was sincere. "Is something wrong?"

"Yes," I hissed. "I don't want her here. She needs to go home." *Where she's safe… and away from Lucas.* My peripheral allowed me to see how he stood up straight when I demanded she be sent away.

"Did I do something wrong?" The hurt in Anna's voice made my stomach turn.

"Of course not," I rushed to assure. "But it's not safe here." I faced Angel again. "And you know that."

"Her mother disappeared a couple of days ago," Angel offered.

"And some guy," Z growled, "came around looking for her."

"He spooked me," Anna finished. "I came home from school today and found the door kicked in. I didn't know what else to do."

Shit. "Anna, I'm sorry." Angel and his family were slowly stripping away the parts that made me human, but rather than blame them, I took my friend in my arms. "I'm an ass."

She nodded with her head tucked into my shoulder. "It's okay. You didn't know."

I still wasn't convinced it was any safer for her to be

here, but there was no way I would turn her away. This may not have been my home, but if Angel wanted this marriage, he damn well better protect my friend.

"We'll put her in the room next to ours," he whispered in my ear. His warm breath skated over my skin. I forced myself to let Anna go before she could feel my entire body tremble for him.

"What about school? She can't fall behind." Anna had dreams of being a doctor and the better school she got in, the better chance she'd one day wear that stethoscope.

"I'll get her schoolwork," Z answered.

"Mian is right," Lucas spoke for the first time. His voice was cool as he said, "She shouldn't be here." My gaze slid to him, and his eyes dared me to challenge him. Anna's gasp was so soft, if we hadn't been standing so close, I would have missed it.

"Exactly what is your problem with her staying here?"

Ignoring me, he faced off with Angel. "We can hide her, but it can't be here."

"Where?" Suddenly, I didn't appreciate Angel's indulgence.

"One of your relatives." Angel seemed to mull it over causing another thread of Lucas's control to unravel. "You know what's coming. She can't stay."

What was coming?

"Maybe he's right." Z's grimace was apologetic. "We're tapped out on risks."

The room was silent while Angel thought it over. "Tell the men I need a detail," he said to Lucas.

"What exactly are we talking about here?" I interject-ed. Lucas was already punching buttons on his phone to make bad things happen so problems disappeared.

"It's not the right time." Angel's tone was dismissive. He didn't even look at me.

"I think—"

"I *said* not now," he barked. His glare was now on me full force, warning me not to push.

Maybe I was as spoiled as he had me pegged because I couldn't keep myself from crossing my arms and saying, "Then if she goes, I go."

I didn't see him move. I only felt the pads of his fingers biting into my nape. "Stop acting like you're still a sixteen-year-old brat. You're a woman—my woman—and I'm telling you, wife, you won't be going anywhere." He had shifted me closer and closer as he spoke until my breasts were flush against his chest.

"You don't own me."

"No, I don't, but I want you safe and safe I'll keep you."

"How am I safer here than her?"

"Because she's not mine. You are." I didn't have a response that didn't include melting, but Anna's gasp quickly brought me back to reality.

Fucking him or fighting him, it was always easy to forget that Angel and I weren't the only two people in the world. Anna's shock, Lucas's grimace, and Z's knowing smile told me they'd heard every word.

"Wife?" Anna shrieked.

Angel's fingers gently massaged my nape where he'd gripped me before letting go. I glanced up for help, but it became clear I'd have none when his eyebrows merely rose. I forced myself to face my friend and confess the magnitude of my father's betrayal. "It seems, Anna, our fathers had a marriage certificate forged three years ago."

"What? W—w—why would he do that?"

"He thought he was protecting me."

"But you can have it reversed, right? What he did was illegal."

And it was exactly why I couldn't. An annulment meant implicating my father, and unlike him, I couldn't so easily sacrifice a person I loved, which left a divorce. Angel would never let that happen. He chose that moment to palm my hip, his touch possessive, a branding of my new life placed on my skin. It made me think of his family crest Angel had permanently inked into my skin.

Anna stiffened when her gaze dropped to Angel's hand on my hip. The atmosphere shifted, the air becoming frigid, as Anna seemed to draw the same conclusion. "Divorce her." Everybody in the room froze at the ferocity in her tone.

"And who will make me?" Angel challenged. I shoved an elbow in his gut, but the pain meant for him shot up my own arm.

"How dare you, Angeles Knight." She charged him as if he weren't twice her size with at least six or seven inches on her. "I'm not afraid of you."

"Good." I felt his fingers grip my arm. "You shouldn't be, and as long as you don't cross me, you won't ever need to be." I didn't fight him as he pulled me to the door. I didn't want to face Anna's inquisition right now. I wasn't ready.

I was going to get out of this marriage one way or another.

"Wait. I can't leave Caylen." His strides didn't slow as he continued to lead me away.

"They'll keep an eye on him," he said when we reached the first floor.

"I really wish you wouldn't make decisions about my

child. He isn't your son."

I nearly collided with his back when he stopped suddenly. He shifted until he faced me, and then his strong arm was like a steel band around my waist. The fingers he shoved into my hair, however, felt like a caress.

"Believe me, Mian. I know he's not my son. I know it every second of the day. I know it every time I look at him. He's not mine." He took a deep breath and closed his eyes tight. "But he should have been."

"We were never meant to be, Angel. You know that."

"Fuck what's meant to be." His head dipped as if he would kiss me. "I only care about what will be."

"Are you going to kiss me?" I was panicking inside, but also high from anticipation.

"I want to." His lids lowered, and the sensual husk of his voice made me shiver. "I really fucking want to."

"What if I don't want you to kiss me?"

He growled low in his throat as he licked my bottom lip. "Then I'm lucky that's not a problem." He then kissed the retort from my lips. I couldn't deny him how well he kissed or how good he tasted or how right his body felt against mine. I was betrayed by my whimper when he ended it. "I want to kiss you in other places." I almost begged him to do it when he let me go. He smiled as if he could read my thoughts. Maybe it was the way I swayed towards him. "Maybe later." He kissed me again, offering his tongue, and forcing his groan down my throat. "Definitely later," he promised.

When he pulled me through the front door, with his arm around my waist, lust was put on hold. Three large black SUVs were parked at the end of the steps with scary looking men waiting around it. I pulled on Angel's hand to stop him, but he only forced me down the steps.

"We're leaving? Why are we leaving?" I dug in my heels, but he simply lifted me from the ground and carried me the rest of the way. "Angel! Manhandling me won't make me like you!"

His chuckle as he carefully placed me inside the middle SUV sounded so sexy that I hated him even more.

"What about Anna?" I questioned when he followed me inside.

"They'll look after her too."

"You mean Lucas? Yeah, he seemed really eager to keep her safe."

"He is." A large hulking man appeared and stole Angel's attention. "Let's go," he ordered. The man didn't hesitate to disappear, and seconds later, we were moving.

"I don't understand how you can allow Lucas to act like such an ass to her."

"He's a grown man, baby."

"I don't trust him with her."

"He doesn't trust himself," he replied matter-of-factly. At my perplexed look, he sighed. "He wants her. If she stays here, she'll be back under him, and he'll hate himself for it."

"Then maybe we shouldn't leave him alone with her."

"He can control himself for a few hours."

I sighed and forced myself to relax. The estate was deep in the countryside of Illinois. For miles, there was nothing but open space whose beauty I couldn't bring myself to appreciate. I was far away from the apartment I was sure I didn't have any longer, and now I was forced to trust a man who caused me to lose everything. Angel drew my attention when he slid out of his suit jacket, leaving him in the waistcoat.

"Where are you taking me, Angeles?" His eyes cut to the side, watching me warily.

"Angeles? You don't call me Angeles."

"Maybe it's time I do." His jaw tightened, making me grateful for the space between us. "Where are you taking me?" I demanded more forcefully.

He forced his gaze from me to stare out the window before answering. "To meet my family."

"Why?" I was genuinely curious why he would do such a thing.

"Because you're my wife."

"In whose reality?"

His head swiveled to face me, and his eyes burned with promise. "Ours."

"You forged that certificate."

He chuckled, but the humor didn't reach his eyes. "You don't believe that."

"I believe you're a criminal who would say and do anything he could to get his way."

"I don't know if you've noticed, wife, but I'm a powerful man. I don't trick. I take." He leaned forward, resting his forearms on his knees. "And fortunately for me, I didn't need to take you. Your precious father handed you to me on a silver platter."

"Because he thought he could trust you."

"He wanted to be *rid* of you."

"He loves me."

He nodded slowly as if he regretted the truth. "I never said he didn't."

Pain clawed at my skin to get inside. "You've had a hell of a time implying it." I stared at my empty ring finger.

"Why do you torture me?" It was an answer I've wanted every day for nearly ten years.

"I wish I knew," he answered after a lengthy silence, his gaze and voice soft, unlike his heart.

"Do you love me?" He jerked. His eyes widened. I held my breath.

Waiting.

It wasn't hope that made me ask.

Once upon a time, I loved him, and he avoided me. Now he couldn't let me go.

He sat back and tilted his head out of curiosity. "Would you believe me if I told you I did?"

"No."

"Neither would I."

"That's not an answer." Wasn't it possible to love and not believe what you're feeling?

The shrill ring of his phone broke the silence. If I were bold enough, I'd chuck it out the window and demand my answer. Instead, I watched as he pulled his phone from his pocket. I was deeply surprised, however, when he ignored the call and tossed the phone on the seat.

"Who was that?"

"Lucas."

"Don't you need to get that?"

"It can wait."

"You sure? Rich men with dirty secrets are waiting."

"Does this mean you don't want your answer?" His lips twitched. "By the way, I have female clients too. Three months ago, I made a wealthy woman richer by killing her cheating husband. He was actually a good guy, I'm told."

"Ironically, it seems beneath you to be a mercenary for disgruntled spouses."

"Her money was good, and she may have been having an affair of her own with one of my biggest clients."

"It's amazing how well you sleep at night."

"Lately, I've had you to thank."

An uncharacteristic grunt came from me. "And the answer to my question?"

"Do I love you?"

"Yes."

"I sold my soul just to have you, and I would sell it again to keep you. Wanting you made me a monster, so tell me, Mian… does love compare?"

"You can't discount how love feels if you've never felt it, and don't kid yourself. I didn't make you a monster. You sold your soul for power, not for me."

He simply smirked and scratched under his chin looking defiant. "Perhaps. Do you love me?"

His question tortured me, and he knew it. "I thought I did."

"I heard good girls like bad men." He grinned. "Tell me the truth. I'll know if you lie. Did it turn you on when I treated you like shit? Did it make your pussy wet?" His smile turned secretive, and damn me for finding him tempting. "All those years, I thought you were the forbidden one…"

"You say you want me to stay, but you do and say everything to push me away."

His smile faded away. "I'm sorry for teasing you," he said surprising us both. I'd never known Angel to be contrite.

"You should know teasing me won't get you back in my pants."

"And do you want me in your pants?" His voice was

deeper now. Lower. *Huskier.*

"Isn't that why you don't want to let me go? So you can fuck me at your leisure?"

"Pussy doesn't move me." His laugh was condescending. "I have women a hell of a lot more experienced than you willing to fuck me *at my leisure.*"

My cheeks heated. I was mortified and didn't want to let it show, but I couldn't help but look away. "Then why the obsession," I whispered to the window.

"You tell me. It was you who cast the spell nine years ago. Not the other way around."

"Believe me, if I knew how to break it, I would."

"You know. You tried. You failed." His words brought my gaze back to him.

He was talking about death. Only death could break the spell. The memory of the moment I plunged that knife inside him replayed, and I knew I could never rip my soul out again to be free of him.

"I don't need to kill you. I'm sure someone will do my dirty work." I didn't tell him the thought of him dead made it hard to breathe.

"You sure you want me dead?"

"You framed my father."

"Fuck your father," he coolly replied. "Do you want me dead?"

"When you say things like that? Yeah… I do."

I wasn't expecting his arm to whip out and wrap around my waist. He pulled me close until I was buried into his side. "You don't belong to your father anymore. Your loyalty should be with me."

"We shouldn't be married. What was my father thinking?" I groaned.

"He was thinking he could protect you by giving you to me."

"Then why am I more afraid than ever?"

"Because you aren't afraid of dying. You're afraid of falling."

For him.

I hated him for being right.

I was afraid of falling for him all over again. "How can you expect me to love a monster?"

His smile drove a blade through my heart. "You become one."

Because loving him, staying with him willingly and wholly meant giving up my soul.

I'd fallen asleep with my head resting on Angel's shoulder and had woken up with my head in his lap and his strong fingers stroking my hair softly.

"You're awake." His fingers stopped moving through my hair. "Good."

I lifted my body slowly and stretched as best I could in the seat. I was aware of Angel's steady gaze. "How long have I been asleep?" I took a look around and realized we were parked in a driveway that could easily fit three cars. "Where are we?"

"You've been asleep two hours. We arrived thirty minutes ago."

"Thirty? Why didn't you wake me?"

He glanced away and murmured, "I think you needed

it." He seemed distant, but I chose to ignore it and stretched one more time. "Ready?" He was watching me again.

"Do I have a choice?"

"There's just one more thing," he answered slowly. I watched as he reached inside his suit jacket and pulled out a little blue box. The same little blue box that had been delivered to me three years ago. "I was planning to take you to dinner and—" He couldn't seem to bring himself to finish. Slowly, he lifted my trembling hand and gently slipped the ring on my finger.

"Is this why you're dressed in a suit?" I remember the first time I laid eyes on him after three years. He had been in a suit then too, playing the part of a high-class criminal.

He didn't answer, and again, I wondered about his mood as he stepped out of the SUV and into the setting sun. His hand reappeared, and I slid mine, now adorned with his ring, into his warm palm allowing him to help me from the car. For once, his gaze wasn't attached to me. He was avoiding me. Looking up, I admired the two-story home constructed of A-lines, stone, and brick. It was modest compared to the estate and reminded me of the homes I once shared with my parents so long ago.

"Who lives here?" I questioned to distract myself from his hand that had fallen on the small of my back. "My aunt lives here with her family."

We climbed the brick stairs to the front porch. "How close is this aunt to you?"

"She's my father's sister."

Now that stumped me. "You never mentioned her."

"I make a habit not to talk about my family since it's my job to keep them protected."

He rang the doorbell, and a second later, the door

opened revealing a girl no more than a couple years younger than me who must have been waiting by the door. She had long brown hair, a heart shaped face, and blue eyes that sparkled. I recognized her from the funeral but had never learned her name.

"Angel!" She jumped into his arms, and he groaned from the weight of her body hitting his.

"Nice try. You can probably bench press a bull."

"How's it going, Tabitha?" He squeezed her before setting her on her feet, and we followed her inside. I looked back in time to see Angel's small security detail posting around the yard. The door closed, leaving me trapped inside with Angel's mysterious family.

"Well, Austin's gone back to school, thank God. One more day with him and I'd have killed him."

"Don't let your mother hear you talk like that. She'll be moving you out of the country next."

"Ugh. Don't remind me, please. She nearly blew a vein when I told her I was thinking of asking you if I can throw a party at the estate."

"I'm cool with it, but you and I know your parents will never be." His voice was no longer gentle when he asked, "Where are they?"

"Dad's office. I heard them say you were coming more than an hour ago before they disappeared in there." Angel's jaw tightened, and I was nervous all over again. This no longer seemed like a pleasant family visit. Angel never looked back as he prowled up the stairs without a word, leaving me alone with his bouncy cousin.

Our gazes met, and I found myself waving awkwardly. I felt extraterrestrial under her stare.

"Hi, I'm Tabitha, Angel's cousin," she finally introduced.

I took her hand when she offered it but was afraid to do more than hold it. I was small by anyone's standards, but even to me, she seemed so fragile.

"Mian, I'm Angel's–" Captive? Lover? Wife? None of them seemed to fit. Red covered almost every inch of her cheeks as she giggled. "What?" I couldn't stop my own smile from spreading.

"It's just… you and my cousin really must be in love."

I felt my smile fall. "Why do you say that?"

"You embraced his claim on you openly, which means you must have claimed him yourself. Angel would never let you unless he was in love."

Something told me this girl spent her time lost in wonderland if she thought Angel and I were in love. "How old are you?"

"Fifteen. I turn sixteen in a few months. Why?"

It was weird seeing someone who was even more sheltered than I had been. "Angel and I aren't in love."

She didn't seem upset by my honesty. Merely skeptical. "Are you sure?"

I fidgeted even though I had three years on this girl. With one question, she seemed more astute than I gave her credit. Or maybe I was just paranoid. "Why are you so sure? You've seen us together for five minutes."

Her bright baby blues twinkled. "You're forgetting the funeral." She walked away, and I found myself following. When we ended up in the kitchen, I watched as she pulled open the refrigerator door littered with magnets and family photos and pulled out a bottle of water. Their home wasn't the symbol of wealth and refine you'd expect from a Knight, and I loved it because it truly felt like a home. "Want one?"

"Sure." I couldn't explain why my mouth all of a sudden felt so dry. I took the bottle and downed a third of it before recapping. She seemed content with the silence while my heart pounded faster. I finally caved when she started humming. "What about the funeral?"

"He could barely keep his eyes off of you."

Because I was his captive.

"Trust me, Tabitha, there was a reason for that, and it wasn't love."

She shrugged as if it didn't matter, but I could tell by the twinkle in her eye that she didn't believe me. "Where's that cute little boy? He was so adorable. Is he your son?"

"Yes, he's my son."

"Is Angel…?"

I almost hated to tarnish the fantasy she was building in her head about her cousin and me. The stars in her eyes reminded me of myself three years ago. "Angel isn't Caylen's father." I laughed at her pout.

"I suppose he wouldn't be. We would have known about him. So where's his father if you don't mind me asking?"

The last thing I wanted to talk about was Aaron, but I didn't want to be rude. "He didn't want him," I answered a little too bluntly.

The fierce look of anger and disgust that twisted Tabitha's delicate features. She looked more related to Angel than ever. "Does Angel know? I bet he'll kick his ass." She stood from the bar stool she had been perched on and looked ready to demand Angel do just that when I grabbed her arm.

"Uhh, Tabitha?"

My touch seemed to bring her back from wherever

she had gone. "Sorry," she exhaled and offered and apologetic smile. "I just hate guys like that. They take what they want and leave their victims behind to deal with the consequences." She then rushed to say, "Not that you're a victim!"

But I was, wasn't I? Aaron raped and impregnated me, and then pretended not to know me, and now his father wanted to kill me. If you looked up the word victim in the dictionary, there I would be, except… I chose not to live that way. I wasn't Aaron's victim. I was his survivor.

"No harm done," I said when her startled face turned worried. "So what do you think they're talking about up there?"

"I don't know. Whatever it is won't be pleasant. He's not exactly welcome here."

"He's not?"

"My mom never wanted any part of Alexander's legacy. My grandfather was furious with her when she married the man she actually loved."

"Why would he be upset about that?"

"Arranged marriages are kind of our family's thing."

I wasn't surprised given how Angel and I came to be married and what drove Victor to betray our fathers.

"No offense, but does your family realize this is the twenty-first century?"

"It happens more often than you think, except it's done in secret. Fathers want to marry their little girls to men, who can offer them the most gain, and sons will do their duty because to them a hole's a hole." I choked on my water. She giggled and patted my back. "Are you okay?"

"I didn't peg you for the cynical type," I said when my throat was clear.

"No?" She giggled again. "I'm sorry. It's just that I've heard it from my mom enough to believe it's true."

"I don't remember seeing you all at the party."

"That's because my mom isn't welcome."

"Really? Why?"

"Well, after my father denied allegiance to my grandfather, and she allowed him to take us away, he disowned her."

"Wow."

"Yeah. Not many people will stand up to my family like he did."

"Your father must be a brave man." *Or stupid.*

She got that adoring look all girls did for their father, and I wondered if Angel hated him too. "He is. He's a cop."

Definitely hates him.

I cast a worried glance toward the stairs and prayed there wouldn't be bloodshed. A moment later, we heard footsteps and exchanged glances. Angel's gaze swept my body the moment he appeared before settling on my face. I couldn't read what he was thinking, but I knew something was at work in that ruthless mind of his.

I hadn't noticed the couple who entered with him until the woman spoke. "Angel, is this her?"

My defenses went up when I realized she meant me. The woman had the same dark hair as Angel, but her eyes were a light shade of blue. She was only about an inch or two taller than I was with curves to envy.

"Michelle, Officer Garrett, I'd like you to meet my wife." Anna's delighted squeal was the only reaction.

"Hello, dear. I'm Angel's aunt. We didn't get a chance to speak at the funeral. It's nice to finally meet you." She offered me a nervous smile, and I returned it.

"Mian," I simply greeted even though it was apparent they knew who I was.

Officer Garrett offered me his hand, and after I had shaken it, he stood back to observe me. He was as tall as Angel was, with blonde curls graying at his temples. He was still wearing his uniform with a shield I noticed was from the Chicago police department, which meant we were either close to Chicago or he had a hell of a commute. "She looks young, Knight."

I was sick of people discussing me while I was in the room. "I'm nineteen. The legal age to marry is eighteen, Officer Garrett…" My accusing gaze met Angel's, his surprise that I was defending him was evident. "…or sixteen if your father consents."

"Just your father?" he replied without missing a beat. "What about your mother?"

"She's dead."

"So you're telling me the two of you have been married since you were *sixteen*?"

"We're telling you that it's legal, and it's done, Garrett." They locked gazes, and some silent battle ensued. Finally, Officer Garrett grunted and scratched his five o'clock shadow.

"Fine. I'll leave it alone…" He studied me as if I were a perp in his interrogation room. "…but only if she can tell me that she married you willingly."

"Dad," Tabitha rushed to defend. "Leave her alone. You're scaring her."

He wasn't, but I didn't like his attention either.

"I want her to tell me she married him willingly because there's no way in hell I'd let my little girl marry someone like Knight."

The room was silent. Every eye was on me as they all waited for me to deny what he suspected or lie and continue this war with Angel. "Then you obviously didn't know my father, Officer Garrett." I moved around him and stood next to Angel, sliding my hand into his much larger one. He immediately lifted it and laid a soft kiss on my skin. Later, I might ask myself if I had made the right decision, but my gut already told me I had. Garrett was a cop who had sworn to protect all, but I was a mother who promised to protect my son, and I couldn't risk him.

Officer Garrett's smile was forced as he took in our joined hands. "I guess we owe you congratulations then."

"Yes, congratulations," Michelle reluctantly added. Our gazes locked, and I could see her disappointment. To Angel, she said, "When can we expect her?"

"Tomorrow." He must have sensed my confusion because he started to rub the back of my palm soothingly. He didn't want me to ask questions right now.

We didn't hang around after that. I think I was as eager to go as they were for us to leave. The goodbyes were stale with the exception of Tabitha, who gave me her cell number. I was too embarrassed to explain that I didn't have a phone. Angel, however, stepped in and told her to call the estate and ask for me when I just stood there awkwardly. All the while, Michelle and Officer Garrett looked on, unconvinced that we were a fated love match.

CHAPTER NINETEEN

ANGEL

USHERED MIAN AWAY AS QUICKLY AS POSSIBLE WITHOUT it being obvious. Coming here and asking for Garrett's help had been risky, but for Mian, it was worth it. She didn't know it and never would, but I'd probably sell the last piece of my soul if she asked.

"Why would you let Anna stay with them if they hate you?" I smiled when she wasn't looking as she climbed into the SUV. Sometimes, I forget how innocent she really is. To her, there was a clear line between love and hate. To her, our emotions were the only factor and were never what we could gain from doing what we wouldn't ordinarily.

"They don't hate me, Mian. They're afraid of me. They're afraid of the danger I could bring to their door-step if they're involved with me." My men had used the other vehicles to block the driveway, keeping anyone from getting in or out without my say so.

"Again… why would you ask this of them and why would they agree?"

"It wasn't easy, especially if threatening them was off the table, but they consider themselves good people who won't stand by and let a young girl fall into my web. They're already kicking themselves for being too late to save you," I added dryly.

"They don't know me."

"It doesn't matter. I won't lie and say my family hasn't chewed up and spit out more lives than I can count. My aunt was always a patron of good, and it shamed her to be a Knight. We aren't good people."

"I gathered that," she agreed caustically.

I eyed her as she huddled as far away from me as possible and felt the malicious need to provoke her until she became unhinged. That was our foreplay. "You fell in love with me anyway."

"I fell," she confessed, "and then I rose again. I'm over it, Angel. I'm over *you*."

"Because I hurt you." It wasn't a question. We both know I did, but maybe it wasn't the reason why. She loved me even when I made it hurt.

I felt the distance between us like a weight on my chest, so I slid across the bench and pulled her into my lap. For once, she didn't fight me. We were battle-worn enemies still fighting the need to love each other.

"I won't hurt you, Sprite. Never again." My hand cupping her face slid down over the milky skin of her throat and rested over her heart. I haven't felt this vulnerable since the first time I laid eyes on her nine years ago. "Do you believe me?"

Her breasts rose under my palm when she sucked in air, and when she released it, I held my breath. "No."

Burying my face in her neck so she couldn't see what she did to me, I whispered, "How can I convince you?" Her shiver when my breath touched her skin tempted me to touch her in other places. My hand left her breast and found her thigh. I was ready to part them and bring her the pleasure her body sought when she stopped me with her hand and shattered my world.

"You choose me."

I lifted my head and met her gaze. The storm in the jade was silent. Everything I've done to her, I did for my family, and if the day came when I'd have to choose, it'd be them.

It would have to be them.

Mian disappeared upstairs the moment we returned to the estate. The ride back had been silent after she gave her ultimatum. My silence had been answer enough, and when she'd climbed off my lap, I let her, needing the distance myself.

I made my way to the kitchen, figuring that would be where I'd find Lucas and Z, but instead, I found Anna.

She sat crossed legged in the breakfast nook my grandfather preferred when he ate, gazing out the window. In front of her was a ceramic bowl full of Rocky Road, Mian's favorite, and the spoon dangling from her fingers while ice cream dripped from the end.

"Mian might never forgive you if she saw you wasting her precious Rocky Road." My attempt at humor fell flat when her indignant cerulean eyes found me watching her.

She took her time setting her spoon in the bowl. "In my opinion, she's far too forgiving."

The chill she delivered had me pondering the advantage of offering her a job. Her natural innocence would make a great disguise as my enforcer. Instead, I took a seat across from her and stretched out my legs.

"What are you doing?" She sat straighter and flattened her back against the wall.

"I think it's time we talk."

She looked as if she'd rather French kiss a snake. "We have nothing to talk about."

"I don't think that's true." Neither of us spoke as we willed the other to give in. When she shot forward and braced her hands on the table, I hid my triumph.

"This marriage is a mistake. She already tried to kill you once. What makes you think she won't do it again?"

"Are you worried about me?"

"I'm *warning* you. It's *my friend* I'm worried for."

"She's safe as long as she's married to me. I won't hurt her."

"You can't really believe that when you're forcing her to honor a marriage made without her knowledge."

"Divorce isn't an option in my family, Anna. Death is the only end."

"You just said you wouldn't hurt her," she accused on a cry. She started to slide from the bench, probably to warn Mian, when I grasped her hands tightly in my own.

"Anna." Her name was a plea. "She's in too deep. The blood in her veins no longer belongs to her. It belongs to

Alexander's legacy. If she leaves, she dies."

"You're saying you'll kill her because your Uncle's book will want it?"

"She'll die even if I don't."

"You'll protect her," she demanded.

My head jerked. "I'll be dead long before they come for her."

"Your own family will kill you if you let her go?" I didn't answer. She'd already pieced it together. She just needed to accept it as I was forced to. "This is sick. *You're* sick. This entire family is sick."

I know.

"We've been this way for two hundred years, and it's not about to change because of one girl. I may rule, but they can still hold me accountable."

"Who?"

"Any eligible heir in my family who wants to take my place." I let her hands go and sat back. I had her attention now, even if she looked ready to bolt. "If I fail to produce an heir, power simply returns to Alexander's line. If I betray this family, however, the first eligible heir who kills me will assume power."

"These rules… can you change them?"

"Never." My family would consider it their right to kill me for even suggesting it.

"What are you going to do?"

"I'll keep her… and I'll protect her."

She nodded, but the distrust in her eyes never left. "Then I guess there's nothing left for us to say."

She took her bowl of melted Rocky Road as she rose from the bench. I watched as she rinsed it out and placed it in the dishwasher. She was leaving, and I was going to let her when she turned back at the edge of the kitchen and hugged her waist.

"Something on your mind?" My voice was casual, but I felt the tension as I waited. She hesitated for a second and then came to a decision.

"Are you only staying married to Mian to protect her?"

I sat back and eyed her. "Would there be another reason?" I mused, even though I knew what she was implying. Everyone except Mian seemed to be convinced I was in love with her... including me.

"Other than the only one that matters?" Her mouth set in a thin line. "No." She pivoted her golden hair flying around her shoulders as she did. I was left alone to wonder if it was more cruel to keep Mian married to me or to let her leave knowing she'd never be safe.

My phone began to ring while I was piling mountains of meat on a sandwich. Checking the caller id, I tensed when I read the senator's name. Lucas and Z must have had a sixth sense for trouble because they walked in the moment I accepted the call.

"For your sake, this call better start and end with something I want to hear." The grins Lucas and Z wore fell as they went deathly still.

"Mr. Knight, as always, speaking with you is a pleasure."

"Cut the shit. When and where?"

"I hold all the cards, son. You may want to watch how you speak to me."

I had forced a deep breath before I spoke. "Are you ready to do this?"

"Tonight, in your family's cemetery. I won't tell you to be there alone because I'll have my own protection with me. So if you're thinking of trying something, don't. It won't end well for either of us."

His warning was fruitless, but I'd pretend to heed it anyway. There was no way in hell I was giving up Mian and Caylen to him, and if he were a smart man, he knew that.

"Don't worry, Senator. As long as you have what belongs to me you'll leave here alive," I lied.

"Good, son. I don't want bloodshed any more than you." That was where he was wrong. I wanted his blood spilled at my feet, and if it was with my last breath, I'd have it.

"I'll see you tonight." I hung up without waiting for his response.

"So, what's the word?" Lucas demanded.

"He wants to meet in the cemetery tonight to trade the book for Mian."

"Do you trust him?" Z questioned.

"No, and that's exactly why we're going to be ready."

"Why would he meet you here? This is your turf. Trapping him will be easy."

"Exactly, which means he has something up his sleeve. Call Augustine and anyone else we don't have a choice but to trust. Tonight, we make war."

CHAPTER TWENTY

MIAN

I was a fool. A humiliated, naïve fool. For a moment, I thought he'd choose me. Finally… irrevocably. Instead, he said nothing and left me to bear the weight of his rejection.

I found Caylen asleep in his crib and Anna nowhere to be found. I was torn between finding her and hiding. She could be tempting fate with Lucas at this moment, but I couldn't bring myself to risk facing my own source of anguish.

It didn't matter, though. Minutes later, a soft knock came. I opened one of the doors to find her on the other side looking like a doe staring down the barrel of a shotgun.

"Anna? What's going on?" I pulled her inside and then fruitlessly locked the door.

"If you leave Angel, his family will kill you." I felt the acidic feeling of doom in my gut. "Did you know?"

Sighing, I sat on the bed and stared at the wooden planks of the floor. "I didn't know for sure, but I suspected that maybe it was a little more complicated than he let on."

"A little complicated? Mian, how can you be this calm? You're trapped!"

I shot to my feet defensively. "I'm *terrified*, Anna, but that's just what they need." I shook my head. "I won't give them that."

"You'll never be anything but a pawn if you stay in this family."

"I'll be a threat if I leave. I'm safer where I am."

"Because that's what Angel told you? Since when do you trust him?"

I wanted to confess that I never stopped being Angel's fool, but I wasn't ready to face the truth. "I don't have a choice. My father took my choice from me when he married me into this family."

"Are you sure your father did this? Angel could be lying to you."

Shrugging, I realized how much I believed he did. I had been holding tight onto the trust I had in my father, but at some point, I let go. One day, I'd confront him, but I knew once I did, and I had the truth, I could never forgive him.

We stayed hidden and talked about everything except Angel, legacies, and my father until Caylen awoke and began crying for food. We didn't run into the guys on the way to the kitchen, but we did run into a long, muscular figure dressed in black and leaning down to peer into the fridge.

His hair was midnight black from what I could see, his

skin tan, and the hand grasping the top of the door large and capable-looking.

"Oh, my God," Anna gasped excitedly in my ear. "Who is that?"

Leave it to her to have an instant crush on a perfect stranger. The stranger's head lifted and turned from inside the fridge, allowing us to see his emerald-colored eyes. His eyebrow quirked when he found us staring from inside the doorway, and then his gaze passed over us slowly. First, Anna, then Caylen, and finally settling on me. He then pushed the door closed and leaned a powerful shoulder against the stainless steel with a grin. "Hello, kids," he greeted condescendingly. "You must be Mian, Anna, and Caylen."

"How do you know our names?" Anna's voice was full of awe as she devoured the full sight of him.

"I make it a point to know everything." *God, this man must have a serious god complex.*

"But you can't know *everything*." She giggled. I was stupefied. They've barely met, yet she was completely taken with him.

"Only what matters," he replied, turning up the charm.

"Who are you?" I had questioned before my friend had a chance to fall in love.

"For once, reality isn't reduced to hype," he observed but left the meaning mysterious. "I'm Augustine, Angel's cousin."

"I'm Anna. This is Mian, and that's her son, Caylen," she offered unnecessarily.

His smile was indulgent as he said, "I know."

"Oh." She giggled again. "Right." I rolled my eyes, which he didn't miss if the smirk was anything to go by.

"Excuse us," I quickly said when he moved closer. I grabbed Anna's arm and moved around the island. There was no way I was letting him get close.

I wondered if he was another one of Alexander's heirs as I handed Caylen to Anna and moved to the pantry. When I turned with a box of cereal and formula in hand, he was gone. Anna shrugged when I sent a puzzled glance her way, so I busied myself feeding my baby.

It was late in the night when I crossed paths with Angel. I had put Caylen down for the night minutes before he had entered the bedroom. There was wariness in his gaze when our eyes met. I was sitting crossed legged in the middle of his bed, the movie I'd been watching forgotten.

"Hey," he whispered.

"Hey." I pretended to refocus on the movie.

I could see him in my peripheral shoving his hands in the front pocket of the black jeans he'd changed into. "What are the chances of me convincing you to take a walk with me without coercion or force?" If I didn't still feel so goddamn raw from this afternoon, I would have laughed. Instead, I unfolded my legs and slipped into my shoes.

"Let's go," I said, my voice deceivingly chipper.

I followed him outside, and I ignored how romantic it seemed when he led me through the gardens. The silence was comfortable even though I could tell something was keeping him on edge. The longer we walked, the deeper the tension became. We eventually came to the edge of the garden, and I followed him down a cobbled path. There was a forest of trees ahead where the path disappeared. We headed forward, and my nervousness grew. Still, I kept following him despite the warning bells. The forest bed was blanketed in red leaves. The wind blew, rustling the leaves and making my body shiver. I was overwhelmed by how far the estate's land stretched when we eventually reached the edge of the forest. He came to a stop. I could feel him watching me, but I was too busy staring at the stone wall that's seen better days but still looked intimidating.

"What is it?"

"That," he gestured lazily, "is just a wall. On the other side is our private cemetery."

"Why are we here?" I could hear the shakiness in my voice and swallowed as if that would steady it.

He looked away, and I watched his Adam's apple bob as he swallowed. "In exchange for the book, the senator wants you and Caylen."

I stumbled backward, but it didn't matter because he followed.

"You son of a bitch."

"Just listen to me. Please."

"Why the fuck would I do that?"

"Because I'm trying to save your life."

"You're trying to save your precious book."

"I can do both but not without your help." He kept advancing.

"Stay away from me." I wondered if I could lose him in the trees if I ran.

"There's nowhere for you to go. If you run, I'll catch you, and we'll just lose time."

"You already made the deal, didn't you?"

"Yes." It sounded painful for him to admit. I even found pleasure in his pain. This was what he did to me. He made every feeling in my bones and in my blood irrational. He was still coming, however, and I knew I could never outrun him. Because I wasn't paying attention, I hadn't noticed the stone before it sent me reeling. He moved quicker, and one minute, I was falling and the next, I was safe in his arms. Except I wasn't safe. Being this close to Angel was more painful than a broken ankle, so I pushed to free myself.

"Let go of me," I growled when he tightened his arms.

"You won't listen unless I force you, so this is me making you listen. I *don't* want to hurt you. Not even close."

"Then what is this? Why are we here? You're going to give us to that—"

"Stop," he roared before I could finish. My chin was in his grip, and I didn't think it was possible, but he tugged me closer. "He won't touch you. He won't touch Caylen. I'll die before I let that happen." His gaze, his voice, his entire being was overrun with emotion. "Will you listen to me?" he pleaded when I said nothing.

"Do I have a choice?"

"Neither of us do."

"If something happens to my baby, I'll kill you." I didn't recognize myself as I spoke my vow.

He lifted my hand and kissed it. "I believe you, baby." He kept a hold on my hand as he led me back to the wall. It seemed out of place even in the backyard of a home as grand as the estate. Some of the wall even looked in dire need of repair. Angel let go of my hand to remove a key from his pocket and to unlock the iron gates. They looked incredibly heavy and creaked when he pushed them open.

He walked through them but turned back when I didn't follow. The air seemed chillier now as I faced my fate. "Come on." He held out his hand while his eyes pleaded with me to trust him. I took his hand and let him pull me through. The cemetery was mostly dark, but around the perimeter were lamps with a dull golden glow. The light fog added to the eerie ambiance as my gaze swept over the graves that belonged to the dead members of Angel's twisted family.

Angel pulled me through the cemetery, and I ignored the chill crawling up my spine. As we neared a small group of trees, Lucas, Z, and Augustine slid from the shadows. Lucas was holding Caylen, who I thought remained safe in his crib, in his arms. I rushed to take him and wanted to scream at Angel for involving my son in this without speaking with me first.

Augustine eyed us curiously and then lifted his chin toward me. "She ready?"

I shook my head. "I'm not doing this with my son here."

"This will end a lot worse without him. If you want to make sure we don't all end up dead, and the senator doesn't burn down the estate with Caylen inside, you'll do this."

Angel always did know how to make me succumb to fear with little effort.

"I'm ready," I reluctantly agreed. Augustine nodded. His game face slipped into place as he slid on a pair of thick leather gloves. He was dressed in a black hoodie and jeans complete with heavy black boots. It was then I realized that Angel, Lucas, and Z were dressed similarly in gloves covering their hands and grim expressions. They looked ready for war.

"Mian," Angel called. My attention shifted, drinking him in. I realized this was the heartless killer that, until now, I'd never met. The monster he unleashed on me was merely an envoy. A show of mercy. *This* was the Bandit. His family's Knight in dark and dirty armor. "The senator will be here any moment. I need him to believe your safety isn't my concern. Can you do that?"

"You've given me every reason to doubt you, Angel. I'm sure I can manage."

His leather-clad hands pulled me close. "You're earning much needed time over my knee, Sprite."

"I'd like to see you try." My tone was equally playful as if the senator didn't exist. As if the threat on my life and my son didn't exist. As if what took place three years ago never happened.

"I hate to break up the lovebird special, but I hear something," Lucas announced. "Sounds like they're here."

Angel's game face slipped back into place. A black town car appeared down a trail I hadn't noticed before. It must have been a service entrance for the cemetery's groundskeeper. The car in the lead was trailed by three SUVs. It was most definitely the senator. His arrival was almost cliché enough to laugh. Angel's hand slid around my arm, and then he tugged me toward his cousin.

He bent low to whisper in my ear as the cars rolled to a stop some distance away. "Whatever happens, stay close to Augustine. He'll get you and Caylen out of here when it's time."

"What's going to happen?"

His eyes flashed with impatience. "The senator isn't leaving here alive, Mian. It's going to get loud, and it's going to go fast. Stay low and stay out of sight, and you'll live."

I watched as the senator and the men he brought to kill me poured out of the vehicles. "There are at least ten men, and there are only three of you."

His smile was rueful. "The senator has exposed his entire hand, but I still have a few tricks up my sleeve. You can't see them, but I assure there are more guns pointing at him than there are at me."

Without another word, he placed distance between us as the senator and his entourage approached, and I remembered I was supposed to be an unwilling party.

Caylen was asleep against my chest unaware of the danger surrounding us. When the bullets started flying, how would I keep him protected? Just then, Augustine moved to stand in front of me, blocking my view, but also providing a wall between them and me.

"Mr. Knight, I appreciate you accommodating me this evening." The senator spoke in his refined voice as if we were hosting a dinner party instead of a deadly trade.

"Do you have it?" Angel's voice was clipped. I couldn't see him, but I felt his anger.

"Where are they?" the senator slyly countered.

A second later, Augustine was no longer blocking me. He was pushing me forward with a heavy hand on my back until I was in view of the senator.

I couldn't see the men Angel hinted were there, and I wondered how many of them were watching from the shadows. Angel's plan was dangerous, but he'd left me no choice other than to trust him. Augustine continued to push me forward until Angel was standing beside me silent and calm with Lucas and Z flanking us. The promise of death in their eyes should have frightened me, but it only made me feel protected.

I wasn't their enemy.

Not tonight.

I almost felt sorry for the senator. Angel said he planned to kill the senator, and the morbid beast who ravaged my soul wondered if he'd make it fast yet hoped he'd kill him slowly.

"Hello, Miss Ross." Hearing my name from him was like a snake wrapping around my body and squeezing.

"Senator."

"I don't know if Angel explained it to you, but you and your son will be coming with my son." It wasn't until he said 'son' that I noticed Aaron standing next to him. He was watching me with unconcealed malice and confidence that I'd be at his mercy soon enough.

"And why is that, Senator?" Before he could answer, the back door of the closest SUV opened, and someone stepped out. It was too dark to see who it might be, but I could tell from the small stature and shape that it was a woman. She strutted on heels too high for the occasion. It was her blonde hair, high cheekbones, and smile meant to charm that seemed so familiar. Another three steps and recognition came like a blow to the stomach. I could do nothing but stare in shock. She was a girl I hadn't seen in three years. A girl a year ago I had called my friend.

"Erin?"

Her bubblegum painted lips stretched to reveal perfect teeth to match the rest of her. She wore tight black jeans, a white silk blouse, and tall black pumps with a black motorcycle jacket. "It's good to see you, Mian, though I do wish the circumstances could have been better." She didn't seem at all bothered by the night time visit to a strange cemetery and scary men ready to kill each other.

"What are you doing here?"

"Oh, we haven't spoken in like a year, so I never got to tell you," she hugged Aaron's arm and grinned, "we're an item now."

"His name is Aaron, and her name is Erin?" Lucas

muttered. "Jesus fuck, they were made for each other."

"And the fact that he raped me doesn't bother you?"

She rolled her eyes to the ceiling without losing her fake grin. "Come on, Mian. You know it didn't happen that way. Aaron told me all about it. I told you losing your v-card was no big deal, but of course, you made it one."

"You were my friend, Erin."

Her smile faltered then. "It's your fault we're not friends anymore. You had to go and get pregnant. Well, I wasn't interested in being someone's godmother or whatever it is you expected from me." I wanted to kill her when she wrinkled her nose at my son.

"I expected you to be my *friend*."

"Poor Mian as always," she mocked.

"How can you date him after what he did to me? He *raped* me."

"He told me what really happened that night. You got plastered and threw yourself on him, and come on... you're sort of hot—so why would he say no?"

I didn't respond. I simply stared wondering what broke in Erin's mind to believe such a lie.

"If Mian gives the word, I'm putting a bullet between her eyes," Z whispered behind me. I heard Lucas's grunt of agreement.

"Enough," Aaron barked. "I didn't come here for a cat fight." He stepped forward and kept coming until he was roughly able to close his fingers around the arm I was holding our son in. "You're coming with us." A second later, Angel had his hand fisted in Aaron's shirt. He lifted him and tossed him a few feet away where he landed at his father's feet. Erin's scream and the sound of weapons materializing and aiming at us filled the quiet night. Caylen stirred in my arms and let out a cry when he became fully awake.

"Mr. Knight?" The senator spoke over Caylen's cries. "I'm disappointed that you'd harm my son. I thought you were agreeable with the trade."

"That hasn't changed, Senator, but your son overstepped. I've yet to see you hold up your end."

"Ah, yes. The book." He snapped his fingers at one of the men with a gun pointed at my head. The man lowered his arm and stepped forward with a briefcase I hadn't noticed before. He handed Angel the briefcase, and then quickly raised his gun toward Angel as he stepped to the side. I didn't realize what was happening until his hand closed around my arm.

Oh, fuck.

I dug in my heels when he began to pull me away. Caylen's screams rose when he felt my panic. "Not so fast, boy scout." Augustine appeared with his gun pointed at the senator's guard.

Angel opened the briefcase stealing everyone's focus. Lying on top of the red felt was a small leather-bound book. The cover looked good to be two hundred years old, and then I remembered Lucas telling me the book had never been touched by anyone other than the Knight.

Angel closed the briefcase and handed it to Z. The senator's guard tightened his grip on my arm.

"I hope you don't mind," the senator spoke, "but I took the liberty of eliminating a few entries."

Angel stilled, and everyone seemed to be holding their breath except Aaron and the senator. "Is that right?" The malevolence in Angel's voice was scarier than the guns pointed at us.

"Did you think I'd let you continue to keep this kind of evidence on me? Fortunately, there are those who can do what you do while maintaining discretion. You understand."

"You mean Victor? I'm not sure how well he can maintain anything while chopped up into tiny pieces."

The senator's chuckle made me uneasy while Angel visibly bristled. "Victor was a pawn, and long outlived his usefulness, so I thank you for proactively taking care of the problem. I really don't like getting my hands dirty."

If Victor wasn't the mastermind behind stealing the book, then who was?

"Who?" Angel's growl made everyone tense.

"You should know. Blood is thickest when filled with deceit."

Augustine cursed, ripped me from the guard's grip, and pushed me behind him. The senator's bodyguard moved to grab me, but Augustine used his gun against his temple to shove him back.

The scuffle didn't escape the senator's notice. "If you're not going to honor your end of the trade and deliver Miss Ross, I'm afraid this will end ugly."

"The deal wasn't that you'd tamper with the book, Staten. You know the rules, and you know what happens when you break them."

"If anyone's death is deserved, it's yours, Knight." The senator seemed to be waiting for something to happen as he looked to the shadows. After a long and tense moment, nothing happened, and when he spoke again, he sounded less in control. "Give me the girl and the child or you and your men die."

"Senator…" Angel's voice was final. "It was very foolish

for you to come here tonight."

"And why is that, son?"

"Because you were never leaving alive."

The next moments were loud and fast just as Angel had warned. Lucas, Z, and Augustine were there shielding Caylen and me with their bodies as gunfire rained around us. I could hear the sound of men dying and bodies hitting the ground and running footsteps. Orders were shouted, and then I was being pulled until I was running on my own. Caylen fought and screamed in my arms. My heart was pounding, my lungs were burning, and my ears were ringing.

The gunshots faded the further we ran, and I fought to keep up with Augustine's long legs. We eventually came near the edge of the cemetery where he stopped, gun at the ready, and checked the shadows for any of the senator's men. I thoroughly checked over Caylen who still fussed and fought me.

"Is he okay?"

I nodded and bit my lip. "Do you think they're okay?" Angel, Lucas, and Z had stayed behind while I fled with Augustine. I didn't know if I was truly worried for them or afraid the final barrier between the senator and me were dead in the dirt.

"They can handle themselves," he answered. "Come on."

I could see the beginning of concrete steps. The trees lining the edge of the cemetery were blocking my view of where the steps led. As we cleared the trees, my footsteps slowed, and I forgot to breathe. The towering mausoleum was a concrete building with an impenetrable-looking entrance. Fixed on both sides of the black painted door were seven-foot statues of Knights with swords drawn and their heads, covered with helmets, turned menacingly toward whoever dared visit. It wasn't until we ascended the steps that I realized the swords were real and held up by a hook attached to the inside of the fists.

"What is this place?"

"The Knight crypt. It's the final resting place for each Knight who served as the Bandit."

"Why are we here?"

"There's a tunnel inside that leads back to the estate."

"You mean we're going in there?" I couldn't help my girlish squeal. His smile, the first since this all started, was faint.

"Yeah, we're going in here."

"Isn't it sacred?" I mocked.

He snorted as he pulled a black iron key from his pocket and stuck it in the door. "I don't know, and I don't give a shit." The sound of the lock turning made my heart skip.

"What?" he questioned after he looked back and found me staring.

"You aren't as dutiful as Angel."

He shrugged, but the muscle working in his jaw told me my statement had a greater effect than he let on. "Maybe I don't care to spend my life following another man's rules." His grunt as he pushed open the door punctuated his words.

"So you are an heir."

"Somewhere down a long line," he confirmed. He swiveled his head to face me. "Unless I kill Angel."

He held the door open, waiting for me to enter. There was nothing but darkness waiting and the unsettling implication that he might be the traitor the senator spoke of.

"Are you the one who stole the book?"

Augustine's eyes narrowed, and his nostrils flared. "No."

"Why should I believe you?"

"Because I'm the one keeping you alive right now. If any of the senator's men slipped past Angel, they'll be heading this way."

"I'm not going in there with you." I was already backing away. Caylen whimpered against my chest. I could feel his tiny fingers gripping my shirt as he fought to get closer.

"We don't have time for this." He let the door slam shut with a growl of impatience as he followed me down the stairs.

"If not you, then who?"

"We'd be here all night if I listed the people who'd gain from killing Angel."

"Which includes you."

"He doesn't have anything I want," he shot back.

I could hear someone in the distance coming this way. Augustine must have heard it too because he stopped dead and turned his head toward the sound.

"You might be telling the truth, and I'm sorry, but that's a risk I can't take."

I didn't wait for him to react. I just turned and ran in the opposite direction at the same time the unmistakable sound of guns firing interrupted the silence. I chanced a look back to see Augustine diving for cover as he fought for his life.

Running toward the forest, I disappeared into the night and hoped my son, and I made it out of this war alive.

CHAPTER TWENTY-ONE

ANGEL

WE TOOK DOWN ALL BUT THREE OF THE SENATOR'S men while the senator himself and his son got away. Mian's friend had taken a fatal bullet meant for Aaron when he used her as a human shield. He and his father wouldn't make it off the property since my men were already blocking every exit, so I concentrated on chasing the men who had disappeared in the direction Augustine had fled with Mian and Caylen.

Augustine should have made it to the tunnel by now, but it didn't keep the fear out of my head that something could happen to them. Lucas and Z kept pace with me as we tore through the cemetery for the mausoleum. When the sound of gunshots reached us, I pumped my legs and arms faster. We reached the mausoleum and found Augustine fighting off two of the senator's men. The third was slumped against the tree with a bullet in his jugular.

Lucas and Z quickly took down the two men while I searched the area for signs of Mian and Caylen.

"Thank fuck," Augustine griped as he walked toward us. "I was running out of bullets."

"That's because you're a shitty shot," Lucas joked.

Augustine flipped him off and said, "What took you guys so long? Staten's dead, right?"

I ignored his question and growled, "Where is Mian?"

He tensed and then expelled a harsh breath. "She took off that way." He pointed toward the path that led to the north wall surrounding the cemetery. "She freaked out thinking I stole the book and was going to kill her, so she ran off."

"Fuck!" I didn't wait around. I took off in the direction Augustine indicated. If the senator realized he couldn't escape before my men got to him, he could be anywhere on the property by now. If Mian kept running this way, she'd reach the wall eventually, and if the senator found her first, she'd be cornered. It could already be too late.

Desperation grew each minute that passed without finding them. I considered changing directions worried she might be lost or hurt when I heard a gut-wrenching scream followed by an infant's loud cry.

I ran in that direction, and for the first time, I prayed.

The forest was too silent after what I'd heard, and I was afraid of what it could mean. I quelled the need to roar her name. If the senator had her, I didn't want him to know I was coming. Taking him down would be safer for Mian and the baby if I caught him by surprise.

My worry that I'd never find them had turned into full-fledged fear when I finally heard them. It was faint—the break of a twig, but it was enough. I kept my own footsteps careful as I closed in on their location. I saw them through the gap between two trees rooted closely together. They faced me, but their attention was on Mian laying at their feet. Caylen sat in the curve of her body whimpering with his fist in his mouth as he stared up nervously at his piece of shit father and grandfather.

"Knight's got to be hot on our heels by now, Father. We need to get out of here."

"No. We take care of them now and leave their bodies for him to find."

"Fine," Aaron grumbled. He bent down to grab Caylen when I stepped from the shadows with my gun aimed at his head.

"Touch him, and I'll kill you slowly." The calculated gleam in his eye was my warning, but I was still too late to react. He jerked Caylen from the ground and used him as a shield. I wanted to lower my gun, but I couldn't risk a second of reaction time if I got a clear shot. When Caylen saw me, he cried out with arms reaching for me. He might as well have taken my heart in his hands and squeezed until it stopped beating. Since my focus had been stolen by him, I hadn't noticed the Senator aiming his gun at my head.

"Mr. Knight, this all could have gone very differently if you had kept your head."

Aaron smirked and said to his father, "I told you he was in love with her."

"Then dying together shouldn't be a problem."

The next moment happened in slow motion. I saw my death in the senator's eyes as he squeezed the trigger. He wasn't quick enough, however, because the bullet that penetrated his shoulder before he could fire caused him to drop the gun. Mian stirred, grumbling as she regained consciousness.

Aaron took off with Caylen, quickly disappearing into the forest. I was torn between pursuing Aaron and seeing to Mian when Augustine, Lucas, and Z appeared at my side. "Go," Z urged. "We'll take care of her." His gaze hardened when he leered down at the senator clutching his shoulder. "And him."

"Take him to the new warehouse." Our gazes met—his pleading, mine promising. "I want to take my time with him."

I didn't wait around to listen as he begged for his life, but his pleas followed me into the forest as I chased after his son. I could hear Caylen crying and followed the sound until it suddenly stopped. The silence felt like death. With a curse, I pushed on not caring if Aaron could hear me coming or not.

I found them in a clearing. Aaron's back was to me, but I could see he was still holding the baby. Raising my gun, I kept my footsteps silent so I wouldn't alert him. I was only two steps away when he said, "I know you're there."

He turned then and rage boiled in my gut when I saw his hand covering Caylen's nose and mouth. He was suffocating him. "Don't take another step, Knight. This is none of your business. He's my son."

"No, motherfucker." I needed to hit him hard. "He's *mine*." My declaration did what I intended. Shock and confusion caused him to drop his hand from Caylen's face.

"That lying b—"

I didn't hesitate.

I put a bullet in his head, cutting off his words, and dived to catch the baby before he could fall on top of him.

Caylen was limp when I took him in my arms. I never felt this kind of terror. Not even in the moments after Mian tried to kill me. Terror had me dropping to my knees and laying him on the forest bed. Terror had me once again praying to a god who had long ago forsaken me.

I did mouth to mouth, my control slipping with each breath I gave him.

"Come on, Caylen." I didn't recognize my own voice. It shook until it broke, but I never stopped. I'd give him my last breath if that's what it took. "Please. Breathe. Please. Please." I couldn't stop my tears—tears I never shed for my father, my mother, or grandfather—from dropping onto his ashen cheeks.

I could hear the running footsteps of someone in the forest as I gave him mouth to mouth. It was only when they broke through the clearing that his chest finally began to rise and fall. My next breath shuddered out of me as I lifted him.

"Caylen?" Mian's terrified gasp as I stood nearly sent me to my knees again. She collided into me and screamed his name again. "Is he okay?" The baby's eyes were still closed as she took him from me. "Oh, God. What did he do to you? What did he do?" She cuddled him into her body and whispered apologies over and over.

There was a large bruise covering most of the right side of her face where they must have hit her. I was tempted to put another bullet in Aaron just because, but Mian and Caylen had been through enough trauma.

"Angel," Lucas called. I forced my gaze away from Mian and the baby and faced my brother. "What happened?"

My gaze cut to Mian. She was now staring with hatred at Aaron's dead body.

Shaking my head at Lucas, I replied, "Later."

I was still pumped up on adrenaline and keeping my rage at bay as I forced myself to stand and watch while the doctor I kept in my pocket checked over Mian and Caylen. Augustine had hung back with the cleaners to clear the dead bodies from the cemetery while Lucas and Z took the senator somewhere no one would ever find him.

"Good news," Doc announced. "Your wife and son will be just fine, Angel."

I glared at Chapman for his assumption while he put away his stethoscope. When he cured Caylen in Chicago a couple of months ago, I never told him he was my son. In fact, I told him very little. I was wondering how he'd even known Mian and I were married until my gaze caught my ring on her finger. In the aftermath of all the drama, I'd forgotten that I made her wear it.

"She's going to need to apply a cold press on her face to help with the swelling and lots of rest. Your son's lungs seem fine, but I'd really feel better if you brought him in at some point so I can be sure there aren't lasting effects. With his young age and the trauma he experienced, you don't want to leave his health up to chance."

I nodded while watching as Mian curved her body around Caylen's sleeping body and stroked the baby hairs on his head. I wanted to join them on the bed and hold them both, but it didn't seem like the right time to stake my claim. I was partly responsible for what could have been tonight. It was going to be hard to live with that.

I forced my gaze away from them when Mian closed her eyes and shook the doctor's hand. "I'll show you out."

CHAPTER TWENTY-TWO

MIAN

WAKING UP THE NEXT MORNING WITHOUT BURSTING into tears the moment my eyes opened was a challenge. I reached out, needing to feel the beat of my baby's heartbeat underneath my palm, but found the spot where I'd left him warm but empty. Flipping onto my back, I sought out his crib and found Angel standing next to it. Through the rails, I could see his hand resting lightly on his chest. His hand was so large, it covered Caylen's entire chest, but something deep inside me knew what he was doing.

He was checking his heartbeat.

Our gazes connected in that next moment when my heart felt full and heat spread through my lower body.

"Hi." His voice was deeper from sleep, which told me he'd just woken himself.

"Hi." He looked away long enough to pull the blanket back around Caylen and then prowled back to the bed.

Slipping underneath the sheets, he reached out for me and pulled me close. I needed his heat and his strength, so I went without a fight. I didn't resist, either, when his lips found mine. It wasn't driven by lust, but instead, the need to soothe.

"How are you feeling?" he whispered after pulling away.

I sucked in air, and then my body shuddered as I released it. "Aaron almost killed my son... didn't he?"

His gaze darkened with leftover rage. "Yes."

"He tried—" My voice cracked, causing my words to lodge in my throat. "He tried to suffocate him?"

"Yes." I could tell it was as hard for him to speak about it as it was for me to imagine. How was it possible to have made something as beautiful as Caylen with a monster like Aaron?

"Caylen is his son," I sobbed. "How could he hurt him?"

"They may share the same blood, but Caylen is not his. He never was."

I cried then, but I didn't cry for me. I cried for my baby who had a father he didn't deserve.

"You were right," I forced through my sobs.

"About what, Sprite?"

"Caylen should have been yours."

Except for his grip tightening on my hip, he didn't react. I began to worry that maybe he didn't want my son after all, but then he unleashed every emotion he was feeling all once when he seized my lips again. This time, there was lust, need, and uncontrollable possession in his kiss. I took his tongue deep and ran my hands over his chest as he rolled on top of me. His weight was like a balm. I wrapped my legs around his waist when he pressed his hips against me. I almost cried out when he broke the kiss and lifted his shirt over his head. My mouth watered at the sight of his abs and chest.

"He's already mine."

"Yes." It was all I could manage when his hands slipped under my t-shirt, and he slowly slid my panties down.

"You both are."

"Ye—oh yes." I lost the ability to do more than moan when his fingers found my clit.

"No one's going to take you away from me. I'll kill anyone who tries."

"Please."

"Is there something you want?" he teased as his finger slipped inside me.

"You."

"Then take me." I hesitated, unsure what to do and how to do it. He bent low and kissed me deeply at the same time he added a second finger and pressed deeper inside me.

"Take me right now," he growled. "Fucking do it."

His skin was hot when my hands found his waist. I slipped them inside the waistband of his gray sweatpants and pushed them down enough to free his cock. He was harder than I'd ever felt him, and it made me nervous as I anticipated having him inside me. I wrapped my fingers around him and enjoyed when his body shuddered.

"Make love to me, Angel." I met his gaze and found him staring down at me with barely controlled lust. "Please."

"I will, Sprite, but first I need to taste you." He slipped

my shirt over my head. I shivered when the air touched my skin or maybe it was because of the way he was devouring me with his eyes.

I watched, dazed, as he took my legs and bent me in half, tilting my hips up until my knees were level with the top of my head, and my pussy was open to him as an offering.

"Angel?"

His eyes found mine through the small gap between my knees. "Don't think." His voice was thick with desire. "Just take, Sprite. Take it all."

His head lowered, and then I felt nothing but his lips and tongue and the burning need to come. I bit my lip to keep my cries from escaping. He'd given me power by letting me take pleasure from him, but when his tongue slid inside me, and his fingers pressed against my clit, all I wanted to do was submit. The hungry sounds he made as he ate me, and the feel of his fingers digging into my ass, heightened my pleasure until I came. Hard. Silent. It seemed to last forever.

I was weak and breathless as he unfolded my legs and gently flipped me on my stomach. "Angel?"

"Shh… it's my turn." I looked back to see him rising from the bed and sliding his sweatpants the rest of the way down his legs. "Have you ever had your ass taken?"

"You know I haven't."

"I just needed to hear you say I'm the first." I was distracted by the curve of his muscular ass when he turned and opened the top drawer of the nightstand.

"You are?" I asked absently. My hips pressed into the bed.

"Yeah." He pulled out a clear bottle and tossed it on the

bed beside me. I read the label and bit down on my lip at the implication. Sensing my unease, he ran his hand down my spine. "We'll go as slow as you like." His hand then skimmed over my ass, curved over my thigh, and spread my legs.

"I—I trust you."

"I know you do." He covered my body with his and slid inside me.

My body tensed as he filled me since I still wasn't used to his size. He shoved his fingers in my hair and turned my head before seizing my lips and sliding deeper. When he ended the kiss, I weakly fell to the bed.

"Relax." After tilting my hips, and arching my back, he then reached out to grip the headboard. "I belong to you. You don't need to be afraid of me." I wasn't able to suppress my cry when he pulled back and slid inside me again. "Quiet, Sprite. You'll wake our son."

My whimper spurred him until he thrust into me deeply, over and over. I was reduced to biting the sheets to bury my cries as his body overpowered mine.

I was tipping over the edge of the world when I felt his finger, gentle and wet from the lube, entering my ass. "You're going to come, aren't you?" His voice was husky and teasing. He never stopped moving inside me.

I cried out when words weren't possible. He pressed another finger inside me and growled, "Come on my dick, Sprite. I need to feel it."

"Oh, God!" I screamed as I came, momentarily forgetting my baby sleeping five feet away. The sensation of his fingers in my ass while he fucked me had me coming harder than ever.

I heard his grunt as he slid from my body. I was still

breathing hard when I felt the head of his cock, slick from my release, pressing against my ass. "Stay relaxed, and I promise to make you come again." He punctuated his words by gripping my hip and guiding his cock head inside me.

I couldn't hide the fact that it hurt like hell the deeper he pressed. I clawed at the sheets while he whispered sweet nothings. I was near to begging him to stop when he finally bottomed out. He didn't move as he praised what a good girl I was and how good I felt.

"You're so tight, Sprite. I'm not going to last."

"You fill me so full."

He pulled back and then gently reentered me. "No one will ever fill you like I do."

He slid in and out easily until I was panting and pressing against him for more. I could feel his control slipping when his fingers found my clit and mercilessly forced me to come again. He dragged my limp body down the mattress by my ankle and bent me over the foot of the bed.

"Grab onto the bed and don't let go. If you let go, I'll stop. If you want me to stop, let go. Understand?"

I nodded, and the moment my fingers touched the sheets, he entered me again without the gentleness from before. My cry mingled with his grunt as his chest pressed against my back, and his strong hand gripped my nape. Holding me in place, he used me for his pleasure. I strained to breathe as he pushed my nose and opened mouth deeper into the bedding, strained to get him deeper inside as he moved with practiced grace, strained to come as I moved my hips back all the while struggling for the air he denied me.

I could feel consciousness drifting out of reach. My fingers itched to let go of the bed and make him stop, but the need to make him lose control had me gripping the sheets tighter. Just as I had begun to fall under, he lifted my head, gifting me air, and came with a grunt, so savage it pushed me over again.

"I want to do it," I announced after our shower. I was still feeling weak and sore in all the right places as I watched from the bed as he dressed. Given the dark, casual clothing and granite set of his jaw, I knew where he was going and why. "I want to be the one to end him."

"No." He stepped into black jeans similar to the pair he wore last night. "I don't want you anywhere near him."

I climbed from the bed, taking the sheet with me. This was not a fight I relished having naked, but by the time I found my clothes, he'd be gone. "That's not your decision. It's mine, and I've made it."

"You went through enough last night."

"And I never want to feel that vulnerable again. It will never be over for me unless I end it myself. My son almost died because of him. If you don't let me end him, then I want to be there when you do. I need to see him die for myself."

He paused from pulling on a clean black hoodie and fixed me with his troubled gaze. I felt kicked in the stomach.

He looked ready to deny me what was mine, and I was

more than ready to fight for it, but then he said, "Dress warm and meet me in the library in thirty minutes."

"Thank you." He didn't respond as he pulled me into him and ripped away the sheet. I was fully naked against his clothed body, but I could still feel his heat.

"I'd give you *my* life if you asked for it." He looked ready to kiss me, so for once, I beat him to the punch. As I played with his tongue, I considered pulling him back into bed with me. That was until he lifted me and carried me back to the bed. I was disappointed, however, when he backed away looking hungry as he bit his lip.

"Thirty minutes," he warned, and then he was gone.

I quickly dressed in a pair of blue jeans and a blue and gray flannel. When I was ready to leave, I crossed the room to Caylen's crib and stared down at him. I almost lost him last night, and I realized there would never be a moment when I didn't fear it happening again.

I forced myself to leave him and knocked on Anna's door moments later. She opened almost immediately as if she had been waiting for me.

"I'd ask if you're okay, but...the wall." Her greeting was glacial, but it didn't keep heat from spreading through my body and ending at my cheeks. "*All* morning."

"God," I groaned. "Tell me you didn't hear."

"Oh, I heard." She blushed, despite her feelings toward Angel. "He seems... thorough."

You have no idea.

"I came to talk to you about last night." I desperately needed to change the subject. She opened the door wider to allow me inside.

"I wanted to talk to you about that too. Lucas, Z, and Angel's extremely hot cousin were particularly tight-lipped at breakfast, though they did notice your and Angel's absence."

Her jaw dropped. "The senator came last night to trade the book for me and Caylen."

"Angel tried to give you up to that creep?"

"No, but he used us to set a trap and Caylen—" I couldn't bring myself to say the words. "He almost died, Anna. Aaron tried to kill him."

"Oh, Mian." Her embrace held my tears at bay though her calm reaction was surprising.

"I thought you'd be ready to storm out that door and call out Angel."

"After yesterday, I kind of understand what's at stake." She squeezed me before letting go. "I still want to kick Angel in the ball sack though."

We burst out laughing even though the look in Anna's eyes promised she most certainly would if given a chance. "I'm glad you're all okay. Even Angel. I thought I heard gunfire, but it sounded so far away I couldn't be sure. When I tried to leave and warn Angel, I found my bedroom door locked. I couldn't get out." She lifted her hands to show me the bruises on her fist. "I yelled and pounded on the door, but no one came." She scoffed and muttered, "Angel must pay the servants a fortune."

"I don't have much time," I said, switching lanes. "I came to see if you could keep an eye on Caylen for a few hours."

"Of course, but where are you going?"

I shook my head, not wanting to get into it. I knew Anna would try to talk me out of it, and for now, I didn't want to give her anything to worry about. "I'll tell you later. I have to go. He should be waking up soon, and he'll be hungry." I didn't stick around for her to argue and hurried down to the first floor.

When I made it to the library, however, I found it empty. I checked the bronze antique clock on the wall and saw I was on time, which meant Angel should have been here. Had he changed his mind and left without me?

Rather than to succumb to paranoia, I decided to wait him out. Angel was the head of a criminal empire and only just last night murdered several people including a senator's son. Maybe he'd been pulled away to deal with something urgent.

My gaze caught something familiar resting at the furthest end of the table and my heart sped up. I couldn't stop my feet from pulling me closer until I was lifting the leather bound book from the glossy hardwood.

Holding the book felt like holding Pandora's Box and opening it would unleash all the evil in the world. I didn't remember sinking into the chair. My fingers caressed the leather nervously.

Did I dare?

With a deep breath, I flipped to the first page. The harshly scripted ink was faded and hard to translate, so I flipped through two hundred years until a date caught my eye.

April 4th 2007.

The day my mother died.

The Parties:
Arturo Knight
Cecily Ross
Victor Castro

The Order:

On this day, April 4th 2007, Arturo Knight orders the death of Cecily Ross as a permanent end to the affair. Such order was executed by Victor Castro.

The Debt:

$20,000 paid to Victor Castro.

The Bandit:

Arturo

The Fifth Knight

I hadn't realized I was crying until the first tear dropped onto the paper, smudging the ink.

Hurt. Betrayal. Confusion.

Each emotion fought for the right to shred my heart until there was nothing left to ruin.

My mom hadn't died of cancer. It had all been a lie.

She'd been murdered by a man who thought his secrets were worth more than her life. A man she loved until he took her last breath. And then he callously recorded the end of her life as if she never meant anything to him or to my father... or me.

I turned the page to see if there was more and there was. So much murder, scandal, and lies, but none of it was about my mother. She was merely a blip in this family's legacy.

The Parties:

Arturo Knight

Theodore Ross

The Order:

On this day, June 24th 2013, Theodore Ross orders the marriage of his daughter. Such order will be executed by the heir apparent, Angeles Knight. Father John Adams and County Clerk Michael Kelley will bear witness to this legal union.

The Debt:

Mian Ross

Angeles Knight

The Bandit:

Arturo

The Fifth Knight

June 24th...

It must have been the day Angel and I had been married without our knowledge. My desire to be Angel's had come true, and my right to be a part of it had been stolen by my father. I flipped the page, no longer able to stand seeing my fate so coldly decided for me with the stroke of a pen. I flipped until I recognized another date.

The Parties:

Angeles Knight

Alon Knight

The Order:

On this day, November 1st 2013, Alon Knight orders Angeles Knight to assume his rightful place as The Knight.

As his duty, he will inherit Alexander's legacy, and become the sixth Bandit. Only by death or succession of a male heir will this Knight's duty end.

The Debt:
His first-born son.

The Bandit:
Alon
The Fourth Knight

His reign began when my life ended.

The day after Arturo was murdered, I was feeling my world turn upside down while Angel had inherited his precious legacy. The Knights tore apart my family so they could continue to feather their nest.

It was time they learned how high the price for losing everything could get. The fireplace beckoned as I pushed away from the table and rose from my seat.

Angel may never forgive me, his family may hunt me, but they started this war.

And now I was ending it.

Turning on the gas, I watched the fire flicker to life and then held the book over the fire. The flames licked at the leather and burned my fingers. I just needed to let go.

The library doors burst open just as I began to let the book slip. Clutching the book at the last minute, I hid it behind my back and faced the intruder.

It was Lucas and Z, and they looked ready to kill.

"I was just—"

"No time, princess." Z slammed the library doors with more force than I'd ever seen from him. Lucas lifted the nearest chair and flung it at the wall. It splintered into pieces before crumbling to the floor.

"What's going on?"

"They took him."

"Caylen?" I didn't wait for them to answer. I was already racing for the door, afraid for my baby, and promising retribution to anyone who harmed him. *I never should have left him.*

Z blocked the door and wrapped his arms around me to keep me from leaving. "It's not Caylen, princess."

Then why did he still look ready to vomit?

"Then who?" As soon as I demanded the answer, however, I knew. "Someone took Angel?"

"Reginald returned here almost an hour ago with the other presumptive heirs and called him out."

"Why would he do that?"

"He said he suspected Angel no longer had the book."

"But he does." I quickly pulled the book from behind my back. "It's right here."

"It wasn't enough to show them. Reginald insisted on inspecting it too."

"The torn pages," I gasped. "They found them."

"If you ask me, Reginald knew *exactly* what to look for."

"Do you think Augustine—" He was the only one with something to gain from Angel's death who would know about the missing pages.

"He's hiding something," Z agreed, "but he's made it clear he doesn't want Alexander's legacy."

"And you believe him?"

"He doesn't exactly stay around long enough for anyone to question him."

"Where is he now?"

"He went with them, but he didn't look too happy about it. He could be our only ally, but right now, I don't trust anyone outside this room."

"Are they really going to kill him?"

"Yes. Reginald has been looking for an excuse for years. This isn't the first time he's challenged him, but this is the first time he's won."

"Won? Are you saying you'll just sit here and let them butcher him?"

"He only has two options, princess."

"Which are?"

"After they execute him, Reginald will turn his wrath on you, and there will be no one to challenge him. We either get you and Caylen to safety now or risk dying as we try to save him."

"And he made his choice very clear, princess."

When I told Angel he'd have to choose, I didn't mean this. "Well, guess what? I'm tired of living my life based on his choices. Where is he?"

"Do you think this is easy for us to stand by and let him die?" Z roared. "It's fucking tearing us apart." He wrecked me when his eyes glistened with unshed tears. "We have our orders, Mian."

Mian.

Not princess.

"He's not your leader right now," I pleaded brokenly as I balled his shirt in my fists. "He's your friend, your brother, and he needs you right now." I couldn't just accept that he was going to die. Not after everything I gave him this morning.

"The crypt," Lucas cursed as he pulled me out of Z's

arms. "They took him to the crypt."

"It doesn't matter," Z argued. "We'll never get in without the key,"

I didn't stop to think about a plan or even if I should rescue Angel with all I had just learned.

I just knew I could never stop my heart from wanting to try.

"It just so happens I know a way in."

CHAPTER TWENTY-THREE

ANGEL

WE WERE UNDERGROUND THE MAUSOLEUM WHERE each Bandit before me, including my father and grandfather, were buried. The main chamber was circular with an altar in the center. The floor was made of black and white tiled marble. Surrounding the altar were six crypts, one of them belonging to me.

"I'm almost disappointed you didn't see this coming," Andrew whispered as he tied me to the pillar. The rope bit into my skin, cutting off the blood flow. "Our family thinks you're a legend yet it was so easy to orchestrate your downfall." He patted my arm once he had finished tying me up. "We've orchestrated a lot of downfalls," he confessed. "It all started with your mother. Your poor, broken mother. Beatrice gave Victor the code to the safe and the tip about the silent alarm. The paranoia Victor implanted

in her head made her think she was saving you from yourself." I kept my gaze forward and didn't react. My chances
of getting out of this alive were slim, but if I did, I needed
to know who deserved my wrath. "Then there was Victor
who was so eager to prove his potential. My father promised him power if he helped us set you up by stealing the
book. When he succeeded, we couldn't leave loose ends, so
we asked him to take your sweet little wife and then you
killed him for us. Just as we wanted."

Reginald and fifteen of my cousins were busy arguing
how best to kill me. His suggestions favored pain while the
others just wanted to get it over with. My family had long
ago divided. There were those who wanted nothing to do
with Alexander's legacy but were too afraid of rebelling.

And then there was Augustine who feigned boredom
as he stood silently within our circle of cousins. I knew my
warning not to interfere had fallen on deaf ears. He was
a calculating player and used every piece in the game of
chess as his personal pawn. He once told me himself that it
was smarter not to trust him.

"Finally, there was the ambitious Henry Staten who
was eager to keep his cozy job in the Senate. We convinced
him to deliver the book to you in exchange for erasing his
indiscretions, and of course, Mian and the kid. Once he
entered those gates, we counted on you making sure he'd
never return." I waited, knowing there would be more.
"We promised we'd show up on a white horse with the
other heirs to bear witness to how a *descendant of Angelo*
broke the rules. But we didn't." He moved closer and whispered, "You weren't the only one laying a trap," he taunted.
"Staten dead means there's no one left to tie us to the book
being stolen and tampered. You remember rules number

five and six, don't you?"

Never sell silence.

Protect the book.

He snapped his fingers. "Almost forgot the last piece of the puzzle. We killed your grandfather, of course. Alon didn't leave us must choice when history repeated itself. He confronted us with his suspicions after that fiasco at the ball." He leaned in close again. "Were you really going to kill that innocent beauty?" I closed my eyes to block the admiration in his voice. What I almost did to Mian would haunt me forever.

"I admire your ability to train your woman better than your father trained your mother. I couldn't get anything out of her during our little chat in the gardens. She was Plan B. Who better to kill you than the woman you love? After we kill you, I think I'll keep her around for a while. Without the kid, of course."

I smiled at that knowing if he did ever manage to get Mian in his bed, she wouldn't hesitate to carve his heart out while he slept.

"Are you thinking about your last words?" he mused when I didn't respond to his prodding.

"I'm thinking if I don't get to kill you, my wife certainly will."

"I'll be sure to keep that in mind when I'm deep inside her." He stood in front of me now. "Maybe I'll even give her my seed."

His grin was triumphant when I growled and fought to free myself from my bonds. If my hands weren't tied to this pillar, I'd carve his heart out myself.

Augustine noticed us first and sauntered over. Reginald called his son away, and I finally relaxed. I closed my eyes and prayed Lucas and Z had followed orders and got Mian and Caylen far away from here.

"What did he say?" Augustine asked me.

"Nothing I haven't already figured out." My eyes opened to find Augustine standing close with his arms crossed. He was using his body to block me from view and kept his voice low.

"Reginald and the kid were in it with Staten."

"They must have offered him anonymity, and Staten must have figured he could control them."

"Those idiots think they'll be gods." His grin was mocking. "Staten would have made them errand boys."

"They'd be dead long before that could happen."

He grunted and then fell silent. A second later, he said, "So how do you want to do this?"

I didn't miss a beat. "You sure about this?"

He shrugged. "I'm not helping to kill the only member of this family I actually respect."

"Two against sixteen…" I've fought those odds before, but I had the advantage of not having my hands tied behind my back.

"Four against sixteen." We shared a look. "I may have left the door to the tunnel unlocked."

"Lucas and Z have their orders. If we die down here, Mian and Caylen won't be safe."

"Then we better make sure we don't die down here."

Over Augustine's shoulder, I noticed Andrew watching us curiously. If we were going to make a move, it had to be fast. Augustine noticed my distraction and quickly drove his fist into my gut. I struggled for my next breath as my body folded as much as my bonds would allow. Augustine may be lean, but he packed one hell of a punch.

"You should know better than to beg for mercy, cousin." He spat the words loud enough for Andrew to hear as he approached.

"Pride is forgotten when one is staring death in the eye," Andrew reflected when he reached us. "Even men who think themselves a god." Augustine faked a laugh for Andrew's benefit and then rolled his eyes when he looked away.

"Has your father made a decision on how we'll end this prick?"

"Actually, it was me who decided to show Angeles the same mercy Adan showed my second great-grandfather."

Augustine blanked. "You want to *behead* him?"

"It seems traditional, don't you think?" To me, he said, "Be sure to thank your grandfather for me when you see him in hell." With a wink, he walked away again and made his way to the long, brown satchel he had brought in. He then made a show of removing an axe while everyone looked on.

Reginald took the opportunity to approach as his son expertly swung the axe through the air. He'd obviously been practicing. "I didn't want it to be like this."

"Really? Because your son says you planned the entire thing." Reginald cast a worried glance at Augustine and stepped closer.

"My son can get a bit carried away with his exaggerations. I long suspected foul play and did my duty to this family by calling you out."

"Whatever helps your crown of righteousness fit better."

"Reginald," Alistair called. "Can we please move forward?"

"Certainly." Reginald fixed his attention on Augustine. "I trust you can untie him and get him on his knees."

Augustine nodded and moved to untie me from the pillar while Reginald and the others circled the altar. Andrew stood alone in the center with an eager gleam in his eye as he twirled the axe.

"Get ready," Augustine whispered as he stealthily untied my hands. I kept them folded behind my back as he led me forward. Beyond the altar, I noticed a dark figure dart into the shadows. I casually let my gaze roam and noticed another moving in the opposite direction. It wasn't until a third, much smaller figure followed the second that my control slipped infinitesimally. "Easy," Augustine whispered. He disguised the order by pushing me to my knees.

I gritted my teeth when my knees hit the stone. I then searched the shadows again for movement, convinced my eyes were playing tricks on me. Augustine had warned me they would come, and I was terrified to believe he was right because if we failed…

"Any last words?" Andrew taunted.

"Try to be tasteful," Reginald scolded before I could answer. "Angeles, please present your neck."

I saw the shadows move again, and this time, it didn't go unnoticed. Benjamin, a cousin from my own line, noticed the gun pointed at his head the same time I did. He backed away, stumbling, and drawing attention.

It didn't matter, though.

It was already too late.

"Actually, I do have last words for you," I announced. I stole Andrew's attention again before he could notice them. "You lose."

Andrew went down after Z delivered a brutal blow

with the butt of his gun.

"What is this?" Reginald bellowed.

Lucas, Z, and Augustine were busy overpowering the armed and stupid when I smelled her soft scent. I didn't know I was already missing her until now. "Why are you here?" I growled as she untied me.

She didn't sound so sure of her answer when she said, "Wouldn't you do the same for me?"

"There isn't anything I wouldn't do for you." Her hands froze from untying me, but it didn't matter. I forced free of the loosened rope and turned to cradle her face in my hands. "But you still shouldn't have come."

"Who would have stopped me?"

I haven't killed them yet even though I *really* wanted to. Reginald and Andrew were tied to a chair at each end of the table while our cousins, who hadn't been injured to within an inch of their life, sat around the table. Lucas and Z stood as sentinels by the door while I leaned against the fireplace, holding the book at my side. The edges of the leather were burned, but I chose to focus on one issue at a time. Tension filled the library as they waited nervously for me to start the meeting.

At this point, there were no sides. Only confusion.

"Someone want to explain what the fuck is going on?" Amir spat. He was a descendant of Meredith and one of the few who hadn't resisted when we stopped my execution.

"Angeles is a traitor and should be put down," Reginald roared.

"It pains me to say it, cousin, but he's right," Liam, a descendant of Angelo, grimly agreed. "You wouldn't have hesitated."

"I wouldn't have been *wrong,* either."

His gaze narrowed. "What are you saying?"

"I'm saying that these two set me up and he," I nodded to Andrew, "was stupid enough to confess his betrayal while I was still alive."

"It's your word against mine, and even if I was guilty, why would I confess to a corpse?"

"Because I wouldn't have still been the Knight." Andrew paled while Reginald glowered at his son. "And as you know my reign doesn't end until I'm dead."

"He's right," Augustine gloated. "As long as he breathes he's judge, jury, and executioner."

The door opened, and Mian slipped past Lucas and Z just as Reginald shouted, "My son is right. Knight or not, you can't prove he confessed anything to you."

"As far as you're concerned, I am your God." I heard Mian's gasp. At this moment, I truly was the monster she once feared. "But if you want proof before you die, I can make that happen." Lucas and Z left on cue. I took the opportunity to meet Mian's gaze for the first time since she had entered the room. She stood by the door wringing her hands. When I held out my hand to her, she hesitated before coming to me. "You don't need to be afraid of me."

"I know."

My frown deepened as doubt stirred in my gut. "Do you?"

"I think so."

I kissed her lips, but she didn't kiss me back. "We'll fix that later," I promised, attempting to soften her. I felt her stiffen in my arms just as Lucas and Z returned. I ignored my cousins' stares and pushed her behind me with a mental note to find out what was wrong with her when we were alone. I felt her fingers dig into my sides when they dragged the senator, crumpled and bloodied, inside. We hadn't had the chance to get him to the warehouse, so we kept him locked in the cellar with instructions to the servants to stay clear.

The senator attempted to stand, but Z's firm hand on his shoulder forced him down. Reginald avoided eye contact while Andrew looked as if he'd pass out. Staten looked around, and when he finally noticed Reginald, his face twisted with rage.

"You son of a bitch! How can you just sit there? You assured me when you stole the book he'd be taken care of. Look at me," he roared. He was a bloodied broken shell of the refined man who wanted me and my baby dead. "My son is dead because of your betrayal."

No one moved or spoke. The only sound that could be heard was the senator's heaving as he attempted to catch his breath.

"I think we have all we need," Alistair slowly spoke. Reginald turned his scowl on him.

"You spit on Alexander when you side with him."

"Alexander is the one who made these rules our family's law. You disgraced him when you tried to frame Angeles."

"I was righting the wrong his line did to this family. Angelo's line has ruled for four generations while we sat back and did nothing. The Knighthood belongs to Andrew.

He should be Alexander's *true* heir."

"I'm afraid that argument won't save you from Angel's mercy," Ronald, another descendant of Alexander's, answered. "If it's all right with you, Angel, I'd like to go home now."

I nodded and silently watched as everyone except Lucas, Alexander, and Z left.

"Angeles." The senator said my name like a plea. "Let me go, son. You can't simply kill a senator and expect no one to ask questions. They'll trace my death to you."

"Senator, I promise you, when I'm done, there won't be anything left of you to find." And my vow was meant for anyone who crossed me. My gaze swept the room, resting meaningfully on my traitorous kin.

CHAPTER TWENTY-FOUR

MIAN

ANNA RELUCTANTLY DECIDED TO RETURN HOME AFTER her mother reappeared. None of us liked it, but it was a decision she forced us to respect.

I hadn't seen Angel in two days, but I didn't regret the space. I was still figuring out how to confront him about my mother and had been focusing on not allowing hurt and anger to consume me. The morning after we saved Angel from being beheaded, I watched a report on the news about the perishing of Senator Henry Staten, his son, Aaron Staten, and girlfriend, Erin Andrews, after the home of the senator had burned down in an uncontrollable fire. Angel's promise to not leave anything left of the Senator to find must have been what kept him away these past couple of days.

I was busy drawing a sketch on a legal pad I'd stolen

from the library, something I hadn't done in months, when Angel stepped out onto the patio looking like he needed a week's worth of sleep.

"Hey," he greeted.

"Hey."

"I thought you might like to know that your friend, Becky, is alive. She was shot in the abdomen, but it went straight through without damaging anything." I felt a tear slide down my face and quickly wiped it away.

"Thank you." My voice shook, but I didn't care. I wanted to see my friends again, but I knew it would never be possible. It was better this way. They were safe.

"Sam also received a package from me this morning."

My lips parted, but no words came. I had to fight for them. "You *paid them off*?"

"I *thanked them* for taking care of you and Caylen," he corrected. "And because she took a bullet for you."

I turned away and ran my pencil over the sketch, darkening lines and creating more depth.

"You're drawing again," he observed as he took a seat next to me. I blushed when he took a peek at my sketch. It was a roughly drawn replica of him during one of those rare moments he never allowed anyone to see. Moments usually spent with me. "Have I ever told you how talented you are?"

I smiled feeling myself blush. "You don't have to suck up. It's just a hobby."

"Have you considered doing nudes?"

"No." I ran my pencil over Angel's eyes, darkening them. "Most of my drawings are of my mother. I barely remember her before cancer so mostly I imagine how she'd look knowing she was going to live." I wasn't looking at him, but I could feel his reaction. When I did look at him, his eyes were empty though his jaw was set. He was never going to tell me the truth unless I made him. "Your father murdered my mother, didn't he?"

"How did you—" His gaze narrowed. "You read the book?"

I slammed the pad down and stood up. "Then I guess we're even." I tried to walk away, determined to leave him once and for all, when his hand closed around my wrist. He was gentle, but his constant betrayal made his touch feel like acid.

"I'm not upset," he rushed to assure me.

"Well, that makes one of us."

I tried again to walk away, but he growled impatiently and tugged me down onto his lap. I was facing him with nowhere to rest my hands but on his shoulder. "You shouldn't have read the book." I squirmed to get away, but he simply tightened his hold. "You would be dead if my family had caught you."

"What happened to you being their God?"

I could hear the humor in his grunt. "I got lucky."

"You wouldn't have let them hurt me."

"It wouldn't have been up to me," he warned unconvincingly. We both know Angel would have forsaken his crown to kill them for hurting me.

It was the very reason I didn't understand Angel bending to a dead man's rules now. It was clear he no longer agreed with them. Maybe he never did. "Augustine doesn't care about Alexander's rules. Why do you?"

Angel's hands squeezed my hips as he leaned forward. His voice menacing as he whispered, "Did you just use another man to emasculate me?"

"I don't think that's possible." I waited until his hold loosened and he sat back to say, "But you aren't their King, Angel. You're their prisoner."

"Maybe. But I'll wear their chains as long as it keeps you safe."

"Don't say things like that." I closed my eyes to block out the look in his eyes. It felt a lot like love.

"Why not?" I didn't answer him. How did I put into words how much I loved and hated him? I felt his lips on me and released a blissful sigh.

"Why did Art kill my mother?" He paused from trailing kisses down the column of my neck and sighed.

"She wanted to be with him, and when he wouldn't leave my mother, she threatened to expose them."

"So he chose to kill her rather than face the consequences?" I pushed against his shoulders and stood to my feet. "I was practically an orphan because of him." With my mother dead and my father avoiding me, there had been no one but Angel. He was the closest thing to family I've had since my mother was murdered. "How did she die?"

He shook his head and stood up. I didn't know what I would do if he walked away from me.

But then he held out his hand to me. "Come on."

"No." His hand dropped. "I'm not going anywhere with you until I have answers."

"The answers you need can't come from me because I don't have them."

"Then who does?"

Angel hadn't spoken since we left Attica. The drive to Chicago had been long and uncomfortable, which he spent smoking. When we sat down across from my father, the tension only multiplied.

"You know how to make your old man's day," Theo greeted. The growth covering the lower half of his face hadn't been there the last time I saw him. His hair had also grown into a greasy shag. Suddenly, I felt all-consuming guilt. Two months ago, I came here asking him to help me steal from the most dangerous man in Chicago and then fell off the grid with no word.

I took his hands in mine. I've missed their strength and warmth. "Daddy, I'm so sorry I didn't tell you I was okay."

"It's fine, baby girl. You're here now." I'd believe that if his hands didn't tremble.

"What have you been doing to yourself? You don't look well."

"It doesn't matter now." His attention shifted to Angel. "What brings you by?"

I didn't want to say the words because saying them meant never being able to take them back. "I—I know about my mother's death." Daddy's eyes flew back to me. "I know Art had her killed because of their affair."

He turned his accusing eyes on Angel again. "You told her?"

"She found the truth in the book." They seemed to have some silent conversation that ended with Angel shaking his head and Theo nodding.

"Baby girl, please understand why I didn't tell you. Her death was hard enough on you."

"And you, but yet I never lied to you." When he hung

his head, I grabbed his chin and lifted until I could see his eyes.

"How did she die?"

"I don't think—"

"No," I ordered before he could deny me. "No more lies. No more secrets. I have a right to know."

He once again turned his attention to Angel, who said nothing, did nothing but wait for my father to prove he was the man I held in my heart. "Victor suffocated her while she slept." His voice was pained as his eyes glistened with unshed tears. I felt pain—not the torpid pain that eventually came because time was sometimes merciful—but the agonizing pain that immediately came because death was sometimes unmerciful.

I didn't *lose* my mother. She was taken from me.

I pulled my hands away and took a deep breath. "And my marriage to Angel?"

His handsome features twisted until he was a broken shell. "I'd hoped that you'd never find out, or at least, not a day before I could explain why I gave you to him."

"I know why, Father." I had never spoken to my father this coldly. "It was easier for you if I belonged to someone else. I wouldn't need you anymore. You told yourself you were protecting me to ease your conscience, but you didn't just marry me to Angel. You sold me to a dead man's legacy. How could you?"

"I'm sorry, baby girl. Please forgive me." Through his eyes, I saw his heart breaking.

But he'd broken me long before I'd broken him.

"I don't think I can, Daddy."

I would no longer be the naïve little girl who would climb on his knee to beg for his love and attention.

"Are you hungry?" he asked after closing the doors of the estate. Angel barely kept his eyes off me during the ride home…here. He sat close, making sure we touched from head to toe. His mood was completely different from the car ride to the prison.

"Not really. Um… can we talk in private?"

He didn't respond except to place his hand on the small of my back and lead me to one of the staircases. I didn't speak, and neither did he as we walked through the east wing until we reached just another of the many rooms. It would be easy to get lost in a place like this. It was exactly the future I feared.

The room he locked us in smelled like leather and smoke. He moved behind the desk made of burl wood, intricately carved edges completed with golden leaf detail, and a rich finish. I sat on a sofa that looked like it belonged in a castle five hundred years in the past.

"What's up?" The casualness of his question was forced. Just days ago, Angel had said he knew what was in my head as well as in my heart. If that were true, then he'd know what I was ready to demand.

"I think it's better for both of us if I leave."

"Why is that?" His voice was empty of curiosity, surprise, or anger.

"Because of all the things you've done to me and all the things you will do."

I could see the first crack in his facade. "You promised

you'd stay."

"I promised I'd *try*. But Angel, letting my father go left a hole in my heart, and I don't know how to fill it. Staying here will only make it bigger."

I didn't miss his flinch. "You know I can't let you leave."

"I'm done being scared! If you have to kill me, do it or let me go."

His gaze narrowed. "What are you so eager to return to, Mian? That pathetic apartment and an empty stomach?"

"Freedom."

"You're not a prisoner," he said through gritted teeth. It was nothing I hadn't heard before.

"No, I'm not a prisoner, Angel. You are. You're chained to Alexander's legacy, and that may be fine for you, but it isn't for me."

"Even if you have to spend the rest of your days tied to my bed. You aren't leaving. Three years ago, I let you go because I thought you'd be better off, and when you tried to steal from me, I found you starving, desperate, and the mother of a baby you can't protect."

"Fuck you."

He scoffed. "You're the same naïve girl you were when you were sixteen, only this time you're *mine*. You're not leaving."

"If you don't let me go, I'll never stop trying to get away from you. Every time you walk out that door, you'll wonder if you're coming back to an empty home because, deep down, you know one day I'll succeed."

"You run, I'll chase. If this is how we spend our lives together, then so be it. I won't let you go again knowing what will happen. I won't let anyone hurt you. Not as long as my ring is on your finger."

With a yank, I ripped off his ring and tossed it at him. It bounced off his chest and fell on the desk. "The only one hurting me is you." I saw his flinch just before I turned and fled. I hated him, not for making me stay but for the reckless part of me that *wanted* to stay.

I was too busy fighting the tears as they came to see him until we collided. Thanks to his quick reflexes, he caught me before I could fall.

"Easy, short stuff. You trying to take me out?" Augustine's blinding smile broke through my tears. "I should warn you that I'm not a cheap date." I was ashamed of the hiccup that escaped when I tried to force a laugh through my sniffling. "Now that was pitiful. I know you can do better than that. That was my best stuff."

"Then you shouldn't quit your day job," I quipped.

"There she goes!" He whooped. My laugh this time was real. "Anyone tell you you're a smart ass?"

"Anyone tell you're rude?"

"I might have heard it a time or two."

"You should work on that."

"Not gonna." His smile was quick and easy, and I had the feeling it had charmed the panties off many women. It was too bad my heart, and my panties were forever wedged under Angel's boot.

"I better go."

"Not until you tell me why my cousin made you cry."

I hesitated. Would it be stupid to confide him in? If anyone would understand my need to decide my fate, wouldn't he? "He won't let us go."

He seemed to contemplate something before saying, "I can understand why."

I eyed him suspiciously until he chuckled. "I didn't

mean you."

"Ouch." I feigned hurt before saying, "I didn't know there was someone special."

He shrugged. "There isn't. I just said I understand." I couldn't tell if he was lying. He was just that good at it.

"You won't live your life based on Alexander's rules. Why should I?"

"I can take care of myself."

"God, you sound just like him." Deciding I was wrong about him, I quickly moved around him. Just when I thought I had an ally...

I didn't get far when his hand closed around my arm. His gaze bore into me, and in the emerald, I could see whatever demons Augustine kept locked away clawing at the walls.

"Running won't make you free."

CHAPTER TWENTY-FIVE

MIAN

ANGEL STAYED AWAY THAT NIGHT, AND I PRETENDED not to miss the warmth of having him beside me. I spent the hours alone until I fell asleep with Augustine's words playing in my head.

I awoke later than usual the next morning. Caylen was already up and standing against the crib railings. He smiled happily when I rose from the bed and babbled at me.

"Mommy's sorry she slept so long," I cooed as I lifted him from the crib. "Are you hungry?" I was partially surprised he wasn't upset. He was usually ravenous with a full diaper in the morning.

"I fed him an hour ago," the deep voice spoke. I spun around with Caylen in my arms and found Angel leaning against the wall with his hands shoved in his pocket.

"Changed him too."

He was brooding, and I didn't get why when I was the one being forced to stay here. "Thank you," I grudgingly replied.

He shrugged his voice flat as he said, "You slept like the dead, and he's been up for a couple of hours."

I kissed Caylen's fat cheek and placed him back in the crib. If he was taken care of, then I'd take the rare advantage of a long shower. "I'm going to shower then."

"I think we should talk first."

"We said all we needed to say last night." I didn't stop moving for the bathroom, but then he was there, keeping me from getting away. *As usual.*

"What about all the things we're afraid to say?" I didn't dare look at him. He was not going to seduce me this time.

"Maybe it's for the best." He was silent for a moment before sighing.

"Maybe."

"Are we done here?" I still refused to look at him.

"You and I will never be done." I felt him move in closer until he towered over me. I let him wrap his arms around me because I couldn't be this close and not feel his touch. "But I'm willing to compromise until you can accept the truth."

My eyes traveled up his muscular chest, past his strong neck, and over kissable lips until I found him staring down at me. "What do you mean?"

"You'll see. Just know it's the only thing I'm giving you. It's the only thing I *can* give you, and not because of the damn legacy." He pulled me closer, and then I let him kiss me. "But because I just don't fucking want to."

He didn't take me back to Chicago. Michelle and Officer Garrett, who insisted I call him Tim, took me in after Angel let me walk away. Bringing me here had been his way of appeasing me so I wouldn't run away and sadly, it worked. I may still be under his thumb, but I no longer felt trapped. I only felt lost.

Angel had packed us up and kissed me on the Garrett's porch as if he would never see me again even though his eyes promised he would. Then I watched him drive away.

That had been a month ago.

"I hope you like vanilla frosting," Michelle said as she burst into the kitchen with a large white box. "I got chocolate cake for the party."

Today was Caylen's first birthday, and Michelle had insisted on throwing him a party. Since tomorrow was Halloween, she suggested it be a costume party, and then promised it would be small and inexpensive when I protested. She had already done so much for us that accepting the above and beyond made me feel guiltier than I already did. She'd wanted a life away from Alexander's legacy, and I had brought her back in by staying here.

"Vanilla is fine. You really didn't have to do this," I pleaded in vain. She waved me off and set the cake on the counter. The house was covered in streamers and balloons with even more decorating their backyard where the party would be held. She had even invited all her friends and neighbors with small kids to celebrate my son's first birthday.

"I keep telling you it's no trouble. I haven't been able to throw a party like this since Tabitha turned twelve. Now all she wants are gifts and a day out with her friends."

"Thank you," I said for the hundredth time since she proposed the idea.

"You're welcome, sweet girl. You and that adorable baby will always have a place here. I want you to remember that." After a teary hug, I helped her finish getting the house ready for the party. Caylen was upstairs napping, but he'd be awake soon. I just hoped he wouldn't be afraid of a house full of strangers. He'd always been good with people, so I wasn't too worried.

The party was in full swing an hour later. I was dressed as Cruella de Vil and Caylen was my little Dalmatian pup. Michelle had promised small, but it was anything but. I didn't mind since everyone was nothing but kind. The two tables not covered with food were piled high with gifts for a boy they'd never even met. It made me wonder how much Michelle had told them, but I decided not to dwell on it. Caylen was happy. It was all that mattered. Michelle, Tim, and Tabitha were dressed as Morticia, Gomez, and Wednesday from the Addams Family. Tabitha had complained to her mom that she should have made her brother, Austin, come home so their getup would be complete.

"These people are so nice," Anna gushed. Tim had offered to pick Anna up and bring her so she wouldn't miss Caylen's birthday, and she'd come as Dany from *Game of Thrones*. "Do you know any of them?"

"Not one. They're all Michelle and Tim's friends."

"To be honest, I'm not sure I know who half of them are either," Tabitha grumbled as she played with Caylen. "But they brought gifts!"

My laugh died in my throat. I felt punched in the gut. I couldn't breathe when the patio door slid open, and he stepped through. His sudden presence arrested me as well as every woman there. He was back in the suit, looking much larger than life and more ruthless than death. Dark shades covered his eyes, blocking out the sun and every curious eye.

"What is he doing here?" Anna growled.

Tabitha, however, handed over Caylen and ran over to greet her older cousin. Tim and Michelle had already hurried over to speak to him quietly. Not once had he looked my way, but he'd know I was there.

"I don't know." I could barely hear myself think over the sound of my heart racing.

"Maybe Officer Garrett will arrest him if he tries to take you back."

We were still watching when Michelle and Tim cast worried glances our way. Their attention, unfortunately, drew Angel's attention. I couldn't see his eyes, but I knew they were on me. I started to think I'd never be free of his trance when Tabitha tapped him on the shoulder, forcing his attention away from me. I didn't stop watching him though. He said a few words to his cousin and then handed her something I couldn't see.

And then he was gone again.

Later that night, when the clock struck midnight, I didn't call to wish him a happy birthday, and he didn't call to make me.

"I hate geometry," Tabitha groaned for the third time. She was sitting at the coffee table suffering through her homework while I fed Caylen dinner.

"Just wait until you're taking calculus," Anna deadpanned. "You'll be tempted to drop out of school." Tabitha groaned and slammed her face in her textbook. Anna and Tabitha hit it off at Caylen's party two months ago. She started sleeping over every weekend after Tabitha and Michelle insisted I invite her over the first time. Today, she was helping Tabitha study for her geometry test the next day.

"It seems bad now, endless even, but when it's over, you'll realize it was worth fighting for." Tabitha lifted her head from the textbook, and they both regarded me curiously.

"Do you think you'll ever go back?" Tabitha shyly questioned. I suppressed a groan. How did we go from talking about high school math to my love life?

"Why? You tired of us already?" I joked to avoid answering.

"Having you here is awesome. It's just so obvious you're in love with my cousin. Why would you leave him?"

I had their attention as they waited for my reason. Saying I didn't love him was an easy lie when the truth was so complicated. "I left Angel because love is war… and we both lost."

Caylen crawled from my lap when he was done eating and headed straight for the decorated tree in the corner. We were a week away from Christmas, and my excitement was nonexistent. Stability was the one thing I wanted to give to Caylen this year. The Garretts had been nothing but welcoming, but I never let myself forget this was temporary.

When Caylen started to pull the ornaments off the tree, I took him upstairs for his bath. "One of these days," I said as I washed his hair, "you and I are going to be just fine."

He responded by splashing the water and laughing outrageously when suds caked my cheeks and hair. After his bath, I read to him one of the books Michelle loaned me until he fell asleep. Downstairs, Anna was packing to leave as Tim waited by the door, dressed in his uniform for his shift. Michelle usually picked her up from the city and Tim would take her back. It was humbling how much they have done for me and how little they asked in return. I haven't known this kind of warmth since my mother died. It often made me envious of Tabitha.

Anna hugged me on her way to the door. "I'll see you in a few days, but call me if anything weird happens."

I pulled back with a frown. "Why do you say that?"

"I don't know," she shrugged. "I just have a feeling. But it's not a bad one," she rushed to assure when my frown deepened.

I promised to call her and settled on the couch to finally watch the scary movie Tabitha's been bugging me about. She was too afraid to watch it alone, and Anna flat out refused, so that left me. Always the lamb and never the butcher.

I wasn't able to concentrate on the move, however, because Anna's words kept ringing in my head. It brought back the fear that returning to the estate was inevitable. No one had ever expected Angel to stay away this long. Tim had already assured me that I wouldn't be going anywhere I didn't want to, but accepting his promise meant putting them at risk. I could never do that.

Anger burned in my gut.

How could Angel ever expect me to call the estate my home? It would always be a prison.

I went to bed afraid for tomorrow, and it was all because of a *feeling*.

Augustine had been right.

Running didn't make me free.

I didn't get much sleep thinking about it, and the next morning I cried in the shower. I hadn't allowed myself to cry since Angel flat out told me I couldn't take care of myself.

My tears had dried, and I was toweling off when I heard heavy footsteps. Tabitha was at school, hopefully passing her geometry test, and Michelle and Tim were both at work. I didn't allow myself time to consider who it might be. I rushed out of the bathroom and to the spare bedroom where Caylen and I slept. I locked the door and snatched the lamp from the nightstand while Caylen was busy pulling off his socks. Of course, the Garretts would be robbed while I was home alone.

I could hear the footsteps on the stairs now. They weren't even trying to be quiet as they reached the landing. When I heard the knock on my door a moment later, my arm lowered as I stared at the door. The spare bedroom was at the end of the hall, which means the burglar had come straight to my room. Did they know I was here? Why would a burglar bother knocking?

"Princess?"

My legs threatened to give out when I recognized Z's voice. I rushed to the door and unlocked it to find both Lucas and Z standing on the other side. They were both dressed in gray suits, Lucas's a slightly darker shade than Z's.

"What are you two doing here?" I screamed.

Z's grin broadened while Lucas's frown deepened. "We're here to pick you up."

"I'm not going anywhere with you. How did you even get in here?"

Lucas snorted. "Really?" he questioned cockily. I forget that their criminal talents stretched so wide that picking a simple lock was child's play. After all, I'd done it myself.

And now, here I am, I reminded myself with a twinge of bitterness.

"Sorry, princess. It's not really an option." They muscled their way into the bedroom. Caylen clapped excitedly when he saw them and lifted his arms like the little traitor he was. Lucas was the first to grab and hold him while Z tickled him. His happy squeals made me forget momentarily that these men were loyal to Angel first.

"We'll be downstairs while you get dressed." I was ready to feign agreement and call Tim as soon as they were out of the room until I realized they were leaving with Caylen.

"Ten minutes, princess. We can't be late."

"Where are you taking us?"

"That's for you to see."

"Dress warm. It's nippy!" Z called as Lucas shut the door. I quickly dressed in jeans and a red blouse. They were dressed in suits, which meant we weren't exactly taking a walk in the park. I grabbed clothes for Caylen before heading downstairs and finding them in the kitchen helping themselves to the Garretts food.

"Seriously?"

Z was dipping celery in a jar of peanut butter. How could they just break into someone's home, terrorize their guests, and eat their food?

"I know," he grumbled. "Normally, I wouldn't eat celery, but they don't have any apples."

"Unbelievable," I muttered as I dressed Caylen. Lucas helped himself to one of Tabitha's blueberry pop tarts. I'd make sure to tell her exactly who the culprit was when she found one missing. That girl does not play about her blueberry pop tarts.

We left a few minutes later, and I grew nervous when we reached the city. I began to think I'd never see this place again. It didn't exactly hold fond memories for me, but it did remind me of a time when I was free. I suppose I should take some responsibility for this new course my life had taken.

I hadn't just looked back into the past. I'd stepped into it.

CHAPTER TWENTY-SIX

ANGEL

I MISSED HER. I MISSED THE HELL OUT OF HER. AND THE worst part of all was keeping the promise that I'd stay the fuck away. I fingered her wedding ring in my pocket and tried to focus on the barrage of questions.

"Mr. Knight, it's been three years since your father's death. No one can ignore the obvious delay in your confession."

My lawyer took a healthy swig of his water as he scribbled furiously on his legal pad. He played his part as the nervous lawyer well, though he had vehemently disagreed with my plan. The prosecutor also played his part. Getting District Attorney Patrick Turner, who had been in my pocket for years, to convince a judge to reopen my father's murder case had been easy. Turner was more than willing to help me prove my guilt since he'd been trying to get out from under my thumb. As a last resort, if I couldn't convince the court, I'd found Milly's substitute from that night and paid her handsomely to testify that I'd threatened her. She'd truly believed Theo had killed Art, but money worked wonders.

"What are you asking?"

"The court would like to know, why now?"

I was ready to answer when the courtroom doors opened, and Lucas slipped inside. His absence this morning had been puzzling, but when he shifted, revealing the reason, my fist balled in my pants pocket. She looked confused as she walked through the door carrying Caylen. Z walked in behind them, and they all found a seat in the front row. It wasn't until Mian started to lower herself on the wooden bench that she noticed me. It seemed as if her legs had given out when she finally sat.

Lucas might have thought bringing her here would make me change my mind, but it only made me more determined. She may not know how to fill the hole in her heart, but I did. It wasn't a change of heart that led me here. It was a change in the rhythm. It now beat for her.

With my eyes drinking in Mian, possibly for the last time, I spoke into the mic.

CHAPTER TWENTY-SEVEN

MIAN

" **F**OR THREE YEARS, MY MOM LIVED IN GUILT because of the choice I had made. She wanted to be punished—to be judged by the law and by God. I wouldn't let her. Four months ago, she went missing, and I don't know if she's dead, but I'm hoping the truth will either bring her home or bring her peace."

I was grateful no one was paying attention to me. I couldn't have hidden my confusion if I had been the one on the stand. Bea had spent the last moments of her life tied to a chair and forced to hear in detail about her husband's infidelity—forced to remember why she'd killed him. The memory of her blood oozing from the sound of her head was still too vivid.

I tore my attention from Angel to lock gazes with Lucas. His eyes warned me to stay calm, but how could I?

Bea wasn't *missing*.

She had been murdered.

And they had discarded her for no one to ever find. My stomach turned while my heart wept for her. It wept for Mom, and even for Art and Alon.

Death wasn't just inevitable. It was endless.

"I was taught by my father to protect my mother at any cost. I knew that night I'd already lost her, but I chose to hold onto her and sent an innocent man to prison."

My breath caught in my throat. I could feel my heart beating hard and fast against my chest.

"And that innocent man is Theodore Ross?" The man questioning Angel gestured toward the table on the right. I gasped when I noticed my father sitting at the table. He was hunched over, his hand covering his eyes, and it looked as if he were taking deep breaths.

"Yes."

What was Angel doing?

I couldn't grasp what was happening. Why was Angel on the stand admitting that he had framed my father for murder? Didn't he understand the consequences?

I wanted my father back, but was I willing to sacrifice Angel for him?

I started to rise, to call out to him, to *stop* him, but Z grabbed my hand, keeping me in my seat.

"So, you're saying your reason for coming forward is simply for moral liberation? You don't stand to gain from your confession?"

"I'm saying the rest my life has been summed up to one choice." Our eyes locked, though my vision of him through my tears had blurred.

"And I've made it."

He chose me.

CHAPTER TWENTY-EIGHT

MIAN

Three years later…

"I HATE GROUP PROJECTS," I MUTTERED TO MYSELF. I'd logged on to check my school email and found a thread of new emails from three of my classmates who I had been assigned to work with. We have to create an interactive media design for the website of an international technology conglomerate that didn't exist. At the end of the semester, we would have to then rebrand the company with a better design. Each project was worth twenty percent of our grade and my teammates were already bickering non-stop on whose idea was better.

Each of their ideas was good, and I saw no reason why we couldn't incorporate them all, so I sent them an email with a proposal. I knew I wouldn't have to wait long for their explosion, but I logged out of my email anyway and headed for the door.

I was already late.

Ten minutes later, I pulled up behind the other long line of cars at the curb and waited. I made it on time with a few minutes to spare thanks to my road rage, so I checked my email. My classmates were surprisingly on board with my proposal for the website. I sent a quick response to their questions and input and logged back off.

The school doors opened moments later, and the small class of preschoolers ran out to meet their parents and nannies. I hopped out of my SUV. I wanted a white Mustang with double black stripes and blacked out rims, but my father insisted I get the four-door tank because it was safer. I met Caylen at the rear door as he ran up the sidewalk.

"Hi, Mommy!"

"Hey, buddy. Have a good day?"

"Yes, but I sort of got in trouble." I paused from helping him into the booster seat.

"Say what?"

"Uncle Augustine said something about butts, so I told Miss Caroline, but she got mad."

I groaned knowing exactly the kind of jokes Augustine liked to tell despite his audience. "Was it supposed to be funny?"

"How should I know? I didn't get it."

My phone rang as I finished buckling him in. "We're going to have a talk when we get home," I warned which earned me a loud sigh. I hid my smile as I answered the phone.

"What's up?"

"I'm starting to think I'd be happier as a full-time

barista," Anna groaned. "Seriously, if I play my cards right, I could be manager one day." Anna currently worked as a part-time barista at one of the campus coffee shops while she was studying Biology.

"You're not going to quit school, Anna, so if you're looking for encouragement, then you should have tried your luck with Tabitha."

She snorted over the line. "I called her first actually. I just knew for sure I'd get her to talk me into quitting, but she called me a trooper and hung up."

"You are a trooper. You've just started your third year. Before you know it, you'll be able to practice medicine. Your dreams are bigger than your woes. Remember that. "

"You do realize that I have at least eight more years before that happens, right?"

"Jesus, Anna, when did you become such a pessimist?"

"Day one of organic chem." She giggled.

I laughed because buried underneath all that bitterness was the lighthearted Anna. We never spoke of it, but I suspected most of her unhappiness wasn't because of school.

It was a broken heart.

A year and a half ago Lucas and Anna decided to give a relationship a try. It had been going well until six months later when Z left Chicago after tracking down his mother. No one could believe she had been alive after all this time. When he left, he wouldn't tell anyone, not even Lucas, where he was going, but he'd kept in contact.

Until one day, the phone calls suddenly stopped.

Anna would never say more than it just didn't work out, but somehow, I suspected Z's disappearance had caused their relationship to spiral down until she finally ended it. Now she could barely look at him, and Lucas never spoke a word to her.

Everyone had the same unspoken fear that Z was dead, but it was Lucas who kept searching.

Anna had never gotten over losing Lucas even though she was the one who left him. She spent half her time excelling at school and the other half complaining about it. Happiness eluded her. Or maybe not just her.

It seemed none of us was destined for a fairy-tale ending.

For three years, I fought to let go of Angel, but no amount of pretending could exorcise him from my head.

With his confession, he exchanged one prison for another, and I never learned how he made it possible. Whenever I asked Lucas, Z, or Augustine for details, they'd only say it was better I heard it from Angel. So for three years, I had been left with the feeling that taking my father's place in prison hadn't been Angel's only sacrifice.

"Mian? Mian? Are you even listening?"

"I'm sorry, Anna. I spaced out for a moment. What did you say?"

"I said I just got a text from Tabitha. She wants you to call her. *Now*."

I didn't call Tabitha until much later that night after I put Caylen to bed. I made a promise to myself when life started to look up that he'd never be my second choice. It was because of that promise that I had nine missed calls and ten messages from Tabitha, Augustine, Anna, and my father. I phoned Tabitha first since she was likely the reason for all the panic.

"Tabitha, what's up?"

"What's up? I'll tell you what's *not* up." I moved the phone away from my ear before she blew my hearing and turned the volume down. "I sick of my parents keeping secrets from me. I'm nineteen, for crying out loud, but they treat me like I'm twelve."

"Tabitha? Can you get to the point?" I didn't want to throw in her face that she was lucky to have parents who put her best interest first. It was something she had to realize on her own.

"Angel's not in prison anymore." My legs gave out, and I sunk to the floor. I kept the phone tight to my ear as I leaned my head against the wall and closed my eyes tight. "He's been out for three months now. My parents and that cretin cousin of mine were keeping it a secret."

"Wait." My eyes opened, and I stared out the window. "Augustine *knew*?"

"It would appear so."

"So… where is he?" I hoped I didn't sound too interested, but he is my husband. The marriage didn't have a legal leg to stand on, but I couldn't risk sending my father back to prison by asking for an annulment. When Michelle informed me there would be a hearing before a divorce was granted, I knew I couldn't risk seeing him again either. So I took the coward's way and continued to live as Mrs. Angel Knight.

"My parents claim they don't know, and Augustine wouldn't tell me when I grilled him."

I sighed and told myself not to make this a big deal. Angel's impending release had been keeping me awake at night lately, but clearly, there was nothing to worry about. He'd been free for months, and he hadn't bothered to pay a visit to his *wife*.

And why should he?

There was nothing for him here. He gave it up on that stand three years ago. He gave me up for *me*.

One day, when I could face him again, I would sever our ties for good. I forgave him for the pieces he carved out of my heart the moment he chose me, but I could never let him return to finish the job.

After Tabitha had finished her rant, I promised to call her tomorrow and hung up. My stomach tightened at the thought of seeing him again. It was as unavoidable as breathing.

I wasn't sixteen with a crush anymore, and I wasn't his prisoner trapped in a marriage I didn't want.

You're just the wife of a man you shouldn't love.

Angel going to prison hadn't waved any magic wands. My life didn't get better once I was free, but I had a village this time who pushed me to get here.

A village I found because of Angel.

My father's release hadn't immediately repaired our relationship, either. I sent him away the first time he showed up on my doorstep, but he didn't just go away after I rejected him. He kept coming back every week for six months until I finally agreed to talk. We took it slow, and eventually, I decided to forgive him by allowing him in Caylen's life.

Undoubtedly, he's been a better grandfather than he had been a father. I made a point not to hold it over his head, but days like these were harder than the rest.

Angel had stayed away this long. A part of me was hurt that he had while the other part of me hoped he never came back.

I lifted myself from the floor and decided I would need a long, soothing bubble bath in order to sleep tonight. I didn't have the energy to talk to the others right now, so I pulled my hair up and ran the hot water.

Just as I started to undress, my doorbell rang.

CHAPTER TWENTY-NINE

ANGEL

Y OU DON'T BECOME A POWERFUL MAN WITHOUT having some strings to pull. Three years ago, I orchestrated my demise, and it had been all for her. When you fall, you want it to mean something. If you rise again, you want to know who you are. I was once the head of a criminal empire two centuries old. Now I was just a man standing on a girl's doorstep, hoping she'd forgive him.

I was so nervous that I had missed the doorbell completely on my first try. After ringing it, I stepped back and waited. I knew she was still awake because I'd stood across the street from her and Caylen's home—the brownstone we had grown up in together.

I bought the brownstone back from the couple I sold it to for twice the price. I could have bought any other place much cheaper, but I wanted Mian to create new memories here, so I gave it to Caylen for his first birthday. According to Lucas, Mian hadn't bothered to open it until six months after my trial. I was just glad she finally had.

I heard her footsteps moving across the floor. They were hesitant as she probably wondered who was ringing her door this late. Michelle told me Tabitha figured out I'd been released. She and Mian had grown close over the years, so I knew she'd warn her.

A few moments passed, and I could no longer hear her footsteps. She was probably watching me through the peephole right now, debating if she should open the door.

I smiled at the peephole and heard her gasp on the other side. Another second later, I could hear the locks turn.

Nothing could have prepared me for this moment.

The door opened, and she stood clutching it, looking as innocent as she always had, with her hair pulled up in a messy ponytail. It was shorter than I remembered. Her skin was soft and slightly flushed as she stared back at me. She seemed to be just as mesmerized.

I was bigger than I was three years ago, almost matching Lucas's bulk. I could see him playing pro football or hockey if he had found the right path. I didn't know if he had the skill, but he definitely had the brawn.

"Angel?"

"Yeah, Sprite."

We fell silent again as we drunk each other in. The silence became stifling after a while, so I searched for something to say, and when I couldn't form the right words, I went for the obvious. "You used the key."

She stiffened and shifted her weight to one hip as she crossed her arms. "I didn't want to, but everyone seemed to think my pigheadedness was denying my son a stable home."

I nodded, sensing it was a sore subject. Agreeing that she was, in fact, pigheaded was a sure way to get the door slammed in my face.

"If anyone deserved stability, it was the two of you," I replied instead. "I'm glad you accepted the gift."

"Before you get any ideas, I made it on my own, and I don't owe you a damn thing."

"I can see that." I was fucking proud and trying not to let it show in the most pleasurable way.

"Can you?" Her eyes narrowed. "Then why are you here?"

"Because we're better than this."

"Than what?" she snapped.

"Pretending that we don't exist to each other."

"That's what you've been doing for three months? Pretending?"

"No," I answered while wondering how long she'd known I was out. "I was fighting to stay away from you."

"So what changed?"

"I realized it was only a matter of time before our paths crossed again."

"Really? I don't see Michelle and Tim inviting you to their annual barbecue anytime soon."

"Maybe not, but we are married." She didn't reply other than to purse her lips and perk an eyebrow. "Can I come in?"

"Why would I invite you into my home?"

She tensed, losing some of her bravado as I stepped closer. "So we can talk," I answered gently. I was so close I could feel each breath she took on my skin.

"We have nothing to talk about, Angel." Her arms loosened from her chest to wrap tightly around her body, and I couldn't help wondering if she was naked under her green robe. "You should leave." Her mask fell, allowing me to see her torment. She looked both surprised and wary when I stepped back.

"This is goodnight then."

I was off her stoop, disappearing down the darkened street before she could respond.

The next morning, I made pancakes. Sure, they weren't my pancakes to make, and I'd broken into the brownstone just before sunrise, but no one could turn down pancakes. My own stomach growled as I turned off the burner and set the table.

I was scooping eggs on each plate when I heard a small voice say, "Are those blueberry pancakes?"

I paused before turning with a spatula full of eggs. Standing in the doorway, dressed in thermal Iron Man pajamas was a three and a half foot tall boy with light brown bed hair and blue eyes watching me curiously.

"Buttermilk," I answered ruefully. "But maybe next time?"

He inched closer, his curiosity getting the better of him while caution kept him back. "I don't like scrambled eggs."

"No?"

He shook his head and moved closer. "You got boiled?"

"Afraid not, but I can make some."

"Mama lets me peel it myself when it's not hot anymore."

"Yeah?" I returned the frying pan to the stove and filled a pot up with water to make his boiled egg. I heard him take a seat while my back was turned and felt him watching me.

"Are you Angel?"

I froze from dunking the egg in the pot and turned to face him. "You know who I am?" He was only one the last time I saw him. He couldn't possibly remember me.

"Uncle Lucas showed me a picture." That would explain why he hadn't been afraid to find me here. "He said... um... he said..." His eyebrows bunched as he fell quiet.

"What did he say?" I prompted.

"He said I couldn't tell anyone because it's a secret."

"Yeah?" He nodded, sure of his answer this time. "Well, Uncle Lucas is my best friend, so his secrets are my secrets."

He fidgeted in his seat as he seemed to think it over. I was ready to turn away and give him time when he said, "So are you?"

It was my turn to frown as I looked back. "Am I what?"

"My dad." His head was down when he answered, and I was grateful. I wasn't sure the look on my face was one any kid should see.

I was going to kill Lucas.

"Did he tell you I was?"

He shrugged his small shoulders. "He said you were the only one I was going to get."

I made a mental note to make Lucas's death slow and painful.

I stepped away from the stove and took a seat across

from him. This was not a conversation I wanted to have two minutes after seeing him again. If I could change the past, Caylen would be mine, but I couldn't, and he wasn't.

"I'm not your father, kid."

"Oh." He looked up and his blue gaze collided with mine. I wanted to erase my words and tell him Lucas had been right. That I would be the only father he ever needed, but I couldn't go behind Mian's back. Getting Mian to agree to a future with me was as unlikely as catching a shooting star. If I didn't win her heart, this kid would still expect a father. I selfishly wanted to claim them both, but I couldn't do that to them.

"I'm sorry, Caylen."

He shrugged as if it were no big deal and looked away. Reluctantly, I moved back to the stove and turned off the boiling pot before draining the water and setting the egg aside to cool. I then slid a pancake on his plate and helped him cut it into pieces.

"Your mom still sleeps late, huh?"

He nodded and shoved a piece of pancake in his mouth, smearing syrup at the corner of his lips as he did and making sounds that told me he like buttermilk pancakes too. "It's Saturday, so I don't have school today. She'll wake up soon to make me cereal."

As soon as he said it, I could hear her moving around upstairs. I forced myself to stay seated, ignoring the light fluttering in my stomach when she called out for Caylen. "In here, Mama! Angel made pancakes."

Shit. The kid was a snitch.

I braced as I heard her coming down the stairs. "Who made panca—" She stopped mid-sentence when she saw me sitting at the table as if I belonged there. "What the hell are you doing here?"

"Mama, you're not supposed to curse."

"Caylen, go upstairs and brush your teeth," she ordered without breaking our stare.

He pouted and stuck his elbows on the table defiantly. "Listen to your mother," I ordered gently. He sighed and climbed down from his chair before running to the stairs.

"No running!" she called out after him. We could hear his steps slow almost immediately.

"Why are you here, Angel? How did you even get in here?"

"Broke in," I said as I stabbed a pancaked. "I made breakfast."

Her laugh held no trace of humor. "I'm still sleeping, and this is a nightmare," she muttered to herself.

"Pancakes might still be warm." I shoved more food in my mouth to keep from saying something else stupid.

She shoved her fingers in her already messy hair, and when she freed them, she looked even sexier than she already did in her small short and thin shirt. Her nipples were poking through the pale pink top, which made it hard to keep my gaze on her face.

"What did you hope to accomplish by breaking in and making pancakes?"

"The pancakes were to get you to talk to me."

"And the breaking in was to make me throw you out?"

"I have about seventy pounds and a foot on you, baby. You won't be throwing me anywhere."

"I can call the police, and they can *throw* you back in prison," she answered sweetly.

I grinned, feeling like a predator, sinking further into our game. "You'd have to make it to the phone first."

She avoided my gaze, looking unsure if I'd really hurt her, and I realized this might not seem like a simple game to her. "I'm sorry." I dropped my fork and stood up from the table. "I'd never hurt you," I said as I moved across the kitchen to where she stood. "If you want me to go, I'll go."

She sighed. "What do you want, Angel?"

"I just want to talk."

"What could we possibly have to talk about that doesn't start and end with divorce?"

"I don't want a divorce."

"It's not up to you."

"I'll contest it."

"And I'll tell the judge you, and I didn't actually consent to the marriage."

"Your father will go back to prison."

I knew I had her when her gaze turned murderous. "Give me one reason why we should stay married?" I started to answer when her finger rested on my lips. "Think about your answer because it better be good, or you're out of here." She slowly lifted her finger from my lips and waited.

"Fate could have chosen anything for us fifteen years ago, and no matter how many times we run in opposite directions, fate always pulls us back. I think we owe it to ourselves to find out why. I can't stay away, and your heart won't stop seeking me. We're inevitable, Mian."

I leaned against the wall while Mian talked quietly with

Anna by the front door. She kept scowling at me over Mian's shoulder as she gave her instructions for Caylen.

Mian had agreed to spend the weekend alone with me, but this weekend was all I would get.

No sex.

No lies.

No looking back after Sunday.

I was eager to start this weekend with her, but as she kissed Caylen and shut the front door, I realized I had no idea what my next step should be. She looked as nervous as I felt as she stared back at me a safe distance away.

"Okay…" She held out her arms and then let them fall back down to her sides. "How should we start, hubby?"

I rubbed my nape and took a deep breath. "What do you normally do on a Saturday?"

"Work," she answered dryly. She had no intentions of making this easy for me.

I nodded and cursed myself for fucking this up already. "I'd like to see what you do."

"Why?" She looked genuinely confused as her brows pulled together.

"I'm interested in you. Isn't it obvious?"

"It's ironic that we spent six years in this house together and you spent most of it ignoring me, and now you're *interested*?"

"Fuck, baby," I groaned. "Cut me some slack. I'm desperate." She relaxed some and started for the stairs.

"My office is upstairs," she mumbled. I followed her up, watching her perky ass twitch in her shorts as she climbed the stairs. At one point, she cast a suspicious glance over her shoulder, and I quickly averted my attention.

We reached her old bedroom, which she'd turned into

a study area. "Caylen has your old bedroom," she said as if she had read my mind.

"Are you happy here?"

"My son is happy, so I'm happy."

"You shouldn't worry so much about making the same mistakes your father made."

She swirled on her foot until we were nose to chest. Her hands planted on her hips as she glared up at me. "Who said I'm worried?"

"You didn't have to. Anyone can see you're afraid of disappointing him."

"The beginning of his life wasn't easy. I'm just fortunate he doesn't remember any of it."

"You protected him."

"I put him in danger. There hasn't been a day I don't regret breaking into your father's home. I had been desperate and didn't think I had a choice."

"You think that makes you a bad mother?" She shrugged and tapped the mouse to wake the desktop. It was clear I wouldn't get much out of her, so I got comfortable in the green cushioned chair and did the pouring instead. "My father risked his life, and it put food on the table, but feeding me was never the reason. He did it to honor his duty, and then he did it for power. I had a place to call home, clothes to keep me warm, and a full stomach at the end of the day, but none of it made him a good father."

I counted the seconds until she took the bait and spoke to me.

"And your mother? What did she do for you?" I couldn't see her face behind the computer, but I recognized the emotion that turned her voice delicate. She knew the answer.

"She stayed." I closed my eyes and saw the graceful lines of my mother's face. She was smiling, and it was real. I couldn't remember a time my mother's smile hadn't been forced. "It eventually killed her."

"Why don't the cops know she's dead?"

"People go missing all the time and bodies would have raised too many questions. I wish I could have buried her even though she wouldn't have thought her life had been worth celebrating." *But she didn't deserve to be discarded, either.*

"I hope they found each other," she whispered so softly I almost didn't catch it.

"Who?"

"Our moms."

I didn't know anything about Cecily Ross, but the love my mother reserved in her heart for her and the adoration in Mian's eyes made me want the same thing. "Me too."

I watched Mian work for a few hours before she grew irritated with my barrage of questions and kicked me out. It was nearing lunch, so I decided to make us grilled cheese since my culinary skills were limited to the most basic of cuisines. When the food was done, I dragged her from the bedroom, ignoring her argument that she needed to work as I did.

"We're supposed to spend time together. That means sharing meals," I said as I pulled her into the living room.

As if on cue, her stomach growled, and I remembered she didn't eat this morning.

She didn't seem to notice as she took a look around. "What did you do to my living room?"

I'd covered the coffee table with the red tablecloth I found and placed a candle in the center with a place setting on each side. "I'm dating you."

"You know you can take me on an actual date." She sat on one side and folded her legs.

"I don't want what's out there to ruin what we have in here."

"But if we can't make it out there, it won't matter what we have when we're alone." Her voice was empty of emotion. "One way or another, we'd be pretending." I handed her a can of soda before taking my place at the other end of the table.

I started to eat when my head replayed her words, making my stomach turn, and my appetite evaporate. Dropping my sandwich on the plate, I sighed. "I can't do this without you, Mian." I spoke so softly I was surprised she'd heard.

Her chewing slowed as she placed her own sandwich back on her plate. "You're the only one who wants to do this at all."

I could feel my ire rising and took a deep breath. "We both know that's not true."

"You invited yourself into my home so I'd give you a chance."

"And it was *your* choice to let me stay." I lost the battle for patience and pushed aside the table until there was nothing but air between us. Her gasp and squeal as I pulled her into my lap and wrapped my arms around her went ignored.

"We said no touching."

"*You* said no touching. I've wanted to touch you since you opened the door last night wearing that thin robe and sent me away. I've had nothing but my right hand and memories for three years, Mian."

"You're trying to confuse me," she whimpered.

"You already know what you want. You're just too afraid to take it."

"How do you know what I want?"

"Because I want the same thing. Possibly more."

Her nose wrinkled as she leaned away from me. She couldn't go far with my arm wrapped around her waist. "It's not a contest."

"Then why are you such a sore loser?" My heart lifted—it fucking lifted—at the sound of her reluctant laughter.

I almost begged to see her smile again when it faded. "I can't believe we're doing this right now. We're wrong for each other."

"You don't know what's right until you've had it, and we've never had the chance to figure it out. There will never be anyone else I'd lose a war for, and if I had to, I'd fall again so you would rise."

I wanted to kiss her when she relaxed against me, but that would be pushing it.

"How did you do it? How did you break free?"

"I rewrote the rules."

"But wouldn't your family have killed you? When you left, I kept thinking someone would come to hurt us while you were safely behind prison bars."

"I gave them all a future they couldn't refuse. Most of my family lived in fear that their sons would inherit a death sentence and their daughters would be sold off to men without morals."

"What did you do?"

"I returned Alexander's legacy to his line and anyone who wanted freedom got it, but they no longer benefit financially either. A bigger piece of the pie was the only way I could convince the others without bloodshed."

"They didn't think it was a trick?"

"After Reginald and Andrew, they were afraid I was trying to weed out traitors, but I convinced them it was legit when I told them my plan to free your dad. The only one I really needed to convince anyway was Aurora. She's Reginald's younger sister and her son was next in line to succeed since I don't have an heir and Andrew was dead."

"I thought only a first born son could inherit?"

"One of the rules I changed was that the ruling Knight could name their successor. Male or female."

"You really picked her?" There was awe in her voice as I rested my chin on her shoulder.

"Aurora isn't just ambitious. She's smart and fair, and it helps that she despised her brother even more than she despised me."

"She sounds like a lovely woman." I could hear the smile in her voice. "So you rewrote the rules. Why would you need her?"

"I wanted you and Caylen to be safe. I needed to be sure no one would come after you."

"You asked her to protect me?"

"Yes."

"And now that she's the Knight, you answer to her?"

"I answer to no one. I'm free, Sprite."

"Really?" The longing in her voice made me hopeful

that just maybe there was still room in her heart for me.

"I guess that would make me an unemployed ex-convict." I was far from penniless, but my joke fell flat when she didn't laugh as I intended. Instead, she turned in my arms to kneel between my legs.

"You really did all of this while we were apart?" It was hard to let my hands roam beyond her waist when she laid her hands on my thighs.

"The only way I could stay away from you was to do everything I could to make things right and to hope that one day, you could forgive me for not doing it sooner."

"You're not playing fair when you say things like that."

I cupped the back of her head, holding her stare as my thumb caressed her cheek. "This isn't a game, Sprite. Not for me."

"Then why couldn't you say all of this three months ago?" There was no anger in her voice. Only hurt that I hadn't come for her sooner.

"Believe me I wanted to. I almost did many times, but Lucas needed me to help him find out what happened to Z. I needed those answers too."

"Oh." She lifted her hands from my legs to wring the hem of her flannel. "What did you find out?"

"Not anything useful. It's like he just disappeared."

"I'm sorry."

"Me too."

We spent the rest of the afternoon talking about the last three years instead of our ambiguous future. I knew most of everything that had happened, but I needed to hear it from her that she had been okay. She told me she used the senator's money to pay for school and then seed money for Rogue Designs. In two years, she'd managed to find over forty clients, ranging from local business owners to national fast-food chains all the while studying for a degree in graphic design. When the conversation turned to Caylen, the pride and love that bled from her were something we had both missed out on as kids. She told me about Anna studying medicine and Tabitha pursuing journalism.

I noticed she steered clear of the subject of her father, and I wisely chose not to mention him, either. Her father and I may no longer be enemies, but there would always be bad blood between us.

When there was nothing left to talk about, I helped her clean the brownstone, something she says she can never accomplish when Caylen was around. After cleaning, we spent the rest of the night watching movies until she decided to call it a night.

I had been staring into the dark and hadn't noticed her return an hour later until the smell of her peach-scented soap reached me. I placed the envelope I'd been clutching on my lap to hide my reaction as she stood in front of me.

"Here." She thrust the blanket and pillow that she'd been holding toward me. "The couch isn't too comfortable to sleep on, but I'm sure it's better than what you've gotten used to."

"Thanks." I made sure my hands touched her when I took the blanket and pillow and hid my smile when she shivered. Her gaze dropped to my lap, out of instinct or desire, I didn't know, but it made me even harder.

"What's that?"

I stood up, forcing her to take a step back to make room for me. What I had to say wasn't something I wanted to do sitting down. "I know I asked you for the weekend, but I think all that needed to be said has been said."

"Really?" She made a sound of disbelief. "Because I think there's just one more thing you still haven't said." I was thrown when her eyes filled with tears, and her voice broke. The last thing I wanted to do was hurt her.

She wanted me to tell her how much I fucking loved her, but I couldn't do it unless she was completely sure she wanted to hear it.

"I never wanted to call what I felt for you love. I saw what love does, and I wanted more with you. I was just too much of a coward to tell you."

I handed her the legal envelope and watched her turn it over. There was no writing on the outside. "What is it?"

I shook my head. "If there's a piece of you left that still belongs to me, you'll know what to do with it." I brushed away her tear. "But if there isn't room in your heart for me anymore, tomorrow morning, I'll walk away forever."

CHAPTER THIRTY

MIAN

I DIDN'T WANT TO BE A GIRL DUPED BY A BEAUTIFULLY worded apology, and I didn't want to be a girl stubborn enough to give up what she wanted for pride. Either decision could one day make me a fool, but which would make me truly happy?

Angel didn't just go to prison for me. He renounced his throne and changed a two-hundred-year-old empire to free his family… and me.

What he gave up, the sacrifice he made—do I just pretend it didn't happen? Loving Angel scared me because no matter how bad anyone hurt me, he was the only one who could ruin me.

I lay in bed staring at the ceiling and listening to the rain as it poured outside. Downstairs, sleeping on my couch was the only man I wanted to love asking me to love him back.

The thing was I could live without Angel and find happiness.

Sitting up, I turned on my bedside lamp and picked up the yellow envelope. My hands trembled as I opened the envelope and pulled out the papers inside. I read the words at the top of the first page and then my teary gaze trailed down to the bottom where I found Angel's signature.

He had filed for a divorce.

I didn't bother reading through the legal jargon. I climbed from my big, empty bed and made my way downstairs. He said I'd know what to do with the papers if I knew what I truly wanted, but he was wrong about having said all that we needed to.

There was still one more thing.

"Angel?" I considered turning around when I thought he might be sleep, but then his voice broke through the dark.

"Yeah?"

I turned on the lamp, which cast a dim glow over the living room. I could see Angel sitting up. He was shirtless and barefoot, but his dark jeans still covered his legs.

"It only took a moment for us to fall, and when we did, I didn't think there was anything that could reverse the spell, but I was wrong." His head bent shielding his eyes from me. "We aren't those kids wanting love for all the wrong reasons." My hand cupped his chin to lift his face. "The thing is we can't rekindle what we never truly had in a weekend. It's not enough." Before he could respond, I scribbled my name next to his and then handed him the papers. "I don't want the marriage our fathers wanted for us."

I held my breath as I waited for him to say something. The next moment, it seemed like all the air expelled from his body, and then he ripped the papers from my hand. I gasped when he tossed them onto the couch and stood up. I felt the fire in his gaze heating my skin, making my heart pound, and my pussy begging for it to consume us. His fingers cupped the back of my neck and pulled me in close. "Then what do you want, Sprite?"

Staring into his eyes, I didn't just see lust. I saw a future I wanted to be a part of. "I want more."

EPILOGUE

MIAN
One Year Later

OMETIMES YOU FIND HAPPINESS, AND SOMETIMES happiness finds you. Right now, happiness was using his mouth to drive me crazy. I gripped his soft locks tighter between my fingers but had nothing to use to bury my moans when his tongue found my clit. My bare ass was slippery against the leather seat of his car as he ate me as if we hadn't just come from dinner and dancing.

Tonight was date night, and Angel had just driven me home from the club. He had barely taken his eyes off me the entire night, so I suppose I should have expected this when I chose the tight black dress with the plunging neckline.

Back at the club, in the middle of the dance floor, he had used his fingers to bring me release, and now he'd chosen the curb where anyone could walk by. He'd also parked the Mustang under a street lamp. I should have said no, but he'd pushed my dress up my thighs and ordered me to lean against the car door there was nothing I could do to resist.

Just then, I heard laughter off in the distance. I cracked open my eyes enough to see a couple walking by on the other side of the street. They never once glanced our way, but I tensed anyway.

"Angel… baby… you have to stop. Someone will see." To my surprise, his head lifted, and I was met with the intensity of his need as his brown eyes met mine.

"Come here." I did as he asked and tasted myself on his lips with a moan when he kissed me. "Do you taste your sweetness?" he asked when he pulled away. His voice was thick with untamed desire. "How can you ask me to fucking stop?"

"I just think maybe we could take this inside," I flirted. His eyes were wide with surprise. We've been divorced and dating for a year, but even though I agreed to give our love a try, I still set some boundaries. Like not staying overnight at the brownstone with Caylen and me. He's been patient, letting me set the pace and make the rules, even though I knew the small space I kept between us was hurting him. I just had to be sure that what *I* wanted was also best for my son. Even without us living together, the bond that had been there between Angel and Caylen when he was just a baby was restored almost instantly. If Angel broke his promise or he left, I wouldn't be the only one heartbroken this time.

"Are you sure?" There was so much hope in his eyes that I was almost sorry I hadn't done it sooner.

"I haven't given you your birthday present yet." I reached down and pulled his gift from my bag. "I think this will show you how sure I am."

He slowly took the small box from my hands. It was the same size as the one he'd given Caylen four years ago. As he untied the bow and tore the wrapping, I held my breath. He lifted the top and lying on the bedding was a replica of the brass key he'd given to Caylen and me for his first birthday.

His head lifted. His gaze met mine. The love in his eyes shone brightly. "Is this?"

I took the key from the box and his key ring from the ignition. "Caylen is ready." He didn't say anything as I slipped the key onto his key ring. "And so am I."

I didn't get the chance to say more when he kissed me hard and deep. "About fucking time," he mumbled against my lips. "You were killing me, Sprite."

My laugh was cut short when a knock on the window interrupted our moment. Angel turned, jaw hard and shoulders tense, to face the intruder at his window. I was surprised to see my dad standing there and also a little worried about how much he might have seen.

"What?" Angel greeted gruffly. I punched his arm, but he didn't even acknowledge my warning as he stared back at my father who was bent over and looking straight at me.

"I asked you to have my daughter home at a reasonable hour."

For the love of God.

It had been a year since Angel came home, and their pissing contest when it came to me wasn't even close to ending. Of course, my dad hadn't actually been serious when he set a curfew. First, because I'm a grown woman.

Second, because Angel would have flipped him the bird if I hadn't been holding his hand and his other hand hadn't been holding Caylen against his side.

Dad's been making an effort, despite trying to enforce himself as the dominant male in my life, to get along with Angel.

Angel has made no such effort.

Although he *did* go to prison so I could have a relationship with my father again. I think he'd drawn the line there four years ago.

"I'll be right in," I said before Angel could respond. Sometimes, it made me sad that they would never get along, and other times, I remember the men they once were and was just glad they weren't trying to kill each other.

"All right, baby girl. I put Caylen to bed an hour ago. I'll be inside." That was his way of letting me know to do what I needed to do. He banged his knuckles on the hood of Angel's precious car to piss him off before walking away. I held in my snicker when Angel's nostrils flared as he watched him walk away.

"I promised I wouldn't kill your dad, but that doesn't mean I won't kick his ass."

"You do know if you ever want to marry me again, you're going to have to ask him for my hand."

His answering grunt was full of challenge as he eyed me. "Your father knows better than that. He'll be lucky if I let him come to the wedding."

It was my turn to make a rude sound. "I think you're both lucky I decided to forgive either of you."

His voice softened as he stared back at me. "I'm now the luckiest man in the world, baby." The butterflies returned, and I was ready to forgive him for being rude to my father when he added, "But my first action as the man of the house will be to make you scream my name." The evil glint in his eyes told me he wasn't speaking about the one his mother had given him.

"I am *not* calling you daddy when we fuck."

The kiss he placed upon my lips was succulent and full of promise. "We'll see about that."

"Angel…" My voice held a warning note.

"Little Mian Ross, it's past your curfew." He leaned over and kissed my lips again. "Now go inside before daddy spanks you."

Oh, God.

I could feel his words deep in my cunt where he should have been. But there was also disappointment when his words registered. "You aren't coming in?"

He shook his head, his face a mask of the same disappointment I felt. "Lucas thinks he has some information about Z."

It's been two years since Z's disappearance, and while we all feared he was dead, none of us was willing to let go of him. It was never far from my mind that if Angel had still been the Knight, he would have probably found him by now or at least uncovered what had happened to him.

"I understand." After all, it was his promise to me that kept him in the dark this long.

He walked me to the door and then kissed me goodnight one last time. My father was waiting in the living room when I walked inside.

"How was your date?"

"It was good, Daddy, but my feet are sore from dancing the night away." I stepped out of the red stilts that were more Brandi's style.

"Glad you had fun." He fell silent, but I had a feeling he had more to say, so I waited. "So, did you give him the key?"

"I did." His face remained emotionless as he nodded and stood.

"Then I'm happy for you, baby girl."

"Are you still going to make it to Caylen's birthday party this weekend?"

"Wouldn't miss it for the world." He kissed my forehead as he passed, but I stopped him from leaving when I wrapped my arms around his waist and held him tight.

"I'll always be your girl, Daddy." It had taken some time for me to trust him again, but I was thankful every day for a second chance with my father. One of the rules I'd established when Angel and I started dating was that he'd accept that my father would be in our lives. Other than an occasional snarky comment from both sides, it's being going really well.

"I know, baby. I don't care what that asshole says," he added good-naturedly. I smiled against his chest and then let him go as I said my good night.

Upstairs, I stopped to check in on Caylen. He was in his usual balled up position with his knees tucked under his chin and his covers and pillows dangling over the side of the bed. I smiled as I fixed his pillows and pulled the covers over him.

After my shower, I found messages from Anna and Tabitha asking if I'd given Angel the key. It hadn't been a spur of the moment decision, but one that had put my head through the wringer for months.

Living together was the next step in our relationship and maybe just maybe, one day, we'd put it on paper again, and this time it would be *our* choice.

I heard myself sigh when I felt the kiss on my shoulder. His masculine scent surrounded me at the same time his heat did as he pulled me into his body. "You came back," I whispered into the dark.

"Did you really think I'd stay away?"

I didn't say anything as his body settled. He was naked from the waist up, and I guessed by the feeling of his bare legs tangling with mine that he was wearing shorts. I'd worn his shirt to bed because it smelled like him, but I found that the real thing was so much better.

"Any news?" His sigh, then the silence that followed was telling. My heart broke for him as I pictured Z's smile. I couldn't believe that it's been two years since he had disappeared.

"It was another dead end."

"I'm sorry," I said as I hugged his waist.

His head dipped, and then he was kissing me. When he pulled back, my eyes finally opened, and I found him staring through the dark.

"I love you."

I've heard him say it a thousand times and each time still felt like the first.

"I love you too."

"Whatever happens, whatever it takes, I'll always

choose you."

"Because you're my knight in shining armor?"

His boyish smile lit up the dark corners of his soul.

"Because I'm yours."

AUTHOR'S NOTE

Stolen Duet ended on a bittersweet note, but I'm hoping you can find some joy in knowing that Z is *not dead*. I'm sure you may have guessed this already. His story came to me very late in this book and unfortunately, for it to happen, his path had to veer from Angel and Mian's story, but don't worry. He'll be back, and Lucas and Anna will be there to help tell his story. I don't have any details yet other than to look for a spinoff or two in the future.

ACKNOWLEDGMENTS

MOM, thank you for not disowning me for the one hundred and eighty times I rushed you off the phone to write.

ROGENA, thank you for being flexible yet again. This wasn't quite the shit show it usually is. Maybe I finally learned my lesson. (Yeah, I laughed too.)

AMANDA, thanks for *two* great covers. My indecisiveness may someday make you a very rich woman.

SUNNY, thank you for putting up with my bitching and moaning for the six months it took me to write this book. One more month, and I think I would have loved you more than chocolate.

LISA, I teased you constantly, bounced some ideas off you,

and as always, you asked some ridiculously hard fucking questions. Thanks for that. I mean it.

READERS who were stuck on the cliff for six months because you couldn't resist my words... You were the motivation to finishing this book.

ALSO BY B.B. REID

BROKEN LOVE SERIES
Fear Me
Fear You
Fear Us
Breaking Love
Fearless

STOLEN DUET
The Bandit
The Knight

CONTACT THE AUTHOR

Follow me on Facebook,
www.facebook.com/authorbbreid

Join Reiderville on Facebook,
www.facebook.com/groups/reiderville

Follow me on Twitter,
www.twitter.com/_BBREID

Follow me on Instagram,
www.instagram.com/_bbreid

Visit my website,
www.bbreid.com

ABOUT B.B. REID

B.B., also known as Bebe, found her passion for romance when she read her first romance novel by Susan Johnson at a young age. She would sneak into her mother's closet for books and even sometimes the attic. When she finally decided to pick up a metaphorical pen and start writing, she found a new way to embrace her passion.

She favors a romance that isn't always easy on the eyes or heart and loves to see characters grow—characters who are seemingly doomed from the start but find love anyway.

Made in the USA
Columbia, SC
17 November 2018